Sunset Ledge

by

Darlene Deluca

Cover Art by *Tina Lynn Stout*

The Wild Rose Press, Inc.
PO Box 708
Adams Basin, NY 14410-0708
Visit us at www.thewildrosepress.com

Publishing History
First Edition, 2024
Trade Paperback ISBN 978-1-5092-5518-4
Digital ISBN 978-1-5092-5519-1

Published in the United States of America

Chapter One

The horse waited patiently. Caroline Tate did not.

Sunshine bathed the grounds outside the barn doors. Time was wasting. Shifting, she crossed her arms and nodded. "Mm-hmm." Finally, when she couldn't stand it any longer, she stepped forward and held up a hand to stop the man droning on about horsemanship. He never even asked if she'd ridden before.

"If you need more—"

"Excuse me, Mister…?"

The man cleared his throat. "Name's Jack."

"Jack, thank you for the refresher." She kept her tone light and friendly. No need to offend the guy—she just wanted to get going. "I appreciate all the helpful tips, but I don't want to take any more of your time. I've ridden horses for almost fifty years."

On sabbatical from her teaching position at Vanderbilt University, Caroline wasn't looking for rules, restrictions, or instructions. She wanted freedom—freedom to set her own schedule, to do whatever she felt like doing when and where the urge struck. She wanted time on her own, and time to explore. And mostly to wipe the voice and face of the smarmy dean of Ecology and Earth Sciences from her mind. Starting right now.

Jack, the ranch hand helping her with the horses,

peered at her, and his ice-blue eyes seemed to register for the first time that he was talking to a person, not rehearsing some lines.

"I see." He handed her the reins then took a step back. "Stick to the roads and trails, and you'll be fine."

Grinning, Caroline placed a foot in the stirrup and swung onto the horse. "Exactly." When she adjusted the camera dangling around her neck, Jack's brows arched.

"Taking pictures, huh?"

"Oh, yes. Photography is a hobby of mine, and I'm combining that with my ecology background to create a book of nature essays. Maybe a low-budget documentary."

Jack let out a guffaw. "Can't imagine there'd be much material for you here, ma'am."

"Call me Caroline, please. I respectfully disagree, Jack. I can't wait to see some gorgeous sunsets and sunrises. And all the little details…grasses, dusty trails, cows, horses, fences." Her favorite subjects usually ended up being small details most people wouldn't even notice.

She studied Jack's tanned face, handsome in a weathered kind of way. Did those stunning blue eyes not see the beauty and art all around him? Maybe he hadn't been there long. Working on the ranch could be a retirement gig for him. Hard to tell, but she guessed him to be in his late fifties or early sixties. Perhaps he'd been there *too* long and didn't notice his surroundings anymore. That'd be sad.

"Not thinking of bringing a crew and a bunch of equipment out here, are you?"

Surprised that he wanted such details, Caroline shook her head. "Not at all. It's just me and my camera."

Today, she wanted to get the lay of the land, and note interesting nooks and crannies she might want to return to later. But she wanted the camera with her, just in case. So often, getting an amazing photo required some luck—right place, right time.

She needed this getaway. She was ready to embark on a new adventure of sensory overload—and she planned to document it all through the lens of her camera.

The small ranch a couple of hours from Dallas offered the quiet solitude she craved and possibly an opportunity to simply hang out with nature. She'd committed to renting a cabin for a week, with the option of extending to four. So far, the place looked promising. The charming cottage had everything she needed, including updated kitchen and bath, barbecue pit, porch, patio, and plenty of windows.

And according to the website, the ranch included acres of scenic open fields, a pond and small stream, a variety of wildlife, and fabulous sunsets. She'd already been greeted by stunning fields of bluebonnets, and she hoped at least a few monarch butterflies would pass through the property on their spring migration. At this moment, the waving tall grasses and chirping birds beckoned from outside the barn.

Jack tipped his unadorned black cowboy hat to her. "Have a good ride."

"Thank you."

Caroline watched Jack's lean form saunter away, his boots clacking against the barn's cement floor. With slightly bowed legs, probably from years of riding, and a plaid shirt tucked into well-fitted blue jeans, he seemed the quintessential cowboy. Funny, when she booked the ranch, she'd been thinking of nature and wildlife and somehow forgot about the people. She let her gaze linger on him a moment. Cowboys might make interesting subjects as well.

Caroline patted the horse and gave the signal to move forward, and her nature adventure officially began as they broke into the outdoors.

The dusty gravel road wound through the property for about three miles, she guessed, with several small trails and a couple of other rutted roads branching out on either side. Looked like most of the land lay to the east, though, and she scanned the fields that stretched like green carpet as far as she could see. Yellow and purple wildflowers, perhaps blooming weeds, dotted the roadside and some of the fields. A few high clouds floated above. Yes, indeed, she saw more than a few photo ops.

Caroline spent the entire afternoon riding the ranch. She knew she'd pay for the hours in the saddle later. Sure, she'd been riding since childhood, but hadn't actually been on a horse for several months, and her protesting thighs proved it. She planned to have a long, hot soak in the tub before bed to soothe any sore and out-of-shape muscles. She'd been thrilled to find the cabin bathroom had a full bath—to soak away dust and aches but also to rejuvenate and invigorate her soul.

As she retraced her path heading back to the barn, Caroline scanned the fields for a good resting spot. Moments later, she let out a gleeful squeal when she discovered the creek had turned and was maybe ten yards away.

She dismounted the horse and couldn't help

smiling at the sound of trickling water—one of her favorite sounds in the world. "This way," she crooned to Star. She led Star through the grasses then rested in the shade of a small cluster of trees. The early Texas spring had been one of the factors that lured her to the ranch. Here, leaves already swayed on the trees and wildflowers colored the fields. It'd be another month at least before Nashville got to this stage.

While Star lapped from the creek, Caroline drank from the extra bottle of water she'd brought. This morning, it'd been frozen. Now thawed, the cold water refreshed her, and she splashed a little on her face. Temperatures had soared in the late afternoon sun, above what she'd expected. She made a mental note to dress in layers tomorrow. And bring more snacks. The sun and fresh air made her hungry. She'd already gone through her nut mix and dried fruit.

Caroline let the horse graze a bit while she fished out her camera and snapped a few photos of the creek. Little more than a wide ditch at this point, the creek was nothing like the rushing brooks she hoped to capture in Colorado or upstate New York as she meandered her way across the countryside, but still waters offered their own sense of peacefulness.

She jotted down some thoughts in the small notebook she kept handy, then resumed her place on Star's back.

"Thank you for a lovely day," she told the horse as they entered the barn doors about an hour later. Dismounting, Caroline breathed in the heavy scent of fresh hay that permeated the barn and looked around for signs that a ranch hand was on deck. She heard only a soft whinny from around the corner. Someone had filled Star's troughs with water and hay. Caroline gave the horse a gentle pat, unsure whether she was responsible for brushing and unsaddling her. Jack's monologue hadn't contained any helpful instructions this morning.

For the horse's comfort, she removed the saddle and blanket and set them on the floor outside the stall, then led Star into the stall and gave her a quick brushing. That would have to do for now. If it was wrong, she'd do it differently tomorrow.

Too bad she couldn't leave the horse at the cabin. Her rental car, which had sat outside the barn all day, would be blazing hot by now. Outside, Caroline glanced toward the large house she'd passed coming in. The house was close enough to walk to from the barn, but not close enough to see activity there. To her right, her gaze landed on a garden plot enclosed in wire fencing. She loved a good garden—and admired anyone who could manage one. In all her years, her only real success had been a few potted tomatoes. Curious about what this rugged land would produce, she was tempted to look closer, but figured it wouldn't be appropriate to snoop around the owners' personal space.

Caroline jumped when something brushed against her. She looked down to find a gray cat pacing at her feet. "Well, hello there." She knelt to pet the cat, and glanced around the yard, expecting to find more. Didn't every farm or ranch have cats and dogs running around the place? Something about the barn cat made the place seem smaller, friendlier, and less imposing.

After giving the feline a quick scratch under the chin, Caroline headed for the car. She climbed inside, tossed her hat and backpack into the passenger seat, then rummaged through her bag and found a napkin to wrap around the steering wheel to keep from burning her hands. She turned the air conditioning to full blast, grateful she didn't have to hike back. The walk from barn to cabin wasn't far, but the road had a definite uphill grade.

As she approached the cheery cabin, she let out a deep, satisfied sigh. This place just might give her the head-clearing she needed. It was a start, anyway. Time to clean up and settle in for the evening. The wine already sat chilling in the fridge. She had a stack of books, plus her digital reader, and some of her favorite scented bath salts. And she'd find out if the ranch delivered on its promised amazing sunset.

****

Jack watched the trail of dust billow behind the car that had turned onto the road and figured the woman had finally returned the horse to the stable. He glanced at his watch. With only a few minutes to spare. Horses were due back in the barn by five o'clock. Roger had underestimated this particular renter—who claimed she'd been riding since childhood—and had already done the evening barn chores. Most visitors didn't keep a horse out longer than a couple of hours.

Jack swiped a hand across his brow and took another gulp of cold water before he placed his hat back on his head and strode to the barn. He found Star in her stall munching hay and looking no worse for the wear. In fact, looked as if the woman had taken the time to brush the horse before putting her away.

How much riding their guest had done, Jack couldn't be sure. Their paths hadn't crossed after the morning. He lifted the saddle she'd left on the floor and opened the tack room to put it away.

As he swung the saddle onto its shelf, the image of Caroline sitting in it popped into his head, and he nearly dropped the damn thing. He swore under his breath. She'd been sitting right there in the gentle curve of the leather. With heat creeping up the back of his neck, he shoved the saddle into place and turned away. That image he could do without. But he acknowledged the unexpected jolt to his system—and a stirring long dormant inside him.

The woman was attractive, he'd grant her that. But she'd been so uppity and impatient, those hazel eyes laughing at him. Had given him attitude when all he tried to do was make sure she'd be all right. He shook his head.

It'd been three years since he'd told Roger and Nora Wheaton, his right-hand man and his wife, they could fix up the cabins and rent them to vacationers. Most days, he regretted it, but he had little to do with the guests, and deliberately steered clear of them. This morning, he filled in for Roger to save time. He wouldn't make that mistake again. Either Roger could deal with her, or she could fend for herself.

At least she'd dressed appropriately in denims and proper boots. That was something. But pearls? He'd nearly laughed when he saw a short strand of pearls peeking from under the collar of her shirt. Her hat, while not a cowboy hat, had a wide brim and seemed to fit well. Never mind the silly red flower on the side that matched the red strap of her camera.

Taking pictures of grass and dusty trails? He shook his head again. Some people had too much time on their hands. For a hobby, fine. Whatever. But a book? Who would buy something like that? Not that it mattered. As long as she paid the rental fee, took good care of the horses, and stayed out of his way, he didn't need to worry about her or what she did with her time.

Something about her had rankled him, though, and he couldn't seem to put her out of his mind. He made a quick tour through the barn to make sure everything was in order, and stopped to check on Penny, their pregnant mare. The vet thought she had a couple more weeks, but Jack knew babies came in their own sweet time.

He pulled out his cell phone and texted Roger.

—*Star's in. I'm closing up for the night.*—

Blowing out his breath, Jack pulled the doors shut and turned toward the house.

Truth was, he didn't know how to act around women anymore. Did they want the assistance of a gentleman, or did they want to be independent and left alone? The cabins attracted a lot of solo travelers. He supposed the quiet space of the ranch with the security of being enclosed with few other people around made it a draw. With security at the main gates, the ranch was secure, safe. No pickpockets or traffic or terrorists lurking around. Good for people vacationing alone.

Sounded lonely to him. But who was he to talk? He spent a lot of time alone. Enjoyed his own company, but to travel alone? Especially a single woman? Didn't seem like a good idea.

Inside the house, Jack poured a couple fingers of his favorite bourbon. Leaning against the table, he took a drink—and grew aware of the stillness. The silence closed around him, reminding him of his own aloneness.

He gripped the glass hard and slammed back the remaining liquid, then pushed off from the table. He yanked open the door, hell-bent on doing something to occupy his mind. With quick, determined strides, he headed for the garden.

Before he could pick up a spade or bucket, his cell phone buzzed with a message from Roger.

—*You coming for dinner?*—

Hand on his hip, Jack drew in a deep breath. Nora and Roger extended the invitation almost every night, and Jack usually ended up at their place a couple of nights a week. He should've let Roger know so he didn't have to check. Wasn't fair to Nora.

If he went, he'd pass right by the Caroline woman's cabin. He'd rather not have another encounter. Besides, he wasn't feeling sociable, which meant he wouldn't be good company, and no reason to subject his friends to that.

—*Nah, I'm good here. Thanks, though.*—

Jack grabbed the spade and turned his attention to the garden. In early April, he was likely to get some new potatoes and the last of the beets. Already, a few tomatoes had ripened, thanks to some early warm weather. The seasons had changed quickly this year. He glanced toward the southeast corner of the house, where a wooden privacy fence atop a short stone wall enclosed the swimming pool. Probably time to get that opened.

He'd quit maintaining the pool for a couple of years when his daughter's visits had become infrequent due to work and having young children. Seemed pointless to keep it up just for himself. But his son and grandson, only a couple of hours away now, came out often, and Dylan enjoyed splashing around. As he dropped potatoes into a bucket, Jack made a mental note to follow up on that tomorrow.

Bucket in hand, he latched the fence that helped keep wildlife from devouring his crops, then returned to the house. He dumped the spuds into a bin then listlessly opened the refrigerator door and stared at the contents. He didn't feel like preparing anything. He wasn't even hungry. He closed the door and opened the freezer where he knew Nora had stocked any number of already-prepared meals. He reached inside and grabbed the first container of soup within reach.

For Jack, eating dinner was just another chore, part of the routine that had to get done. He washed up the few dishes then made himself a cup of coffee and took it out to the porch that stretched along the back of the house. As he sank into a chair, facing west, his thoughts turned to sunsets—and a certain woman interested in them.

Didn't look like tonight's display was going to be anything for the record books—or a photo book. No cloud formations to add interest. Would she be watching from the cabin? All she had to do was look out the front door. He thought of "the ledge," an outcropping of rock up behind the cabin. He'd bet money she'd notice it—without a doubt the best place on the ranch to watch the sun set.

A familiar pang wracked his chest. He and Rosalyn used to go… They'd watched so many sunsets from the ledge. After they had a glass of wine, he helped her down from the rock, and holding hands, they picked their way back along the faint trail they'd worn over the years. He swallowed hard. Sometimes it felt like yesterday, and some days, like today, it seemed a vague dream that had never been real.

Part of him hoped their renter wouldn't find her way up there, to that place that held so many memories. But from what he'd seen, the woman was adventurous enough to explore on her own. Would she be wanting a horse for an evening? Was she going to take off and wander the ranch alone at night? Jack rolled his neck then took a final swallow and emptied his mug as visions of her roaming around the property, twisting an ankle or tumbling off the ledge came to mind. And did he need one more thing to worry about?

Chapter Two

"Knock, knock!"

Caroline bolted upright at the sound of a woman's voice. A morning visitor? Quickly, she slipped her bare feet into her kick-around flip-flops. At the same time, she grabbed her sweater and attempted to shove her arms into the sleeves to cover her braless pajama shirt. Enjoying a quiet morning on the patio, she hadn't expected company.

A woman sporting stylish short gray hair and bright pink glasses that matched her blouse appeared in the yard carrying a wicker basket covered with a cherry red dishcloth.

"Caroline?" the woman asked. Flashing a wide smile, she approached the patio, hand outstretched.

"I, um, yes. I'm Caroline." She moved forward and grasped the woman's hand.

"Pleased to meet you. I'm Nora Wheaton, caretaker."

"Nora! Hello." Caroline returned the smile. "So nice to meet you. I was hoping I would. Can you sit for a minute?"

"I think I can sit for a spell. Thank you." Nora set the basket on the patio table then settled into the opposite chair.

"Let me get you something to drink. Coffee? Do you have time for a chat?" She wanted to pick Nora's brain and pick up an anecdote or two about the ranch to add some additional flavor to her essays.

"I'd love a cup of coffee if it's made."

Caroline grinned. "Got a whole pot."

"Just black," Nora told her.

Caroline returned with one of the ranch's sturdy mugs. "Here you go."

"Oh, thanks, hon."

Caroline returned to the cushioned wrought iron chair and curled up her legs. "Did you know your niece, Gabby, and my daughter, Lauren, are friends from college? Lauren Hendricks. I use my maiden name because that's how I was known professionally. We heard about the cabins for rent here on the ranch through Gabby."

"That's wonderful. We love word-of-mouth referrals."

"Same. Seems the girls belonged to the same sorority in college."

"Such a small world sometimes. What's your daughter doing now?"

"She does environmental-impact assessments for building projects. Sometimes for private businesses, sometimes for city governments."

"How fascinating." Nora leaned forward. "How are you liking the ranch so far?"

"Love it. Had a fabulous ride yesterday. Really spectacular. Perfect horse—once I managed to convince the ranch hand that I can ride. The guy was mansplaining me all about riding and swaggering around like he owned the place."

Nora's brows pulled into a puzzled frown, and Caroline belatedly realized she might be tattling, or worse, insulting a friend of Nora's. "Oops, sorry. That was tacky," Caroline apologized. "Never mind."

"No worries. We have a confident crew around here. Did he say his name?"

Caroline cringed. Now she didn't want to tell, but Nora was waiting for an answer. "Um, yeah. Jack. Older guy. Well…" She shrugged. "Probably about our age."

Nora burst out laughing.

Caroline cocked her head. "I missed the joke."

When she came up for air, Nora reached out and put a hand on Caroline's arm. "Oh, I needed that. You must mean Jack Armstrong. He was probably swaggering around like he owns the place because he does."

"What?" Caroline's mouth dropped open. "You're kidding. Why in the world would he be in the barn getting a horse ready for me? Aren't there ranch hands for that?"

"I'm sure he and my husband, Roger, talked about it, and Jack decided to help you since it was the weekend. The barn is a lot closer to the big house than our place, though Roger is technically in charge of overseeing the horses. We do have a few employees, but they work the ranch, not the rental business."

"I see. Well, Jack was thorough, I'll say that."

"Which horse did he give you?"

"Smaller one named Star. She was good, gentle, and responsive. And, thankfully, didn't want to stop and eat all day. Should I make a request to reserve her? If I'm going to be here a few weeks, it'd be nice to stick with a single horse so we can get used to each other."

"Right. I'll see what Roger says. The only problem

might be that Star is the horse Jack's grandson rides."

"Oh, really? So, the family lives here? Multiple generations?"

"No, no. Only when they visit. Jack's son, daughter-in-law, and grandson live in Dallas. They're here every couple of weeks or so. I'll check their schedule. I'm guessing they'll be here for a few days sometime while you're here, if you stay the full four weeks."

Like well-oiled gears, a memory clicked into place. Now she remembered Jack was the owner and had lost some family members in a car crash a few years back. Lauren had mentioned it when she told Caroline about the cabins. She'd have to look up the circumstances later, so she didn't accidentally put her foot in her mouth.

"Sure. Just let me know," she said. "I'm flexible." Caroline took a sip of coffee and caught a whiff of something sweet as a light breeze swept through. "What have you got in that basket? It smells heavenly."

Nora quickly set down her mug. "Oh, we need to get these out. Fresh eggs from my chickens, homemade cinnamon rolls, and a loaf of sunflower bread with honey butter. I love to bake."

"My word." Caroline nearly drooled over the tray of glazed rolls Nora waved in front of her face. "Those look amazing. Let me get utensils."

She made a second trip inside and returned with small plates, forks, and a knife. She intended to indulge, but she'd be cutting one of those sinful sugar-and-fat rolls in half.

The first bite went down smooth and easy. "Mmm. Absolutely delicious, Nora. Thank you so much."

"You're welcome. Now, I don't want to keep you if you have things to do."

"Not at all. This is lovely. Tell me more about the ranch."

"There's not much more than what we put on the website. It's a working ranch. Small staff. My husband's been working for Jack for years. His wife, Rosalyn, was my best friend until she died from a sudden heart attack." Nora's voice softened with sadness. "I guess it's been seven years now."

"Oh, I'm very sorry, Nora. So, he lives alone in the big house?" Caroline hadn't been inside, but passed the sprawling residence on her way in. It was a lot of house for one person. A sense of sympathy—and guilt—rolled over her. She should've kept her big mouth shut. Jack Armstrong had a lot on his shoulders besides getting horses ready for visitors. That explained his aloof, unaware behavior yesterday.

Interesting. She'd swear the man who helped her wore a wedding band.

Nora blew out her breath. "He does. I help with cooking and some housekeeping, but he's been alone a long time now. He'll go into town for supplies occasionally, but other than that, he hardly ever leaves the ranch."

"That's so sad. Maybe I should invite him for dinner." *Oh, brother.* The words had just popped out. He probably had a rule against fraternizing with the guests.

Nora's eyes widened. She opened her mouth as if to say something, then shut it again, and stared at Caroline.

Seconds ticked by.

"What? Doesn't he eat?" Caroline asked with a little chuckle.

"I— Well, of course he does. He...um...doesn't socialize much."

Caroline sensed Nora's uneasiness as the woman looked away and fidgeted with the buttons on her blouse. Perhaps Jack had withdrawn into a shell and didn't want to come out. Or maybe he was off limits. Fine. She hadn't come looking to socialize anyway. "Got it."

"Still..." Nora finally met her eyes. "You know, I think that's a nice idea. It's kind of you to suggest it. I'll warn you, though, I keep his freezer stocked pretty well, so don't be surprised if he says no."

"No worries. If he wants company, I'm sure the food in the freezer can keep. If not, that's okay, too."

Nora sat forward, rubbing her hands together as if struggling with her thoughts.

Caroline waited. Maybe she was treading into muddy waters and should mind her own business. Jack hadn't made any friendly overtures, and she certainly didn't need to take on a cause.

A moment later, Nora clapped her hands and shot Caroline a bright smile. "I leave it up to you. Now tell me, what's the news of the outside world?" She gave a light laugh. "I don't get out much either."

"But you've been here a long time. Do you love it?"

"Most days I do. I love being surrounded by the beautiful, wide-open space. There's always work to be done on a ranch, but I enjoy keeping busy. I've got my garden and my chickens. And it's a great place to raise a family."

"I appreciate the fresh eggs. Do you sell them? Or the produce from your garden?"

Nora shook her head. "No time for that. I've always got projects. Canning, knitting, cooking, you name it. Last fall I got Roger and the boys to build me a new chicken coop, and I just finished painting it pink and purple."

"Seriously?"

Nora's eyes sparkled. "Oh, yes. It's adorable. Looks like a chicken cottage." She leaned forward. "I make my own fun around here."

Her laugh was infectious, and Caroline joined in. Nora clearly had the right energy and personality for life on a ranch. "That sounds amazing. Can I see it from the road?"

"No, it's around back. That's the only way I could get away with it. You'll just have to come for coffee, and we'll sit out back."

"I'd love it."

Caroline settled into her chair and listened to Nora's tales of the ranch for almost an hour. Many of the stories were too personal for her book, but her account of the monarch butterfly migration sounded magical. Her enthusiasm spoke of a deep tie to the people and the place. And Caroline felt as if they'd been friends for years.

When a truck rumbling down the road interrupted their conversation, Nora rose. "I guess I've yammered on long enough." She lifted her mug and headed for the door.

Caroline followed then walked Nora to the front porch. "Hey, Nora?"

"Mm-hmm?"

"Stop by anytime you feel like company. You don't need to bring a thing. I've got tea and coffee. It's been fun chatting with you."

A smile spread across her face. "It sure has. Nice to have another woman-of-a-certain-age around. I'll see you soon." She turned back a second later. "Also, let's keep that earlier conversation between the two of us, okay? What I mean is, Jack doesn't need to know it ever happened. I think it might be nice for him to have some company, but I wouldn't want him to feel setup. I might suggest, but I don't push."

"I understand. My lips are sealed."

After Nora left, Caroline opened her laptop and did a quick Internet search on Jack Armstrong and the car accident. It probably wasn't any of her business, but she always felt better armed with more information rather than less.

A number of news stories populated her screen along with a few horrific photos. She swallowed hard and clicked on an article. What a terrible tragedy.

If she followed the reports correctly, Jack had suffered great loss. His daughter, son-in-law, and granddaughter were killed. His grandson, Dylan, was the only survivor. Jack's son, Reed, was assigned guardianship of the boy. Apparently the six-year-old had sustained some injuries. She hoped he'd healed in the three years since the accident. That Dylan could ride Star was a good sign. She'd gladly switch to a different horse.

Caroline couldn't stop shaking her head. She couldn't decide whether her next move should be to give Jack a wide berth or extend an invitation. Probably best to go about her business and see what the next few days brought. The information helped round out the picture of the ranch's owner, but those details weren't the kind of anecdotes she could put in her book.

****

On Tuesday, Caroline opted to drive rather than ride horseback. Driving would give her overworked legs a break and make it easier to take photos. Star had been great both days she'd ridden, but without a sure place to tie her up, she could easily wander off while Caroline was busy with the camera. Chasing down a runaway horse—or having to explain to its owner why she hadn't returned the horse—did not make her top-ten things-I-want-to-do list. She could only imagine Jack Armstrong's disdain.

She kept the car at a crawl along the main road, watching for the "road" that led to the pond. Bracing herself for the bumps and shimmies, she turned the car and hopped out to unlatch the gate. After she drove over the threshold, she shut the gate and then jostled across the field, hoping she didn't have any close encounters with cows. She wouldn't mind seeing them, but she didn't care to be in the same pasture with them. This time of year, surely a few calves had been born on the ranch. And baby close-ups were always cute, no matter the species. Would it be presumptuous to ask Jack or Roger if she could tag along for a few pictures? Maybe she'd drop a hint and see what happened.

She parked the car then set up her folding chair— another advantage to driving—and grabbed her camera, backpack, and brown-bag lunch. All around, birds chirped and insects buzzed, signaling she'd found a good spot. Today was all about them and their watery habitat. When a dragonfly zipped past Caroline and skimmed the surface of the pond, she shoved her half-eaten apple into the bag. Looked like a Great Blue Skimmer, one of the earliest spring species.

Crouching in the grass, she steadied the camera on her knee and snapped photos in rapid succession as the bright-blue insect put on a spectacular show. When the dragonfly moved on, Caroline traipsed through the grasses around the pond where cattails and other water-loving plants offered one photo opportunity after another.

"This is amazing," Caroline said to no one but herself. "Exactly what I envisioned."

Pleased with what she'd captured, Caroline scanned the vast fields for her next location. Maybe a little farther up the road, closer to that rocky area. She packed up her things, tossed them into the backseat, then rounded the back of the car—and came to a dead stop.

She knew that sound.

Heart pounding, she slowly turned her head in the direction of the sound, careful not to make any sudden movement. *Oh, holy mother of nature.* There it was. Looking straight at her. Pointed straight at her. Coiled, and ready to strike. She'd seen rattlesnakes before, but never up close and personal in the wild—alone. She'd already tossed her bag in the car, but if the snake struck, and hit skin, she could reach the kit before she passed out. *Breathe, Caroline.* This situation demanded patience, and she forced herself to stay calm. All the dozens of "Keep Calm and whatever" memes she saw regularly on social media ran through her mind, and hysterical laughter almost bubbled to the surface. Keep Calm and what? Wait for the snake to calm down?

Pretty much.

In slow motion, as stealthily as possible, she raised the camera still dangling around her neck. She had to try to get this image. Thankfully, her shutter was set to silent. Caroline focused the frame and hardly took her finger off the shutter button, snapping frame after frame. Finally, the snake pulled back a little. She held her breath as the tail relaxed. After what seemed like hours, but was probably seconds, the snake slithered into the grass away from her.

On quaking legs, she yanked open the car door then sank into the driver's seat. She grabbed her water bottle and practically guzzled the remaining liquid. With that little episode still giving her shudders, she considered calling it a day, but after several deep breaths, she started the car and put it in gear. The rocks loomed just ahead. Might as well check out the area while she was close by. She took a moment to regroup before getting out, then reached for the camera to check her shots. Could anything possibly be in focus?

Caroline gasped as the photos loaded on the back screen. *Oh, yeah.* The shots were worthy of publication—and the several minutes of sheer terror the poisonous beast had put her through.

****

Jack spotted the car first. But as the road curved around the creek, he saw the woman. He watched as she set up a tripod then pulled a bag from her car. No equipment, huh?

She tossed off the hat she'd worn the day they'd met and moved up to the camera, hair blowing around her.

He signaled Charlie, his trusted Appaloosa, to

move forward. As far as Jack could tell, she was taking pictures of rocks. He didn't much care what she was doing, but he wanted her to know he saw her and all the stuff she had strewn about.

As they approached, she turned, shading her eyes with her hand.

Jack tipped his hat. "Afternoon, ma'am. I understood you weren't bringing equipment." He wished he knew her last name so he could address her properly. Ma'am seemed too formal but using her first name didn't feel right.

"Good afternoon, Jack. It's Caroline. Do you mean the tripod?"

What else would he mean? He nodded toward her set-up.

"I understood you didn't want a crew of people and video equipment. All I have is a single tripod for a single camera used by a single person. It helps steady my hand." She held up a hand and added with a light laugh, "I prefer my pictures to be in focus." She gestured toward the rock. "These little guys move so fast."

Jack squinted. "What guys?"

"I've got three or four lizards running around here."

"Ah." Jack adjusted on the horse, feeling a bit foolish. Probably best to move on and leave her to it.

"I got a great shot of a rattler a while ago."

Alarm pulsed through him. "You did? A rattlesnake here on the ranch?"

"Yes. It was amazing, but a little…rattling. Pun intended."

She let out that soft chuckle again.

"I admit it gave me a scare for a minute, but after a short standoff, we gave each other our space and went our separate ways. Want to see?"

She fiddled with the camera a moment, and Jack was compelled to swing down from the horse. *He did want to see.*

When she held it toward him, he peered into the back of her camera, and found the cold-blooded face of a rattlesnake staring at him at close range. "God almighty." His heart bounced. He turned his gaze back to the woman beside him—and wondered if the ranch had adequate insurance to keep her on the property.

She'd captured one hell of a shot. The snake, obviously alerted to her presence, sat tensed, partially hidden beneath a rock, but its rattle erect and sending the telltale warning to the intruder.

"What do you think?" Caroline asked.

Jack shook his head. He couldn't say what he really thought in the presence of a lady. He blew out his breath. "Caroline, we try to keep our guests out of harm's way on the ranch and would appreciate it if you'd help us out in that regard by not doing something foolish. How close were you?"

The hand she placed on his arm sent unexpected—and unwelcome—jolts of heat through Jack.

"Don't worry. It's a long lens. I wasn't as close as it might seem. Ten feet away, I suppose. Also, if it gives you any comfort, I carry a snake kit in my backpack. And I know how to use it."

Disbelief rolled through Jack. That sounded like a line of bull to him. He stared hard. He'd better make sure they had a fresh supply of the kits just in case. It'd been a while since he'd seen a rattlesnake around.

"Remember?" Caroline prompted. "I'm a biologist. I've taught biology and ecology at Vanderbilt University for twenty-five years. Technically, I'm Dr. Tate."

She added a saucy smile that crinkled around her warm eyes.

Caught off guard, Jack cleared his throat. "No, I don't think you mentioned that." The information explained the hint of arrogance in her attitude. Well, fine. No need for him to worry about her then. "Very good. I should let you get back to your picture taking."

He put his left foot into the stirrup and swung his right leg over Charlie's back.

"Hey, Jack."

He would've moved along had she not called to him. Instead, he turned back. She didn't seem to have any trouble with his first name. In fact, it rolled from her lips as if they were old friends. He squirmed in the saddle. "Yes?"

She dusted her hands against her jeans before meeting his eyes. "I understand you're all alone in the big house. Would you have dinner with me tonight? I'd love to learn more about the ranch."

A hot flush crept to Jack's collar. She had to be kidding. Who had she been talking to? And why would he want to have dinner with her? Sweat rolled down the back of his neck. Because he could use the company? And she was an attractive, interesting woman?

She glanced at her watch. "I'm ready to wrap up here. It's been a full day, for sure. Want to say around six-thirty?"

He hadn't said yes.

"I've got coffee, iced tea, and wine. So, if there's

something else you'd prefer to drink, feel free to bring that along. Otherwise, I've got it covered."

Jack almost laughed. Sounded as if she didn't expect him to say no—or wasn't taking no for an answer. Speech still evaded him as she began loading her things into the car. The polite thing to do would be get off the horse and help, but by the time he thought of it, she'd almost finished.

He cleared his throat. "Why don't I go ahead and open the gate for you?"

Shielding her eyes, she looked up at him with a smile. "That'd be great, thanks."

He turned and led Charlie to the gate at the road, then waited a couple of minutes for Caroline to arrive. And in that time, his foggy brain hadn't come up with one plausible excuse to decline her invitation.

As she approached the gate, she rolled down her window and waved. "See you at the cabin at six-thirty."

Lifting his hat, he nodded. What had he gotten himself into?

Chapter Three

Jack was still kicking himself for his backbone collapse when he arrived at the cabin for dinner. But resigned to his commitment, he climbed out of his truck and stood straight, squaring his shoulders. Not that big of a deal. He could eat dinner and talk about the ranch—whatever that meant—then go home.

Caroline opened the door at his second knock. Her thick straight hair, a natural-looking mix of gray and shades of blonde, was pulled back from her face, and she'd changed into a bright green shirt and scarf. She looked...soft...and casual, relaxed.

She greeted him with a wide smile. "Hey, Jack. Come on in."

He held out the plastic bag in his hands. "Brought you some potatoes from the garden."

She stepped back to allow him inside. "Fantastic, thank you. Nothing better than fresh produce. I've got some asparagus marinating. And I see you brought your own beverage."

"It's what I usually have in the evenings." No reason not to. In fact, he appreciated that she'd suggested it when she spelled out the options earlier.

"Well, let's get you a glass. I just poured myself some wine."

He took the glass and poured a moderate amount of the mid-grade bourbon. Just enough to take the edge off for now.

As soon as he lifted the glass, Caroline tapped hers against it.

"Cheers!"

"Cheers," he murmured, aware that his voice sounded strained and awkward.

Caroline turned and gestured toward the back door. "Want to sit outside? I started the grill a few minutes ago."

"Sure." Grilling was a good sign. He could eat almost anything grilled. Jack followed behind, glancing around the cabin at the same time. Seemed to be in good shape. Though he owned them, he seldom ventured inside the two rentals on the property that once housed married workers. Roger and Nora handled the maintenance and upkeep. He didn't mean to snoop, but he noted a stack of books on the side table and a vase of wildflowers, probably picked from the fields, on the counter. Looked like Caroline had settled in just fine.

"Have a seat while I check the temp on the grill. I've got chicken kabobs. Hope that's good with you."

"Sounds fine. What can I do to help?"

She waved a hand. "Nothing at all. Please, have a seat and relax. My camera's on the table if you want to take a look at what I've shot so far."

When she picked up the camera and moved in close, Jack stiffened. What happened to tending to the grill? He'd prefer some personal space, but he shoved his free hand in his pocket, and watched while she turned the camera over and adjusted the settings to load the images.

"Hit this button to flip through," she said.

"Got it." At least it'd give him something to do. He started through the pictures but kept an eye on Caroline as she went back inside and returned with a platter of colorful kabobs.

"Like I said earlier," Caroline told him as she placed the skewers on the grill. "The ranch is full of amazing photo opportunities."

"You have a sharp eye for detail."

"Thanks. It's been really fun. It'll be hard to narrow down the images and choose the ones for a book."

"You've already sold the proposal?"

"I'm pretty sure the university press will publish it." She laughed as she spoke. "They almost have to. I'm a tenured professor."

Her laughter seemed to bubble into the air. Sometimes women as vivacious as Caroline had loud, cackling laughs that set his teeth on edge like nails to a chalkboard. Hers was light and…he searched for a word…happy.

"Nice position to be in," he said. Jack continued looking through the photos while Caroline moved back inside, and he found himself visualizing the finished product. He reversed his earlier opinion. Her thoughts and expert insights combined with the nice photos would probably make an interesting book.

A few minutes went by before she joined him outside again.

"Speaking of photos, I'd love to get some pictures of little calves. This is the season, right?"

"Sure. We've got twenty-three."

"Really? May I see them?"

"They're in the south pasture now, farther from the

main road. You'd need to take the far cut-off and go left about a mile."

"Would you mind?"

He hesitated while a dozen unpleasant scenarios blasted through his brain. Surely, she wouldn't go into the field with the cattle. So far, she'd proven herself smart, but… But he'd agreed that guests had access to all roads on the ranch. "No, that's fine. Just don't cross any fences. For your safety," he added.

Her brows shot up. "Something tells me you don't completely trust me not to break the rules, Jack Armstrong."

He had to laugh. So much for his poker face. "Not completely sure you have a healthy appreciation for the potential dangers of the ranch, that's all."

"I promise I'll be careful. Are the calves scattered all over?"

"No. We keep the moms and calves in one area. We're out there every day right now making sure they don't get separated from each other. Gotta keep a close watch on them when they're first born. At night, they go into a safe pasture that's got an electric fence around it to protect them from coyotes."

"Oh, dear. Is that a big problem?"

"Big enough to worry about."

"How do you know which baby goes with which momma?"

"They know. Plus, they have matching ear-tags."

"Oh. You've already tagged them all? Not sure I'd want that for a picture."

"We do that as soon as they're born."

"Ouch. Does it hurt them?"

"Nah. It's just a little poke. Happens fast. Kind of

31

like getting your ears pierced."

"Hmm. We'll see." She turned her attention to the grill. "Almost ready. Would you prefer iced water or tea with dinner?"

"Water's fine, thanks."

"Let's eat inside so we don't have to battle the bugs."

"Good idea." He stood, and she handed him a plate. "Would you put these on the table?"

When he glanced at the plate, his mouth watered. The chicken held a golden glaze on the outside, and a hint of crispness along the lines where it had rested against the grill. "These look great," he told her.

"Let's hope they taste that way, too."

Caroline followed with another plate and something wrapped in tin foil, leaving Jack to stand awkwardly while she bustled around the kitchen area.

He glanced at the square table, relieved to see she'd put the two place settings opposite each other.

She added a platter of asparagus and a steaming bowl of wild rice to the table, then handed Jack a glass of water. "I think we're ready. Have a seat."

He stepped up to the table and pulled out a chair. "After you."

She looked up at him with surprise on her face. "Well, thank you."

Maybe she appreciated the gesture, or maybe she found it silly. To him, it was automatic, but her reaction made him feel old—old-fashioned, anyway. He sighed inside. He was set in the ways of a different time.

Jack filled his plate with food, suddenly eager to dig in. Each item looked done to perfection. From all appearances, Caroline was a woman of many talents.

He waited for her to take a bite, then popped a hunk of chicken into his mouth. And savored it.

"This is excellent," he told her.

"Thank you. I'm glad you like it. Thanks for joining me tonight, Jack. I enjoy cooking, but don't do much these days. Cooking for one is often too much trouble."

"I know what you mean." Jack swallowed a few more bites while he tried to think of some interesting conversation starter. "Where are you going next for your photo project?"

She swished the wine around in her glass a moment, then took a sip. "Not sure yet. I'm debating whether to do regions of the U.S. or divide the book into a couple of sections and maybe do land and water. I could go to the lake areas in Minnesota or the Finger Lakes region in New York. And, of course, a beach. I'll probably head to a beach next. I need some sun and sand time where I can sit and read, recharge."

"You prefer beach to a pool then?"

"Love them both. I'll look for a place on the beach that also has a pool."

"Our pool man's coming tomorrow to open ours."

Her eyes widened. "Really? There's a pool on the ranch? I don't remember seeing that on the website. Where is it?"

Jack groaned inside. Why did he even mention it? "It's, well, it's at my place."

"Oh." She gave a light laugh. "Got it. Not for guests."

"We don't advertise it for guests." Jack wished he'd kept his mouth shut. But he couldn't back down now. "No lifeguard, but there's no reason you couldn't use it if you'd like."

She looked at him thoughtfully over the rim of her glass.

"Do you mean that? I'd love to, if you're sure. But I don't want to cause any issues."

He shook his head. "It's my pool. My invitation." He winced inside, hoping the words hadn't come off as pompous and arrogant as they sounded.

She flashed him a wide smile.

"Well, thank you, Pool Czar. Let me know if there are any dos and don'ts or times you keep it for yourself. I don't want to be in the way."

Jack caught his breath as an image of Caroline in a swimsuit popped into his head and wouldn't budge. He took a big gulp of water. "Come whenever you like."

"Do you like the beach, too, or is the pool more your style?" she asked.

Jack shrugged, but memories crashed in. Memories of taking a moonlit dip with Rosalyn...and friends visiting around the pool deck. He looked down at his almost empty plate—maybe he should go before this got any more personal. But Caroline was looking at him expectantly.

"Didn't get to the beach. Running a ranch is a twenty-four-seven deal. Hard to take vacations." Why did everything she asked remind him of what he missed so much it hurt deep in his bones or make him wonder if they'd done enough for the kids? They'd had a lot of great family times, but not a lot of family vacations.

"Of course. What about now? Any trips on your bucket list?" Standing, she reached for his plate.

"Now?" He rolled his glass between his palms. "Doesn't seem to be much point now."

Plates still in her hands, Caroline swung around and stared at him.

"Are you serious? What about retirement? You don't have a bucket list? Things you want to see or do, places to go before you die?"

She looked at him as if he'd sprouted a third eye.

"Not really. Travel was never important to me, and now, well, without my wife…" he let his voice trail off.

"I understand," she said softly. "My husband died ten years ago. I wasn't sure about traveling on my own at first. It took some time to get comfortable with it. I did my first solo trip, a safari, with a group from Vanderbilt. For that, I was glad to have a professional guide, but I have to say, I discovered I had a different agenda than most of the other people."

With a quick hike of her shoulders, she gave a sassy grin. "I like doing my own thing on my own schedule."

Jack couldn't help laughing. "I can see how you would."

"You know, if you don't want to travel alone, there are all kinds of group excursions you could look into."

Did she not hear him say travel wasn't important to him? "Sure, but I'm not looking to go anywhere." He hid his scowl behind his glass but couldn't help an edge to his voice.

"Ah. Well, to each his own, of course. I've got a couple of ice cream choices for dessert. Pistachio-almond or a vanilla-caramel-swirl with walnuts. Which would you like?"

He didn't need dessert at all, but he couldn't decline her expectant smile. Besides, a little ice cream didn't sound half bad. "Whichever you're having is fine."

"Anyway," she continued. "I have a long list of places I want to go—and it keeps growing." She withdrew an ice cream scoop from a drawer and gave a light laugh. "Guess I caught the travel bug. I want to sit on a hill in Italy and watch the sun set, and I want to hang out on the French Riviera with a glass of wine."

She set a bowl of caramel ice cream in front of him. "That'll come later, after I visit some of these places in the States."

He stared at her. "You're going to do all that by yourself?"

For the first time, her smile faltered, and her eyes became distant.

"Well, I don't know. Maybe. My daughter travels a lot for work, and I've got friends who enjoy traveling. I like a good girls' trip occasionally. The thing is, I've been tied to a calendar and schedule for a lot of years. I reached my career goal of achieving tenure, and I've helped others achieve their goals. Much of the traveling my husband and I did before his death was related to his business." Her glance flicked back to Jack. "This might sound selfish, but honestly, I'm ready to do my own thing."

"Not at all. Sounds like it's your turn," Jack said. He'd hardly taken two bites of his ice cream while he listened to Caroline talk. Her words made him wonder if Rosalyn had ever regretted being tied down on the ranch. She'd never said so. Would the two of them have taken up traveling if she were still alive? Nora and Roger had begun taking some trips in the last few years. Guess they'd hit that stage. He swallowed hard, imagining the four of them going on vacation together if Rosalyn hadn't died. No doubt in his mind they'd have had some fun times. They always had, even doing simple things like playing cards at the ranch on a Saturday night.

He took an oversized bite and let the brain-freeze crowd out those thoughts. It did no good to dwell on the what-ifs.

Caroline pushed aside her bowl and leaned forward. "Jack, I should probably tell you I know about your wife's death and the accident that took your daughter and granddaughter. I'm so sorry for your losses. And please know we weren't gossiping—it came up when Nora and I were talking about the horses, and I said I hoped I could continue to ride Star. She told me Star is the horse your grandson likes."

Jack didn't even try to speak. The sympathetic sincerity in Caroline's voice and eyes clogged his throat. Nodding, he picked up both bowls and carried them to the kitchen sink. While he appreciated her honesty and candor, her eyes seemed to penetrate right into his soul, leaving him raw and exposed.

A moment later, she placed his glass on the counter and reached for the bottle of wine. "Why don't we check out tonight's sunset?"

Jack drew in a deep breath. He needed some space. "I think it's probably time for me to get on home."

"Well, thank you for a lovely evening, Jack. I enjoyed the company." Picking up her glass, she walked with him toward the front door. "Oooo, look at that," she said as she stepped onto the porch. "It's going to be a pretty one."

Jack glanced at the westward sky, the sun already dropping toward the horizon. Several lines of purple clouds streaked like runways through the deepening orange-and-pink palette. He stopped short. Caroline was right. And there was nothing he needed to rush home for. "Just a minute," he told her.

He retraced his steps and poured himself a fresh bourbon, then joined Caroline on the porch again.

Her brows lifted, but she offered a smile and waved toward the west. "See? How could anyone resist that?"

Jack set down his glass and lifted one of the rocking chairs. "Let's sit out here so the porch railing doesn't block the view." *The view*. He practically bit his tongue to keep from mentioning the ledge. He moved the other chair to the grassy area in front of the cabin, and motioned Caroline to sit before he could change his mind again and bolt.

The still evening enveloped them, and Jack absorbed the peacefulness. The only sounds were the constant buzzing of the seasonal insects and the occasional clinking of ice cubes in Jack's glass. In his peripheral vision, he saw Caroline sip her wine. She seemed content to watch the transformation of the sky without conversation.

The hues changed from vibrant pinks and orange to dusty blue and finally a deep cerulean. Each new phase garnered quiet oohs and aahs from his companion.

Minutes later, when the sky grew dark, she turned toward Jack and let out a long breath. "That was spectacular."

"It was, indeed. You didn't take any pictures."

She waved a hand. "There'll be another one, I'm sure." She reached for his glass. "I'll take that. And let me get your bourbon."

A vague disappointment settled in Jack's stomach. Of course, the alcohol belonged to him, and she probably wouldn't touch the stuff, but for some reason, it bothered him. As if he were "taking his toys and going home." And wouldn't be invited again.

He moved the chairs back to their place on the porch and accepted the bottle when Caroline returned. "Thanks for dinner," he told her. "I had—" He cleared his throat. "I had a nice time."

"Me, too. I'll probably see you around the barn or out on the road."

Jack nodded. "Take care, now. Especially if you go see those calves."

He sounded stiff and formal, but he couldn't help it. They were barely acquaintances. In a few weeks, she'd be gone, and he'd likely never see the woman again. What more was there to say?

Chapter Four

The next morning, Caroline stood on the back patio, coffee in hand, and pondered her options for the day. She'd missed the sunrise, but the sky still held an early pinkish hue, and a soft breeze whispered against her skin. If she wanted to catch Jack or any other ranchers working with the cows—she hesitated to call them cowboys, as that conjured a whole different image—morning was her best bet.

She figured it would be twelve to twenty-four hours after the service man arrived before the pool was usable. If the temperatures stayed this warm all week, she'd be ready for a refreshing dip. For now, she'd drive into the pasture areas and see if she could find the calves. Riding and taking photos at the same time turned out to be difficult. Without knowing how close she'd be able to get to the animals, she'd need all her camera lenses on hand.

Loading the car took only a few minutes, but she still needed to get herself put together. Even on a dusty ranch in the middle of nowhere, she had her standards. She slathered sunscreen over her face then reached for foundation. Only a little, and some powder... Caroline laughed at herself. Okay, maybe she anticipated running into the "cowboys" today and didn't want to resemble a scarecrow.

****

If the men were working in the same field where the calves grazed, she'd love to get pictures of them, too. She could decide later whether to include the cowboy species in the book. She remembered Jack's hesitation last night when she asked about photographing the calves. She needed a low-key approach—that meant staying out of the way.

Moments later, she pulled the car onto the main road and jostled over the gravel ruts toward the pastures. Last night, Jack told her to go to the far road, but how would she know which one was farthest unless she went to the very end? She should've asked for more details. Or, he could have offered some. Maybe a landmark? Or why not number the turn-offs? She couldn't help wondering if he'd neglected the specifics on purpose.

No, that wasn't fair, she chided herself. Though the man had a curmudgeonly shell, he'd been polite and gentlemanly at dinner last night. Almost friendly. She had no reason to believe he'd do anything underhanded. Besides, he was pretty direct.

Caroline drove past the first road, straining to remember any other details Jack had mentioned, then resigned herself to driving to the far gate and counting the number of roads in between. Turned out there were only two others. Muttering, she pulled the car around and started down what she hoped was the correct road—or rutted trail to be more precise. By the time she returned the rental car, it might need some service.

She scanned the fields on either side of the road and saw a whole lot of nothing. She'd have to get out and walk to discover where the cows and calves were. Movement to the left attracted her attention, and she stopped the car. There, only a short distance from the fence stood a small black calf. Caroline lifted her camera and climbed out of the car.

"Hey, cutie," she called softly to the calf. "Where's your momma?" She remembered Jack's goal of keeping the babies with their mothers. The calf looked in her direction but showed neither fear nor interest and didn't budge from its spot. Shading her eyes, Caroline wandered up the road a bit in search of the mother. No luck. The poor little thing. Back at the fence, she squatted close and snapped a few frames. From this angle the ear tag didn't show, which was best for her pictures, but if she reported the lone calf to Jack, she'd better make sure she had the details. She moved farther down until she could see the tag then zoomed in on the ear until the number was legible. Little number twelve gave a pitiful sound that could hardly be called a "moo."

"Come here, sweetheart," Caroline coaxed. "Are you out here all alone? How 'bout we call you Lona? Or Lola?"

The calf took a couple of steps and bleated again. Caroline took more pictures while the young animal looked right at her.

"You're going to have to get louder if you want Momma to hear, Lola girl." Again, she scanned the fields. No other cows, and no cowboys. With a heavy sigh, she stood and returned to the car. She'd better see if she could find someone to help the creature, probably still nursing.

After another mile or so, several more cows dotted the field. That didn't seem too far out of range for the little one. Still, Caroline would feel terrible if the poor thing died and she could've helped. She stopped the car and climbed out again. She took the next curve on foot and spied two men among the cattle inside the fence.

She couldn't see their faces, but one looked like Jack's silhouette. And she thought she recognized the horse he'd ridden yesterday.

"Jack!" she called. "Hey, Jack!" No response. She took off her hat and climbed on the lowest rail of the fence, waving the hat in the air. "Jack!"

The other man turned, shaded his eyes, and said something to Jack, who immediately looked her direction. He started toward her.

As he came closer, Caroline saw his mouth was set, and he didn't look pleased to be interrupted. Well, too bad. She figured he'd want this news.

"Caroline. Do you need something?"

At least he'd taken to calling her by her first name, though the addition of the Texas drawl took some getting used to. He drew out the third syllable as if he were singing the popular Neil Diamond song. She almost expected to hear *bomp, bomp, bomp* after her name.

"Good morning!" she called. "Hey, I want to take some pics, but first I wanted to let you know that I saw a calf back a ways." She jerked her thumb back toward the road. "I know you said you wanted to keep the moms and babies together, but I didn't see the momma."

Jack's eyes narrowed as he looked west. "You sure?"

As if she didn't know what a calf looked like? "Um, yeah. I even have proof." She held up her camera. "Want to see?"

Darlene Deluca

He stared at her. "Did you get the tag number?"

She flashed him her best no-duh look. "Number twelve." She found the photo and held it up to him.

"Well, damn. Didn't realize one had wandered off. We've been dealing with another one reluctant to nurse." His gaze rested on her for a moment before his lips turned in a wry smile. "Good work."

A silly jolt of pleasure shot through Caroline. Well, now. She'd just received a compliment from Jack Armstrong, and she guessed him to be stingy with those.

"Thanks. Mind if I take my reward in photos?" She was sure his lips twitched, but this time he held back a smile.

"Can you take them from that side of the fence?"

"I'll see what I can do." The long lens would probably work. No need to antagonize the man. Although she had to admit she rather enjoyed nudging the stoic Jack Armstrong out of his well-worn comfort zone. The man was in desperate need of lightening up.

She was about to take her leave and let him deal with the lone calf when the other man drew his horse toward them. As he came nearer, Caroline could see he looked about the same age as Jack. Weren't there any young men on the place? Ranching was hard, physical work.

The man brought the horse to a stop then tipped his hat. "Howdy, ma'am."

Caroline barely kept from laughing. She felt as though she'd stumbled into an old John Wayne movie. "Good morning." She offered a polite smile and looked at Jack for an introduction.

It took him a minute to figure that out.

"Uh, Caroline, this is the ranch manager, Roger. I believe you've met his wife, Nora."

"Oh, of course. Nice to meet you, Roger."

The man's eyes lit up. They held a sparkle that was sorely missing in Jack's eyes. But Roger had sweet Nora, and they'd begun traveling. Those two things must make his life fuller and happier than his taciturn friend's.

Roger regarded her for a long moment before his glance flickered to Jack then back to her. "Hope you're enjoying your stay."

"Absolutely. It's beautiful country, and the cottage is lovely, thank you."

He nodded. "You be sure and holler if you need anything."

Before she could respond, Jack motioned to the other field. "Looks like we got a straggler separated from the herd and its mother."

"That so? I better give it a look-see." Roger tipped his hat at Caroline and turned the horse away.

"Pasture's all yours," Jack told her. With a word to his horse, he also turned and trotted after Roger.

Midday lighting wasn't ideal, but Caroline couldn't resist a few cowboy shots. She raised her camera and snapped several of the two riders. Only took a moment for Jack to catch up with Roger, and the two rode side by side. She wondered if Jack had mentioned to Roger that he'd had dinner with her. Probably not. She'd bet he kept all personal information close to his chest.

She snapped a few more frames then turned her attention to the cattle and their babies. Less complicated subject matter.

****

"Nora told me about the new visitor in cabin one," Roger said over his shoulder when Jack caught up. "Said she was a nice lady. Guess she forgot to mention the gal was quite a looker, too."

Jack refused to take the bait. He adjusted his hat and scanned the horizon for the missing calf.

"She seems awfully friendly," Roger continued. "Sharp eye, too. Nice of her to tip us off about that lost calf."

With a shake of his head, Jack swore under his breath. He would not put up with this nonsense for long. Spring had obviously touched his friend with fever.

"I hear she might stay for a whole month. That's long enough to get a feel for—"

Finally, Jack swiveled in his saddle. "Could you shut the hell up? We've got work to do." He signaled Charlie and picked up the pace, brushing past Roger and his horse. But he still heard his friend's low chuckle. A dark thought clouded Jack's mind. Was this a setup? Had Nora deliberately set out to find a single woman to rattle his cage?

He'd never gotten crosswise with Nora, and didn't want to now, but he wouldn't let anyone meddle in his personal life. She'd been Rosalyn's best friend. Why would she— Jack heaved a sigh. Of course, she missed Rosalyn, but she probably missed having a female friend on site, the camaraderie of a woman. Her boys were grown and had moved away. He hadn't considered it before, but maybe the cabin guests helped fill a void for Nora. After all she'd done for him, he'd let it go—for now.

His cell phone buzzed in his pocket, and he paused

a moment to look at it. A text from Reed.

—*Looks like we can get away early and be there Friday afternoon.*—

Good timing. The pool would be ready, and their presence might save him from any awkward encounters with the ranch guest. It wasn't that he disliked the woman. In fact, he admitted she had some intriguing qualities. But those were of no particular interest to him. He wasn't looking for a date, for Pete's sake. He'd had the love of his life for thirty-five years. And that was that. He'd been smitten with Rosalyn Billings since the day she'd slipped into the empty desk beside his in tenth-grade homeroom. And he'd understood long ago that she was irreplaceable.

He glanced over at Roger. "Let me answer this message, then let's get moving."

—*Sounds good.*—

"Damn, Jack, look at this." Roger clicked his tongue and moved the horse to a canter.

Jack followed and saw the black lump lying in the thick grass. Adrenaline rushed through him as they closed the last few yards to the cow on its side. Jack swung down from Charlie and rushed to the cow. "Better call Doc," he told Roger.

He quickly examined the cow. Still alive. He pulled out his cell phone. "I'll call. You get the truck and bring water. Fast."

Roger mounted his horse.

"And have Denny bring a bottle for the calf," Jack shouted after him.

Roger signaled with a hand in the air as he sprinted in the other direction.

****

Caroline straightened at the sound of hooves beating on the ground. She turned to see Roger and his horse barreling across the field. As they passed her, she gaped and held onto her hat. What in the world? Dust filled the air and, coughing, she quickly closed her mouth. That didn't look good. She sensed an emergency with the calf and its mother.

Her glance followed horse and rider toward the building in the distance, a working utility building, she guessed. She wasn't a veterinarian, but she'd spent time on her grandparents' farm and had a background in biology, so she knew a little something about animals. Should she offer to help? If nothing else, she could hold onto a horse or fetch supplies or hold a bottle to feed the baby if necessary. Maybe—

"Don't be ridiculous," she muttered. These men had worked this ranch for decades. They were experts in animal husbandry and knew all about their livestock. The last thing they'd want is some big-city stranger in the way no matter how well-intentioned. She shook her head and dusted her hands on her jeans. She knew from personal experience that men like Jack Armstrong didn't take kindly to unsolicited help or advice— especially from women.

What was she thinking trying to get involved, anyway? She'd come to Texas for wide-open spaces, to be surrounded by peace and nature. The best thing for her to do was simply stay out of the way.

She turned to make her way back to the car. A moment later, a truck bounced onto the road and sped past her. When another truck followed, spitting gravel into the air, she flattened against the fence and tugged down the brim of her hat. She let out another cough. Of all the potential dangers on the ranch, being in the way of the cowboys seemed to be the most hazardous.

Flapping a hand to wave away the fog of dust in the air, Caroline headed for her car. This time, she watched the road closely so she could swerve to avoid the bigger ruts. At the cabin, she climbed out and scanned the sky. The cloud formations hinted at a great sunset ahead. This might be the best evening for one so far. Inside, she kicked off the dusty boots and headed straight for the bathtub. First, a long soak, then a light dinner and a fabulous sunset.

She hoped the cow crisis would be done by then and Jack would get a chance to enjoy the sky's artistry. Would he even notice? Ugh, she needed to get a grip. It wasn't her job to help some poor widower open up and break out of his shell, to notice the beauty around him.

Determined to put Jack Armstrong out of her mind, she opened her music application and started a favorite playlist then dumped a packet of lavender salts into the tub. "Ahhh," she let out something between a moan and a groan as she sank into the warm water. The lovely, scented liquid washed away the dirt and grime of the day and left her feeling limp and languid.

She considered dressing in leggings and slippers for the rest of the night, but Jack's words rang in her ears. "…not sure you have a healthy appreciation for the dangers of the ranch." With a heavy sigh, she pulled on jeans, clean socks, and boots. If she were outside shooting photos for even a few minutes, she couldn't risk stepping on a snake or scorpion or fire ants. Yes, she'd done her research. She knew about the myriad hazards that could plague her.

A little before eight o'clock, she stepped onto the

front porch. Golden yellow mixed with blue, outlining the clouds with a shimmering glow. She raised her camera and began shooting. Frame after frame, she watched the yellow blend into orange then pink, the clouds like soft pillows suspended above.

Then a sound broke the quiet evening. She raised her head and stilled her finger on the camera to listen. The clip-clop of a horse's hooves grew louder, nearer. Caroline stepped onto the gravel driveway and looked up the road. Sure enough, a horse moved toward her. Jack sat atop Charlie, and the horse's steps sounded slow and tired.

"Jack!" She hurried to the road. "Oh, my gosh, have you been dealing with the lost cows this whole time? Is everything all right?"

He brought the horse to a stop and lifted his hat, then swiped his brow with his sleeve. "It's been a long day, I'll say that."

Caroline took hold of the bridle. "Stop for a minute. You can tie Charlie to the porch railing. Climb down and let me get you something to eat. You must be starving."

Even with the shadows deepening, she could see the grim lines on his face. They tugged at her heartstrings—or her fix-it instincts.

"Thanks. I appreciate the offer, but I think I'm ready to get home and call it a night." He looked across the field and nodded. "Got yourself a real pretty one tonight, didn't you?"

She glanced at the horizon. "Yes. It was gorgeous. What happened up there? Are the mom and little Lola okay? I've been worried about them all day."

Jack's brows pulled together. "Little who?"

Oh, shoot. That was a slip-up. Her face warmed, and she gave a light laugh. "Oh, I...I gave the baby a name. When I was talking to her. She looked so sad out there all by herself."

"Ah. Well, we don't usually..." He shook his head. "Calf is fine. She'll need bottle feeding for a while. Mom's not out of the woods yet. Looks like she got hold of something poisonous. Gonna have to bring in a field botanist to check all the pastures."

"Oh, no. That's too bad. I sure hope she recovers. You know, I'm not a botanist, but I know a lot about plants. I'd be happy to help look for the culprit. In fact, I'd love to."

"Somehow that doesn't sound like a vacation for you."

"I could see what all is growing in the fields. Maybe pick up a snippet or two for my book." She patted Charlie while she thought about the situation. Why did she feel compelled to offer her services anyway? A lump formed in her throat. Because she knew stuff—and her most recent boss discounted her expertise? She sighed inside. It'd been a long time since she'd put her knowledge to good use in a real-world situation.

When she took sabbatical from the university, it had been her choice, but in some ways, it'd felt as though she'd been put out to pasture. The leave had been strongly encouraged by the new dean, and several people knew she was testing the waters of retirement. But here was an opportunity to make herself useful—and she admitted it energized her.

"Let's talk about it tomorrow, okay?"

Weariness laced his every syllable, and she

dropped her arms and stepped back from the horse. "Sure," she murmured. "Goodnight."

He nodded. "Goodnight, Caroline."

She lifted the camera again and watched as the two figures moved in perfect sync, nearly a silhouette against the dusky sky. She almost felt as if she were intruding on a private, personal moment.

Would they talk about it tomorrow? She didn't see how unless she got up early and just happened to be hanging out on the front porch when he went by. She didn't have his phone number, and as far as she knew, he didn't have hers. He could probably get it from Nora, though.

Well, she'd be ready. She had a few hours to brush up on her knowledge of good and bad pasture plants. Inside the cabin, she set the camera aside and opened her laptop. She didn't intend to be unprepared—or look a fool in front of Jack Armstrong.

Chapter Five

Sunlight streamed into the room, and Caroline opened one eye. Had she forgotten to close the blinds last night? The windows faced east, but it seemed much sunnier than the previous mornings. She rolled over and lifted her phone from the side table to check the time. *Nine-ten?* Nine-ten in the morning?

Obviously, Jack hadn't made any effort to touch base with her after all. She sat up. Then, with a groan, she flopped back against the pillow. No use hurrying now. She'd missed any chance of catching him before he headed to the pasture or to check on the sick cow. What a waste of time staying up last night and researching poisonous plants. It was her own fault. She'd stayed up too late and hadn't set an alarm.

Well, she'd enriched her mind and refreshed her memory of some plant information from earlier studies. And no learning was ever a waste. Even if she didn't use the material to help out on the ranch, it might come in handy in her other nature travels. She threw back the covers and padded to the kitchen. So, a leisurely morning it would be. After all, she hadn't come to work the ranch.

With a little more vigor than necessary, she yanked up the coffee carafe and added water. She started the coffee then moved around the cabin, opening blinds and curtains. Looked like another warm, sunny day. Maybe a good day to scope out the pool and check in with Lauren.

When the coffee pot gurgled to a finish, Caroline poured a cup then fetched her phone and punched in her daughter's number.

"Mom!"

"Hey, sweetheart, can you talk?"

"Yeah, I have a few minutes. How's the ranch? What you expected?"

"It's lovely. Better than I expected, really. I've already had several encounters with creatures outside. I'm starting to tan, and today I think I'll lounge by the pool and read."

Lauren laughed. "That sounds good to me. Are there any other people around? Did you meet Gabby's aunt?"

"Oh, yes. Don't worry. It's not that remote. I've met Gabby's Aunt Nora as well as the owner of the place, and a sweet mare named Star. Nora's delightful. Brought me some baked goods and fresh eggs the very first morning." Only the fact that the place came recommended from a friend had kept Lauren from freaking out over Caroline's solo journey. Her daughter sometimes forgot who was the child and who was the parent in their relationship.

Caroline sipped her coffee and filled Lauren in on the setting, complete with baby calves and beautiful sunsets—and avoided the subjects of rattlesnakes and poisoned cows.

"Hey, Mom, there's a chance I need to be in Dallas in a couple of weeks to look at some property. What if I came out there for Mother's Day? Is there any place we could go for dinner?"

"Not that I've found. You'd need to pick up some groceries on your way out. Then we'd have to cook."

"People live there, right? Isn't there a town nearby?"

"I think it's a tiny speck of a town. Not sure if there are any restaurants. But we have plenty of time to figure that out. I'll ask Nora." Now that she thought about it, a small town might be fun to explore. Might be worth a side day trip. See what kind of community structure they had out here. Surely, they had schools and a bank and post office and a dry goods store of some sort at the very least. Where did the vet come from? She figured the botanist must come from Dallas.

"But you know, honey, I might not stay that long."

"Well, if that's your last weekend, we could meet up in Dallas. Maybe have a spa day."

"Sure. That's a great idea." By then, she might be ready for a night on the town, shopping, and socializing among people again. Her daughter didn't know how much the trip to the ranch was also because Caroline needed a break from people. She'd kept the level of drama in the science department and her own discouragement from her daughter. Lauren didn't know about the dean's passive-aggressive behavior and the snide comments in meetings that he pretended were jokes. She thought her mother had earned a long overdue sabbatical—not that the dean was looking for any way to get rid of Caroline, even short-term.

Caroline was used to people liking her, and the dean's animosity hurt. Embarrassed her. Not something she wanted to share with her daughter.

****

"Next week?" Jack clenched his phone while he

kicked his boot into the gravel outside the center pasture building that now acted as animal infirmary. That was not the answer he wanted or needed from the state's agriculture agency. The mother cow was alive, and the vet was doing everything he could to keep her that way, but she was seriously ill. "No one who works emergencies?" He did his best to keep his voice steady, but inside he was about to explode.

"Sorry, sir. By the time we get a call, they're almost all emergencies. I'll get someone out there as soon as I can. In the meantime, keep your stock out of the pasture where the sick animal was found. Walk the fields and see if you spot anything that doesn't belong there. You have a field guide?"

"Yeah. Thanks." Jack ended the call and thought of the thick manual of plants complete with detailed drawings and photos back at the house. He hadn't looked through it in years. Then he thought of Caroline's offer to help. She seemed awfully confident in her abilities. But could she possibly know anything about poisonous plants in this region? He needed real answers, not some biologist playing sleuth and stabbing in the dark.

And he sure as hell didn't need a guest getting into something dangerous on his watch. The number of reasons to nudge the woman off the property were piling up.

Roger met him outside. "Any luck?"

Jack shook his head. "Can't get here until next week."

"No kidding?"

"We're going to have to keep all livestock in the other pastures until then. And alternate fields so none of them get overgrazed. That'd just make things worse."

"No problem. Momma Twelve seems stable. We may have caught it soon enough to save her. Damnedest thing, something like this hits out of the blue."

Jack pushed off from the fence and adjusted his hat. "Yeah. Look, you and the boys move 'em all this afternoon. I'm heading to the house for my field guide. May not come back up today. Tomorrow we'll search the other pasture on our own. I'm not waiting around on the state."

"Sounds good, Boss."

With colorful language bouncing around in his head, Jack strode to the pickup. He pulled the truck into the driveway at the house and came to an abrupt stop. Caroline's car sat there, too. He glanced around. Why would she park down here to get a horse?

When he climbed out, he looked over again and realized her intent. The large tree in the yard provided a nice canopy of shade over her car. Made sense. The weather had been warmer than usual all month so far.

Nora met him at the door.

"Hey, Jack. How's everything? Roger told me about the sick cow. Is she better?"

"A little. I've got some research to do."

"I'm about ready to head home. There's lasagna in the fridge for tonight. What kind of research? Anything I can help with?"

He had the presence of mind to stop and smile at her. Her first reaction was always to pitch in. It struck him that Caroline did the same thing. Maybe the two were a lot alike, and that's why they'd hit it off.

"Nah, thanks, though. Just need to get a book out of the library."

"By the way—"

A door sounded, and he whirled around. "Is someone here?"

"Caroline."

"Caroline?"

"From cabin one."

"In the house?"

"At the pool. She, um…" A look of uncertainty flashed across Nora's face. "She said you told her she could use the pool."

He sucked in a deep breath. That explained why he hadn't seen her around today. And why her car sat at the house, not the barn. Apparently, she'd decided against making herself useful.

"Yeah, I did. No problem. That's…that's fine."

Nora rested a hand on his arm. "That was nice of you, Jack. Let me get you a cold drink while you find the book."

He shook his head and braced against the table. "Nora," he tried to infuse his voice with humor. "You're not up to something here with Caroline from cabin one, are you?"

She crossed her arms. "What's that supposed to mean?"

"Do you know her?"

"Met her this week, same as you. I like her. Seems sharp, you know? Adventurous, spunky…just the kind of gal we like."

Straightening, he pushed off from the table and squeezed Nora's shoulder. "If you say so. See you later."

Jack flipped the light switch inside the library and took a step inside. He stood a moment taking it in. This was where they kept all kinds of books and reference materials. But more than that, it was Rosalyn's room. Memories assaulted him every time he walked through the door.

He walked past her desk and searched the bookshelves for the heavy manual. Didn't take long. It was exactly where he'd always kept ranch-related books. He pulled it from the shelf then let his gaze land on the desk that still held several framed photos. One of the things she liked most about the room was the window seat with a view overlooking the garden and pool area. Swallowing hard, he moved to the window and pushed back the light curtain.

The clear blue water shimmered. Around the pool was a small green patch intermixed with rocks and garden beds. Once, it had been a private oasis. Some shrubs and perennial flowers still gave the impression of some landscaping, and a few white daisies bloomed now. A figure stretched out in one of the lounge chairs on the pool deck, her long, slender legs tanning in the sunshine. He sucked in his breath. The swimsuit confirmed what he already suspected—Caroline maintained a fit and toned physique. She'd traded the floppy hat for a sun visor and appeared to be reading a book.

Well, at least someone was having a nice, relaxing day. He couldn't explain why he felt annoyed seeing Caroline lounging as if she hadn't a care in the world while he dealt with a serious problem. After all, he'd rejected her offer to pitch in.

She suddenly rested the book on her stomach and glanced around as if she sensed him watching her, and he stepped away from the window.

He turned and caught Rosalyn's image inside a simple silver frame. "You aren't being a good host," she whispered. "A gentleman is kind and gracious. I always loved that about you." It wasn't the first time he'd felt her presence in this room. Or the ache deep in his chest. He glanced back at the window and let out a long sigh then picked up the book and switched off the light, closing the door behind him.

An invisible force drew him toward the pool.

****

The back door to the house opened, and Caroline looked up.

Jack, fully dressed in long-sleeved shirt, jeans, and boots, emerged on the pool deck. He'd removed his hat. With his short but full head of salt-and-pepper hair uncovered, he looked younger, perhaps a smidge more approachable.

She sat up and tucked her bookmark into the book on her lap. "Hi, Jack." The sun was still too high in the sky to be the end of the workday, but he'd put in long hours yesterday. "Are you taking off a little early today? You worked so late last night."

He gave a short laugh and shook his head. "No. Looks like we've got a puzzle to solve."

She fiddled with the bookmark, unsure what to say. Did he stop by just to say hello? Did he expect her to offer her assistance again? That wasn't happening. But he was looking at her as if he expected her to say something. *Or leave?*

She swung her legs to the side of the lounge chair. "Let me gather my things, and I'll get out of your hair."

He waved a hand. "No. You're fine. Stay put. I didn't come out here to run you off."

The comment begged the question, why did he come out?

"How are momma and baby doing today?" she asked instead. She lifted her insulated cup and took a sip of iced tea to keep from fidgeting under his scrutiny.

"About the same."

"Glad no one's taken a turn for the worse," she said lightly. "Can you take a break? Have a cold drink?" *Oh, jeez*. Offering him a drink at his own home?

To her complete surprise, he nodded, his lips quirking up in a faint smile.

He reached toward her insulated tumbler. "I think I will get something to drink. Let me refresh yours. What are you having?"

"Oh, gosh, you don't need to do that."

His brows lifted. "What are you having?"

"Iced tea," she murmured. "Thanks." She relinquished her hold on the cup.

He set down the book he'd been holding then turned for the door.

She glanced at the book. Ah, a plant guide. She almost got up to take a look but managed to stop herself. Instead, she walked to the pool steps and dipped her legs in to cool off.

When the back door opened again, she emerged from the pool and met Jack halfway.

She'd swear his eyes flickered from her face down to her toes and back again. She couldn't help wondering if he was beginning to see her as a woman rather than just a renter. Did she want him to? She certainly hadn't come to the ranch to start any romantic entanglements, but something about the man made her want to shake him out of his stupor. She'd never met anyone so stuck in the past—alive but barely living.

"Thank you." Caroline took her tumbler and sank back onto the lounge chair then gestured toward the book. "Have you definitely concluded the momma cow ate a poisonous plant?"

Jack lifted the book and sat down with it on his lap. "It's looking that way. Now we need to find where it is and get rid of it." He looked past her and shook his head. "Could be like looking for a needle in a haystack."

"Well, I suppose you'd start where you found her. Was she far from the baby?"

"Not too far. Same pasture." He leaned forward and rubbed his palms together. Then his eyes met hers. He cleared his throat. "So, you know something about dangerous plants?"

She sucked in her breath and nearly choked. "I…yes, some. I know about ecosystems mostly. Not an expert on the plants found in this region, but I did some brushing up on poisonous plants last night."

His eyes widened, and he stared at her a moment. "Did you now?"

She sent him a cool, pointed look. "I did."

His glance dropped to his hands. "I don't suppose you'd…do you…"

So hard to ask a little thing. She finally put him out of his misery. "Jack, if you'd like me to help, I'm happy to see what I can do."

His head jerked up, and he nodded. "Do you have good work gloves?"

"Not with me."

"I'll find some."

"Okay. Do you want to go now? I can be ready

in—"

"No, it's too late for today, and I want to look at this book." He met her eyes. "Do a little brushing up."

"Excellent idea. Tomorrow morning then?"

"I'll stop by the cabin at seven-thirty."

"Sure, that's—" Another thought hit her brain. "Joe!" She clapped her hands and shot up from the chair. "I should call Joe. Oh, my gosh. He would love to help with this."

"Who's Joe?"

"A professor friend. Naturalist. Botanist. Knows everything there is to know about plants. Seriously. I bet he could sniff this out in an hour."

"He probably couldn't get here any faster than the state's guy."

"I don't know about that. For an opportunity like this, he might drop everything and board the first plane out here. Or charter his own."

Jack's brows drew together. "If he was that interested, couldn't he do this on a daily basis? Looks like the state agency might be hiring."

"But he wouldn't want to be stuck in the same place. He travels all over the world, giving talks and advice. Grows all kinds of interesting plants in his lab. He's like the Einstein of botany."

She snatched up her phone. "I'll call him right now."

Jack held up a hand. "Whoa. Hang on. How much is this gonna set me back?"

"Likely nothing, if it's a legitimate environmental issue. This is what he does."

Only took a second to find his number and connect.

"Well, well, a call from Miz Caroline Tate. This

must be my lucky day. How are you, Caro?"

"Hey, Joe. Doing well. And you?"

"Great. Getting ready to stink up the place with my titan arum."

"Oh, my gosh, is it blooming?"

"Just a few more days."

"Good. I've got a proposition for you." She glanced at Jack in time to see a sardonic smile turn his lips.

"And I'm all ears."

She launched into an abbreviated version of the situation. "Of course I thought of you."

"I'm delighted. Is there an airstrip close by?"

"Hang on." She lowered the phone. "Jack, is there an airstrip around here?"

"Are you serious?" A look of disbelief crossed his face.

"Yes."

He smiled and shook his head at the same time. "Sure. Over in Stockton, a twenty-minute drive from here. No rental cars, though. We'd have to arrange a ride or send someone to pick him up."

"Yes. Get to Stockton. Let me know when you'll be here, and I'll pick you up."

"Sounds good. See you tomorrow."

Caroline ended the call and grinned at Jack who appeared to be speechless. Her heart unexpectedly stuttered. That looked an awful lot like gratitude in his eyes. Maybe mixed with a dash of admiration?

Excitement surged through her. "He's in."

Chapter Six

As soon as he heard the car, Jack swung a leg over the fence railing and dropped down on the other side. He'd searched the field for about an hour and hadn't found anything unusual. But he's been distracted all morning waiting to hear from Caroline. He hoped this guy she was bringing had the amazing powers she claimed. Must be a pretty good friend to drop everything and come when she called.

As the car came to a stop, he lifted his hand in a wave. Both front doors opened, and Caroline climbed out of the driver's seat wearing a wide smile. She certainly had spunk. Today, she'd pulled her hair back and tucked it inside a bright-pink baseball cap. She looked ready to roll up her sleeves and go to work. Well, not literally. There would be no rolling up of sleeves that would expose skin to poisonous plants. He moved forward to meet botany's Einstein.

A tall man sporting a white ponytail and dressed in khaki work pants and a white shirt stepped forward. Caroline hadn't mentioned the guy's age, and Jack was surprised to discover he looked to be in his seventies. Like an old Harvard hippie.

Caroline made introductions, and Jack held out a hand to Joe.

He gave it a vigorous shake. "Pleased to meet you, Jack."

"I've filled Joe in on the situation," Caroline said. "He's got some ideas on how to get started."

"Good deal." He hesitated a second when he had the absurd notion to kiss her cheek. As an expression of thanks. Instead, he nodded and left it at that.

"You're lucky this smart cookie happened to be staying on your ranch," Joe said.

"Yep." Jack flicked a glance at Caroline, surprised to find a worried expression on her face. "I've got a couple of other men on standby. Wasn't sure how many you'd want to start with. It's a big field."

"One more could be useful," Joe said. He knelt and opened a small suitcase and pulled out gloves and an electronic tablet.

Jack stepped away and tossed his gloves into his truck then texted Roger to join them.

When he moved back, Joe handed him a pair of gloves. "These are great for handling small specimens." He turned to Caroline. "Petite ones for you, my dear. Unless, of course, you'd rather have a parasol."

With a laugh, she swatted his arm. "Oh, Joe, you know me so well," she said in a falsely sweet voice. "Did you bring one?"

He hooked an arm around her shoulders. "I know better."

Jack assumed this was a shared joke and had something to do with Caroline not being one to sit on the sidelines.

But they didn't clue him in, and Joe held out the electronic device. "Now, here are what I think are the top five most-likely bad guys."

Jack moved closer to peer at the small screen at the same time Caroline did, and her shoulder grazed his arm. He took a step back and placed a hand on her shoulder to allow her to move slightly in front of him for a better view.

Naturally, Roger chose that moment to show up. Jack dropped his arm and kept his eyes on the screen. He was relieved to see that four of the five plants displayed were ones he'd seen as he studied the reference book the prior evening. Maybe he'd recognize them if he saw them.

The group listened to Joe explain his theories and process then moved into the pasture. "Remember," he added. "The poisonous plant is probably mixed in with other plants, and the cow ate it accidentally. Yell 'stop' if you find something."

Jack nodded and started to put on his gloves. When he pulled the left glove over his hand, it caught on his ring. He stopped tugging and looked at the gold ring. And for the first time in years, he wondered about the consequences of taking off his wedding band. Would it feel like burying her all over again?

He shot a sideways glance at Caroline. He'd noticed earlier that she didn't wear a ring. Did that mean she didn't miss her husband? Hadn't loved him as much as Jack had loved Rosalyn? Did it mean she was looking for a new relationship? Or simply that she'd closed the book on that chapter of her life?

His throat tightened, and he yanked on the glove then forced himself to take his place in the field. He wasn't sure he even wanted to consider finding answers to those questions.

****

Caroline stuck her small orange flag into the ground to identify her starting point then turned her attention to the plants covering the pasture. Or tried to. With Jack on one side and Joe on the other, she had trouble concentrating. What a crazy turn of events. Of all the people she worked with at the university, she would miss Joe the most if she decided to retire. He'd been one of her staunchest supporters during the tenure process. He'd seen her ability to connect with students as a huge asset to the university—equal to, if not more important than, the work done inside the labs.

On her other side, Jack hunkered into the grasses, focused on the task at hand. She breathed a sigh of relief. When Joe first began issuing instructions, she'd been concerned that Jack might not be able to let someone else take charge. But he seemed to be all right with letting a plant expert call the shots for now.

They were nearing the two-hour mark when Jack hollered, "Stop." He shook his head when Joe and Caroline started toward him. "I haven't found anything. Just wanted to tell you lunch and fresh drinks are on the way."

"All right. Everyone drop a flag so we know where to pick up again," Joe hollered. "Jack, are we getting close to the pond?"

Jack gestured ahead. "Close. Just over this ridge. Want to stop for a bite or keep going?"

"Let's recharge then start again."

At the fence, Caroline waved to Nora. She'd set up a table and some folding chairs and already had a jug of something waiting for them.

"Nora, you are amazing," Caroline told her. "Thank you so much. What can I do to help?"

"Absolutely nothing. Grab a chair and a sandwich, hon."

She stepped back and watched Roger sidle up beside his wife and drop a kiss on her lips.

"Thanks, love."

It was a sweet exchange, and a lump formed in Caroline's throat. Something about the ranch had her feeling melancholy. Was it the vast expanse of the green pastures? Or being alone on vacation? Or the lonely widow? The scene had her wondering where she and Andrew would be if he were still alive. Still happily married? Traveling?

The weeks before he died in that plane crash had been hectic. Both of them busy with their own jobs and activities, they'd hardly seen each other. He'd been following up on some problem with one of his redevelopment projects. Caroline had moved her mother into a nursing home for memory-care patients. At seventeen, Lauren had her first real boyfriend, which had been a source of concern since she was driving on her own and in charge of her own schedule. The way Andrew had simply disappeared from Caroline's life still felt surreal. But the ache deep inside her heart was very real.

In the last couple of years, her daughter and several friends had urged her to take up new hobbies, get out more, meet people—single men in particular. They'd even suggested online dating. But Caroline hated that whole idea—putting herself out there to be judged and considered. Like shopping for a man. The thought was enough to send her running to a secluded cabin on a ranch all by herself.

Ironically, she'd run straight into close contact with a single man. She shot a sideways glance at Jack. The man oozed confidence. He might be a little rough around the edges, but he was the most interesting man she'd met in years. She compared Jack's presence to the fool of a dean trying to drive her away from the university and almost laughed. The man desperately wanted to be seen as strong and in command. He had no idea.

Jack and Joe were deep in conversation. Caroline chatted with Nora for a few minutes then pulled a chair beside Joe.

"I'm taking photos of each different plant species I encounter," he was telling Jack. "We can catalog them later. So far, everything looks completely normal."

"I've got my camera in the car," Caroline told him. "I can snap some pics for you."

"That'd be great. Let's see what we find first. Ready to get back to it?"

"Still want all four of us?" Jack asked.

"For the pond? You bet."

They helped Nora clean up then headed back to the field. At the pond, they fanned out. Caroline took her cues from Joe and knelt into the thick grasses near the water.

"Watch out for snakes," Jack shouted.

She shot back up. *Ugh.* Her earlier snake encounter was enough for this trip. Gingerly, she parted the grasses and peered closer.

Couldn't have been more than five minutes when Joe shouted, "Stop."

"You found something?" Caroline called.

He pulled the tablet from his backpack. A moment later, with a grin on his face, he motioned to them. "I think I've got it."

Caroline got there first and knelt to examine the

specimen and then the photo. The telltale purple splotches were a sure sign of poisonous hemlock.

Jack and Roger joined them.

"Right here." Joe pulled back some other grasses. It's well-hidden. Fortunately, it's a small patch. Shouldn't be too hard to wipe it out."

"Should we keep going around the pond in case there's more?" Jack asked.

"Absolutely. Let's do that, then we need to dig out everything we can see and get a chemical treatment down," Joe said.

"Oh no," Caroline clutched Joe's arm. "Seriously? Even if we dig it up, it'll still need chemicals?"

"I'm afraid so." He leaned into her and covered her hand with one of his. "I know you hate that, Caro. I do, too. But this is tough stuff."

Jack looked at her. "Our first priority is the livestock," he said, his tone matter-of-fact.

As if she didn't know that. "Yes, Jack. I realize that." The double-team put her on the defense. "But the chemicals aren't good for living creatures, either. What if they get into the water?"

"For poison hemlock, you're probably looking at a couple of weeks before you can put cattle back in here," Joe added.

"So what's the point of digging? Why not just let the chemicals take care of it?" Caroline asked.

"A combination is most effective. If we get the primary plant, the chemicals can finish off any of the roots we miss. Might not have to use as much. I've got shovels and disposal bags."

"We'll handle the digging," Jack told Caroline. "No need for you to risk getting any on your hands."

71

Her cheeks flushed. Was that a misogynistic this-is-a-man's-job statement? If not, wouldn't he be concerned about all of them? Caroline held up her gloved hands. "That's what these are for."

"We'll mask up and double glove when we start digging," Joe said. "When we're done, everyone should shower and change clothes right away. And don't touch your face. Ingesting it is the bigger concern, but we should be cautious about skin contact as well. Let me get the supplies."

"I'll help you." Roger jogged after Joe.

Caroline shot a glance at Jack, and he scowled back at her.

"Remember how I told you we try to keep our guests out of harm's way?"

"Oh, now I'm a guest? I think you use that line when it's convenient."

"Now don't get huffy. I didn't say you *aren't capable* of doing it, I'm saying it's not necessary."

She crossed her arms and glanced toward the road, wishing she'd gone with Joe. A touch on her arm startled her, and she jumped.

Jack's eyes met hers. "Look, I'm just saying I'd hate for your reward for helping with this to be getting sick."

Okay, fine. That sounded a little better. Top of mind at the moment, though, was that he'd touched her for the second time today. That he stood only inches away from her. That his sky-blue eyes could sparkle like blue diamonds. She sucked in a deep breath then took a step away and examined some grasses. "I'm not looking for a reward. Let's just…let's wait for Joe."

She hurried forward when Joe and Roger headed

back through the field.

Still grinning, Joe took her hand and swung her around. "Sweet success!" He leaned close. "Do me a favor, Caro. How about you spend some time looking for any more of this stuff while I start digging?"

She rolled her eyes, but somehow, the request sounded different coming from Joe. "Sure."

Jack stepped in beside her.

"Then you can get a head start on shower and clean clothes," Joe continued. "I'll let my pilot know we're heading out tonight."

"Oh, do you have to? I was hoping you could stay tonight. I could fix dinner, and there's plenty of room at the cabin for—"

"He can stay at the big house," Jack interrupted. "There's only one bedroom at the cabin." *Oh.* Blood pounded in his ears. Maybe she wanted Joe to spend the night with her? He cleared his throat in the awkward silence. "Where's your pilot? I've got room for him, too. Least we can do."

Caroline cocked her head at Jack. "How do you know the pilot is a him?"

He opened his mouth then closed it and shook his head. "There's room at my place for you and your pilot, regardless of whether it's a him or her."

Joe laughed. "You two stop squabbling. My pilot is in Dallas. Now, we've got work to do, then I need to have a shower and catch a plane."

****

Jack carefully dropped the last plant into a bag and sealed it up.

"How many ponds like this on the property?" Joe asked.

"Three, plus the stream."

"It'll take some time, but my advice is to go around all of them two or three times from now until fall. Keep looking. Make sure we caught it all. Best to catch it now before it can bloom and spread."

Jack nodded. And people wondered why he didn't take vacations. Obviously, he'd still need the state's people to come out, and he'd need to apply the chemicals immediately. There was always work to be done. He extended a gloved hand to Joe. "Can't thank you enough for coming out on such short notice, Joe."

"My pleasure. I was glad Caroline called me."

"You're a good friend."

Joe pulled off his goggles. "I'd do anything for that sweet gal. She helped several of my students over the years. She's a great mentor—got that tough-love attitude with a kind heart and a lot of smarts. I sure miss her on campus." He stopped talking and stared into Jack's face. "You two a thing?"

Jack's heart slammed against his ribs. He hadn't been prepared for this line of questioning. Maybe he shouldn't have let Roger leave earlier. "I, uh, no. We just met. I thought maybe you two—"

Joe let out a chuckle. "Heck, I'm at least fifteen years older than her. Nah, me and my Lisa have been together almost fifty years. Caro's a special lady, though. Like a little sister to me."

"She's only been on the ranch a few days, and—"

"But you like her?"

Prickly heat spread up Jack's neck. He swallowed hard. "Of course. I—"

"Her last couple of years at the university have been rough. Got a new dean who wants to make a name for himself. Wants all the professors to do more community work, publish more papers, get their research out there, have active labs. Doesn't give her enough credit for her teaching and mentoring." He shook an index finger. "That gal is a damn fine professor. Beloved. Look up any of those professor-rating websites sometime and see all the great comments. You ask me, the numbskull is jealous of Caro's popularity." He swung his pack onto his back.

"I imagine so." Jack picked up the remainder of the bags and began walking toward the road alongside Joe. "She takes good pictures."

"She sure does. I can't wait to see this book of hers. I'm gonna buy a bunch of them and put one on Dean Hanson's desk and all over the department."

Jack laughed with him. As they approached the fence line, Jack saw Caroline standing outside the car with her camera. Her hair was uncovered. Probably still drying, and she'd changed into fresh clothes. A smile widened across her face as they approached. And he wondered if any of it was directed toward him.

Chapter Seven

Caroline pulled the soft-sided cooler she'd purchased in Dallas out of the cabin closet, ready to set off for the small town of Stockton. There hadn't been time to explore yesterday when she was picking up and dropping off Joe, but the glimpses she'd gotten intrigued her enough to warrant a second look.

Might as well refresh her supplies while she was there. Or she might head on over to Abilene, the next "real" town in the area and see what it had to offer. She figured it was best to stay out of Jack's way today. He had a lot on his plate and probably wouldn't appreciate any questions about the momma cow or hemlock clean-up.

He'd been gracious to Joe, but she had to admit, she was surprised he hadn't shown her more appreciation for making Joe's assistance happen. Not that she needed great praise and adoration, but a heartfelt thank-you would be nice. Basic manners, at least. She picked up her car key and stopped short. Speaking of manners…she was going into town…should she call Jack or Nora? See if anyone needed anything? Did other guests do that? Or would it seem weird and intrusive, as if she were butting into their personal lives?

Maybe for today, she'd keep her nose out of their business. They'd survived on the ranch for a long time without her.

She added a layer of sunscreen to her nose and hands then picked up her camera bag. This was a bumble-around day, and she planned to stop and look at anything potentially interesting.

The first thing that came into view as she approached the town was an old silver water tower declaring in huge red letters it was the home of the Stockton Sergeants. By the time she made it to the sign announcing the city limits, she needed refreshment. She drove slowly through town, craning her neck to peer at the storefronts. There was a bank and a post office. A faded-yellow building caught her attention. General store. She slapped a hand on the steering wheel and grinned. An honest-to-goodness general store. Exactly the kind of place she'd hoped to find.

She parked the car in a diagonal spot out front and opened the car door. Her camera came with her, even though she'd stand out as a ridiculous tourist. Large pots of bright-red geraniums on either side of the weathered wooden steps made for a cheery welcome. She couldn't help snapping a few pictures.

As she approached the sky-blue wooden door, a sign taped inside the glass panel made her stop for a closer look. The sign advertised a town street dance. Live band performing. Caroline guessed it might play country or light pop music. Hmmm. She might still be around. That could be fun. Maybe Nora and Roger would attend. If she asked Nora about it, maybe they'd invite her to hang out with them.

She pushed open the door and stepped inside. After her eyes adjusted to the lower light, she scanned the shop. Rows of shelves and barrels of goods crammed the space, leaving little spare room. The air held the scents of fresh-ground coffee, maybe some baked goods, and spices. The whole atmosphere was warm and inviting. Charming, even.

"Hello there, ma'am. What can I do you for?"

The man behind the counter had a friendly tone, but curiosity in his eyes. She obviously stood out like a sunflower in a wheatfield.

"Just looking around a bit first, thanks."

"What brings you 'round our fine town today?"

"I'm staying on the Armstrong ranch for a few weeks. Out exploring today."

He stared harder. "Is that right?"

If he'd been a dog, she had no doubt his ears would've shot straight up.

He extended a hand across the counter. "Well, welcome to Stockton, Miz…?"

She took his hand. "Tate. But please, call me Caroline."

"Pleased to meet you, Caroline."

"And you're Mister…?" Her voice pitched up in question.

"I'm Bill, ma'am. Owner of this establishment. You let me know if I can help with anything."

She smiled and turned to wander down an aisle.

"We've got groceries on the other side, and a couple of cooler cases if you need anything like that. Over here, you'll find dry goods, personal items, cleaning supplies, office supplies…a little bit of everything."

She waved and focused her attention on the shelves. "Thank you." She stopped in front of a display of nuts and dried fruit. A large handmade sign drew her attention to locally-grown pecans.

"Those are straight out of San Saba, only a few hours from here," the man hollered at her.

Jeez, was he watching her? She lifted a bag of the nuts. She had no idea Texans grew and harvested pecans as a crop. Joe might've been interested in that. Heck, Joe probably already knew all there was to know about Texas agriculture. She grabbed another bag to send to him. As she made her way back to the front, her stomach rumbled, reminding her it was lunchtime. "Are there any restaurants in town, Bill?"

"Got Stella's Diner just up the street a ways. Best beef burger in west Texas, ma'am. She'll be busy about now. I can offer you a cold beverage and a snack." He gestured sideways, and she spied the counter where several stools invited customers to stay a while.

And then she saw the dispensers along the wall. "A soda fountain!" She grinned and moved toward the stools.

"I can fix you up a root beer float, a cherry limeade, or a pineapple-peach fizz."

"They all sound delightful." A glass box on the counter held a selection of baked goods. "Ooo. These look heavenly."

"Arlene, my missus, bakes muffins and cookies fresh every day," he said proudly.

She glanced around again. "I wonder if I should get some lunch first and come back for dessert." If she bought any groceries, she should do that right before she went back to the ranch. She set down the nuts. "You know, I think that's what I'll do. I'll be back for these. Thanks so much."

Another woman entered the store, and Bill turned

and greeted her by name.

Caroline couldn't help but smile. She imagined Bill knew everyone in town and the surrounding areas. Such a different lifestyle from what she was used to in Nashville. A lot of people recognized her on campus, and she was a regular customer at a couple of restaurants, but nothing like this. It had her wondering whether she'd enjoy the familiarity or whether it would feel invasive over time. She appreciated the friendliness anyway.

Only took a couple of minutes to locate Stella's Diner. Caroline stepped inside and glanced around for an open table—and discovered nearly every eye in the place was focused on her. She smiled and made her way to an empty spot at the end of the counter. Perfect. This way, she'd face the dining area instead of having her back to it.

She picked up the printed menu from the counter and read the options.

A woman slid a glass of water in front of her. "Something to drink, hon?"

"Iced tea, please."

"You got it."

The tea arrived, and Caroline ordered a BLT sandwich. She picked up the glass but stopped her hand midway as snippets of conversation reached her ears.

"You should've seen this guy. Old man with a long, white ponytail. Doesn't say where he's going or anything. Gets out of the plane and gets a good long hug from some broad I've never seen before. They get in a car and drive off."

Caroline took a sip and glanced sideways at the men.

The one speaking shook his head. "Then, he comes back late in the day. The gal drops him off, plane picks him up, and he's gone again."

The other man shoved a french fry into his mouth. "No idea where he come from?"

"Logbook said Nashville."

"No kidding? Hope it's not one of those developer types nosing around again."

"Seems like they'da got the message last time."

"You'd think."

"And they show up in highfalutin suits and ties. This guy had on a hat and getup like he was going on a safari."

The other man burst out laughing. "Sounds like he was lost."

Caroline hid her smile behind her glass. Andrew would've enjoyed the description. He'd owned many "highfalutin" suits and ties. How fun to supply the locals with mystery and intrigue. Where had this guy been during all the comings and goings yesterday? She hadn't seen anyone. Typical small town, she supposed. *Careful what you do and say because someone's always watching*, her grandma used to say.

The waitress placed a plate in front of Caroline. "Need mayo?"

"No, thank you. This looks great." She bit into the sandwich and recognized the sweet flavor of homegrown tomatoes. *Mmmm*. She needn't have worried about fresh produce out here in the middle of nowhere. Homegrown was fresher than any grocery store.

When the woman stopped to refill Caroline's tea, she hovered a moment then gestured toward her camera. "You visiting relatives, hon?"

They certainly weren't shy about approaching strangers. And was everyone "hon" around here?

"Nope. Just visiting. What a cute town." She made a point to look at the woman's nametag. *Donna.* It suited her.

"How in the world did you come across Stockton? Are you lost?"

Caroline couldn't help a light laugh at the puzzled look on Donna's face. "No, I'm just exploring. I'm visiting at the Armstrong ranch."

Her brows shot up, much like the man's had at the general store. "Is that right? Jack's place?"

Caroline shifted on the stool. "Yes. One of the rental cabins," she clarified. "So tell me, what are the sights I shouldn't miss while I'm here?"

Donna cackled. "Oh, sweetie. If you've driven down Main Street, you've seen it all."

"I'm photographing nature, or interesting tidbits of small-town ranch life."

The woman gave a blank stare. "Only things around here are fields and cows."

"Native trees, flowers? An old cemetery or schoolhouse would be interesting, too."

She laughed again. "You must be a city girl. Where you from?"

"Nashville. I'm a biologist." In her peripheral vision, she saw the man at the counter swivel her direction. Oh, boy. The tongues would be wagging today. "Could I get an iced tea to go?"

"Coming right up."

The woman brought the tea and check and gave Caroline a few brief directions.

As she walked to the door, she could feel the curious stares that followed her. An older gentleman tipped his hat and opened the door for her. "Ma'am."

She smiled and stepped into the sunshine. For an hour, she wandered the town and snapped pictures of storefronts, flowers, and details of small-town life. Then she returned to her car and drove to the outskirts of town. She found the cemetery enclosed within a white picket fence and stopped the car.

Old-fashioned yellow rosebushes flanked the stone entryway. She stepped past them and a sense of calm stole over her. Peacefulness permeated the quiet, shaded grounds.

She walked along the perimeter road, looking for old markers. The place was tidy and well-kept. Bluebonnets and wildflowers lined the edges, and Caroline snapped photo after photo, capturing the striking pop of color against the white fence.

On her way back to the entrance, a tall, rose-colored, obelisk marker drew her attention. Set several feet away from others, its specks of mica sparkled in the sun. Caroline walked between the graves and approached the headstone. Then gasped. Her heart pounded as she stared at the inscription etched into the stone.

Rosalyn Billings Armstrong
Beloved wife, mother,
daughter.
—The greatest happiness in life
is to love and be loved—

Her throat clogged. A bouquet of wildflowers filled a small container at the base of the headstone. Did Jack come to town and keep flowers on the grave after all this time? But Nora said he rarely left the ranch. Maybe she did it? More likely, Jack paid the caretaker to keep it adorned with flowers. It was a lovely tribute to his wife.

Caroline's eyes strayed to the next marker, and she nearly fell to her knees. Oh, dear lord. These were the graves of Jack's family members killed in the car accident. Flowers decorated them as well. Tears blurred her vision as she ran a hand across the little girl's stone. Only a toddler. So much loss. No wonder Jack was withdrawn and aloof. The man had endured so much.

Her thoughts ping-ponged all over the place—thoughts of Jack, Andrew, grief, the future. She let out a long, shuddered breath. If all you felt was pain, was it better to not feel? To go numb? What about Jack's son and grandson? Did he have anything left for them, or had he shut down on them as well? Different people in different circumstances handled adversity in different ways.

She'd lost her husband and her parents, but she'd never had to bury a child. That was the worst. At the time of her husband's death, she'd still had a job, still had a daughter to get through high school and college and launched into the world. Had to keep going. In the past few years, she'd only visited Andrew's grave on special occasions…birthdays and anniversaries. Over time, the pain dulled, and she'd transitioned to being single again.

A wave of sympathy for Jack washed over her. She sniffled and wiped her eyes. Now she wished she hadn't come. It felt as if she were prying into his family's life. She should've stayed on the ranch and started on her essays.

Avoiding the names on the gravestones, she raised her camera and snapped a picture of the flowers. Then she turned and slowly walked back to her car. She sat with the door open and let the light breeze cool her face while she guzzled the last of her iced tea.

Feeling drained, she considered skipping the second stop at the general store. She pushed back her hair and heaved a sigh. But she said she'd be back and had left the pecans on the counter. And now she could use a fresh drink. Maybe it would revive her spirits.

Inside the store, she retrieved the pecans then headed for the refrigerated cases. Might as well restock her fresh produce. A large bin caught her attention. The attached sign read "Critter Carrots." What did that mean? She peered closer. The bags were full of misshapen carrots. Oh, fun—horse treats. Thinking of Star, she lifted a bag. Hmm, maybe a bag of peppermints, too. She'd seen some earlier but hadn't thought of the horses. She retraced her steps and grabbed the mints.

"Looks like you've got a soft spot for horses," Bill said at the counter.

"Guilty as charged," she told him. "They deserve a little spoiling."

"Caroline, this here's my missus, Arlene." He took hold of a plump woman wearing an apron and swung her around.

"Pleasure." The woman regarded Caroline with keen eyes. "I hear you're at Jack's place."

Caroline smiled. She was impressed. Even for a small town, that news traveled lightning fast.

Arlene took a step forward and looked over the counter. Then she nodded. "Good for you. Nice boots."

Though her tone was gruff, a friendly light sparkled in her eyes.

Caroline crinkled her brow. "Thanks."

Arlene leaned closer and whispered in a loud voice. "Last week we had a gal in here visiting her grandparents and wearing flip-flops. I kid you not. Flip-flops." She threw her hands in the air. "Can you imagine?"

Caroline couldn't hold in a laugh. *Whew.* Glad she passed that test.

Half an hour later, she'd met half the town and was still trying to leave the Stockton General Store. Arlene had come in with fresh-baked cookies and insisted Caroline sample every variety.

"Please take these, too. On the house." She shoved a bag of cookies at Caroline.

"Thank you. They'll be a nice treat in the afternoons." Good thing she was getting in lots of steps on the ranch.

"Here, take these to Jack while you're at it. I know he's a fan of my snickerdoodles, and we don't see him in here much these days." The woman pressed another bag of cookies into Caroline's already laden arms.

"Oh, well, I don't know if—" When would she see Jack next?

"Sure is nice to meet you, hon. Have a safe trip back."

Caroline gave a little laugh at the woman's friendly but brisk goodbye. "Nice to meet you, too. Thanks, again."

With her cooler stocked full of fresh groceries and a pineapple-peach fizz drink from the soda fountain in her cup holder, Caroline turned the car back toward the ranch.

At the gate, she punched in the code and waited for the heavy wrought iron to pull back and allow her inside. She drove in and looked to the east to check for activity at the big house. Should she make a point to stop at the house and drop off the cookies? Somehow, she felt awkward about stopping with no invitation. Maybe she could leave them on the porch. No, some wild animal could get to them before Jack did. She glanced at her car clock. Only four. Too early for Jack to be home. Probably too late for Nora to be there. She'd just have to wait for an opportunity.

****

After a light supper, Caroline loaded the carrots and peppermints into the car and headed to the barn. She missed seeing the horses today. The girls-and-their-horses bug that bit her at age seven nipped at her again. Horses were magnificent creatures. It'd been years since she'd owned one. That dream had been fulfilled in high school. Then college got in the way. And then marriage. And then a child. Caroline had introduced Lauren to the equine world, but she'd never taken to it the way Caroline had.

She had time on her hands now. When she got home, maybe she'd contact some of the local stables and see if any horses needed a new owner. If she bonded with one… But no. She couldn't do that if she intended to travel.

She pushed back the heavy barn door and went inside. Then, one by one, she visited the stalls and presented the animals her offerings. Charlie gave her a wary stare that reminded her of his standoffish owner. But after some coaxing, the horse moved forward and accepted a carrot. He turned his nose up at the peppermint.

Caroline laughed. "All right then, big guy. To each his own."

With a satisfied smile, she gave Star one last pat and another mint, then meandered back to the car.

Later, as had become her nightly routine, Caroline slipped into her kick-around-the-house pajamas, poured a glass of wine, and stepped onto the patio. She inhaled the soft breeze and stared at the clear night sky, full of twinkling stars. Vast and beautiful. A nice end to a full day.

She sipped the wine and listened to the night sounds, knowing she was surrounded by wildlife she couldn't see—owls, frogs, and all kinds of mammals that rustled through the brush under cover of darkness.

An occasional whinny from the horses also added to the nighttime melody. The cabin sat around the bend in the road from the stables, but not far as the crow flies, and the barn noises floated up the incline. She closed her eyes—and the whinny came again. Caroline bolted upright. *Oh, shoot.* Had she left the lights on?

She set down her wine glass and thought hard. She'd shut the door, she remembered that for sure. The lights…hmmm. Maybe she should go down and check. It might unsettle the horses if they were used to a dark space, and she'd left on bright overhead lights.

Groaning, she exchanged her comfy pajamas for jeans and boots then grabbed her car keys.

As soon as she turned the car onto the gravel area that led to the barn, she could see a light glowed inside, though it was dim. She rolled her eyes. *Nice job, Caroline.* Good thing she'd come down. She didn't need one more thing to annoy Jack.

She hurried to the barn door, pushed it open, and stopped in her tracks. Was someone there? She'd swear she heard someone talking. Standing still, she listened. That horse sounded—*oh, the pregnant mare!* Caroline ventured farther into the barn. A moment later, she gasped and clamped her hands over her mouth.

Chapter Eight

Jack sat on his haunches near Penny. The mare lay on her side in the hay.

"Oh, my gosh!"

Jack turned. His eyes narrowed for a moment, then he motioned her forward.

"The baby?" Caroline whispered. "It's time?"

He nodded. "Guess so. A little early, according to the vet. I've got to watch her to be sure everything is all right."

"What are we watching for?"

"Any signs of trouble, stress. She might seem agitated, but right now it's pretty routine."

Caroline searched his face and didn't detect anything out of the ordinary. As usual, he seemed sure and confident. "You've done this before?"

"Many times."

Caroline crouched beside Jack and patted the mare. She'd seen a foal born before, but it'd been a while, and her memory was sketchy. "What can we do to help?"

"Not much." He held up a roll of gauze tape. "Gotta get her tail out of the way."

"Sure. How long will it take for your vet to get here?"

"Twenty minutes, if he's needed. Hopefully that won't be until morning."

Jack's brisk voice told her this was business as

usual for him. His hands deftly wrapped the mare's tail, and she wondered if he'd mind the company. If the birth was routine, she could stay out of the way. If there were problems, she could lend a hand. She wished she'd thought to grab her camera before she dashed down to the barn.

Glancing at Jack gave her no incentive to stay or go. The man was focused on his task. Probably preferred no company, but Caroline's inclination was to stay. Besides, she'd been wanting to see an Armstrong Ranch sunrise. Maybe this would be the morning. She hadn't pulled an all-nighter in a good long time.

Inspiration struck. "Hey, Jack. I think I'll run up to the cabin and grab my camera and a thermos of coffee," she said. *Tell, don't ask.* "Be right back."

"Caroline, this might take all night."

"I'd like to watch, if you don't mind."

"I can let you know when it's about to happen."

Uh-huh, the way he let her know about the poison-plant hunt? No way. He'd be busy and would get caught up in the moment and not even think of her until it was all over.

Argue or let it go? She sucked in a deep breath. "I could be a second set of hands if you need anything."

"Roger can help out if needed."

Ugh. He was difficult. "I promise I'll stay out of the way." She tried to infuse her voice with brightness.

He didn't answer but spared her a nod.

She took that as acceptance and didn't give him time to reconsider.

Inside the cabin, Caroline went straight to the kitchen to start the coffee. Then she took a minute to put on a bra and real shirt, grimacing at her appearance in the mirror. At least she hadn't dashed down to the barn with night cream all over her face. Thank goodness for small favors. She ran a brush through her hair then clipped the front so it was out of her face. Jack Armstrong probably couldn't give two hoots how she looked, but she had her standards.

By the time she gathered her gear and a couple of mugs, the coffee pot gave its last few gurgles. Nearly all of it fit in the steel thermos she traveled with. Good, they might need it. She was betting Jack took his coffee strong and black, but she scooped up some small packets of sugar and powdered creamer just in case. She grabbed a towel and some hand wipes then started for the door. *Oh, wait.* She ran back to the kitchen. Talk about a perfect opportunity to give him the cookies from Arlene. Smiling, she loaded the car and headed back to the barn.

She moved quietly to Penny's stall then scooted a small bench to the center of the walkway and draped it with a sunny yellow kitchen towel. Then she set out the mugs and thermos.

Jack turned, and a frown furrowed his brow. "Don't think I'm gonna have time for a tea party."

Caroline's face flushed hot. It was probably a good thing she hadn't already poured the coffee, or the man might be wearing his. She sucked in a deep breath and did not wait the advised ten seconds before responding. "Wow, Jack. It's just coffee. A simple thank you would suffice."

She poured herself a cup then stepped back and dropped to the floor with her back resting against the wall of another stall where she still had a view of Penny's. Maybe the barn cat would wander in—might be better company than her current option.

When Jack stood, Caroline took a sip of coffee and avoided his eyes. What the heck was his problem? After spending all day in the fields together trying to solve an issue for his ranch, she thought they were warming to some kind of friendship. Apparently not.

****

Jack flicked a glance at Caroline. Color stained her cheeks, and her face was set, her lips a thin line. He'd obviously offended her. If he'd said something like that to Rosalyn, she probably would've laughed—and put her boot to his backside. Caroline didn't know him well enough for that.

He shoved his hands in his pockets and let out a deep sigh. "Sorry if I hurt your feelings."

Instead of looking at him, she stared into her mug. "You know, Jack, I wonder if you've been doing this Lone Ranger thing so long you've forgotten how to act around people. Decent people do small kindnesses for each other as a matter of habit."

She met his eyes then, and the look in hers was like a sucker punch to his gut. This was the first time he'd seen this strong, capable woman look the least bit vulnerable. Something lodged in his throat. Swallowing hard, he turned and headed for the tack room. He pulled a few clean horse blankets from the shelves then returned to the aisle outside Penny's stall.

He placed a couple of blankets on the floor beside Caroline. "Not exactly luxury accommodations around here, but maybe these will make you more comfortable." He hoped she'd accept them as an apology and one of those *small acts of kindness*.

She crouched and adjusted the blankets then sat on

93

top of them. "Thank you."

"You're welcome." He knelt behind the bench and lifted the coffee carafe. "Thank you for the coffee."

With brows slightly raised, she nailed him with a cool look just shy of a glare.

"You're welcome."

He nodded and cleared his throat. "I could run up to the house if you need cream or sugar."

"I brought some." She tugged one of the rugs forward and tucked it under her knees then dug around in a small bag and produced packets of creamer and sugar.

She let out a short "oh," as he dumped an entire packet of sugar into his coffee.

He looked up. "What?"

"I…uh…nothing. I'd pegged you for the strong-and-black type, that's all." She opened a packet of creamer and sprinkled a little into her mug. "Oh, I forgot spoons."

Jack reached over and snapped a stalk of straw from a nearby bale and began stirring his coffee.

"Ick."

He let out a short chuckle. "I'll live."

"Hope so. I'd hate for you to miss out on these." She pulled something else from the bag. "It's starting to look like you have a sweet tooth. According to Arlene at the Stockton General Store, you have a soft spot for her snickerdoodles." She set the cookies in front of him. "With her compliments."

Jack couldn't help grinning as he reached for the cookies. "I do, indeed. These are mighty tasty. Have one." He opened the bag and nudged it closer to her. Maybe she'd take it as a peace offering. He waited for her to select one of the cinnamon-sugar-dusted cookies then withdrew one for himself but hesitated before taking a bite. "We good?" he asked gruffly.

Looking down, Caroline broke off a piece of cookie and seemed to consider his question. When she looked up again, she nodded with a faint hint of a smile. "Sure, Jack."

"And I don't think I thanked you properly for your help getting Joe out here yesterday. That was…well, thank you. It's lucky we have you here."

"You're welcome." She leaned forward. "How did today go? Did you check the other ponds?"

Jack breathed a sigh of relief, back on solid ground. "We did. Thankfully, didn't find any more of the hemlock. We'll start up and down the creek tomorrow."

"Did you get the chemical application done?"

"Roger went into Abilene to get the mix. We'll put it down first thing tomorrow."

Caroline's glance moved to Penny's stall. "Oh, gosh. I sure hope Penny has her foal by then. Might be a long night for you."

"She's making progress. Roger can take over if necessary."

"Oh, right."

"So, you went back to Stockton today? If you needed supplies, Nora—"

She waved a hand. "I didn't really need anything. I was exploring. It's a cute town. Friendly people."

"Yes, lots of good people around here."

When Penny let out a whimper, Jack turned to check on her. Nature seemed to be taking its course. And was in no hurry.

"I had lunch at Stella's. Did a little shopping at the

General Store and walked through the cemetery."

His head snapped around. "Why would you do that?"

"Just taking in the town. Sometimes cemeteries have interesting histories, famous people buried there." Her voice dropped. "I saw your family's section."

Was that a deliberate punch? He stared at her.

"They have the prettiest markers in the whole place. Beautiful. And lovely that they are kept with fresh flowers."

Jack studied his nails, unsure what to say. Unsure he wanted to have this conversation. "I don't get over there much. Special occasions." He'd never missed a birthday, Mother's Day, or anniversary.

"Did you consider a family cemetery on the ranch?"

He looked at her then. "I did. But everyone advised against it. Problems with access if the property was sold down the line."

"That makes sense. Well, the caretaker seems to be doing a nice job."

Jack swallowed hard and nodded.

Caroline gave a sad smile and touched his arm. "I don't mean to pry. I just thought you might like to tell me about them. Some people like to talk about loved ones they miss. If you don't, that's okay."

He searched her face a moment. Her soft eyes held sincerity, kindness, compassion. Jack's chest tightened, and he barely resisted the urge to brush back the loose strands of hair from her face.

Penny's whinny drew his attention, and he broke the eye-lock. Standing, he moved into the stall again and helped the horse upright. He spoke softly to the mare as they walked around the stall. "Sometimes walking helps," he said as they passed Caroline.

When Penny stopped and knelt, Jack examined her. "Water hasn't broken yet."

He washed his hands and joined Caroline again. "I imagine we've got a few more hours. This stage usually takes a while." He picked up his coffee and took a drink then met her eyes again. "The little girl, my granddaughter, was just two. I'd only seen her a handful of times."

"Hannah."

"Yeah. Cute little thing." He pulled another stalk of straw and began twisting it.

"I'm glad your grandson was spared."

"He's a good kid." Jack gave a short laugh. "Acts like he kind of likes me sometimes."

Caroline crinkled her brow. "Oh, Jack, I'm sure—"

"I'm not good with young kids."

"Not everyone is."

"Got another one on the way. My son's wife is expecting."

"That's wonderful. A new baby is something to cherish, for sure."

"You have kids?"

"A daughter. Lauren's twenty-eight, living on her own in Nashville."

"Only one?"

"Yes. I thought we might have two or three, but it didn't work out."

He raised his brows in question.

"I had a couple of miscarriages. We thought about adopting, but we were both busy with our careers, and we…well, we decided it wasn't meant to be."

"Life throws curveballs, and some last forever."

"Yeah." She reached for the coffee and refilled both mugs.

Jack was quiet a moment, digesting the information. She wasn't just trying to pry information from him but sharing as well. She'd faced plenty of tragedy in her own life.

"I saw some pictures in the tack room of a girl with horses and blue ribbons. Your daughter?"

"Mm-hmm. Amy. She loved the horses. Sometimes I'd swear she was a horse whisperer, could communicate with them and understand their feelings and personalities."

"That's very cool. I'm so sorry for your loss, Jack."

"Thank you."

They lapsed into silence, and when Caroline covered a yawn with a hand a few minutes later, Jack gestured toward the opposite stall. "You might as well sit back and try to get some rest. I promise to wake you if anything happens."

Jack moved quietly, helping the mare up as needed, adding fresh straw around her. He reheated the water in the bucket standing by and knelt alongside the horse. He smiled when he peered back around the stall. Caroline's eyes were closed. While he watched Penny, he also kept an eye on Caroline to make sure she didn't fall over.

She slept right through one of Penny's agitated spells. When he finally settled on the floor across from Caroline, he took the opportunity to study her features. She was an attractive woman, no doubt about that. Her hair was a pretty mix of honey-colored strands and gray that disguised her age. The few wrinkles around her eyes and lips smoothed out in her sleep, and she looked peaceful. She had a quiet beauty to her.

At the sound of a bang, Jack started. He blinked to get his bearings, then scrambled up. He must've dozed off. Sounded like the mare kicked the stall. He knelt to examine her. Okay, almost time. He whirled around to wake Caroline and found her hovering behind him.

"Is she ready?" she whispered.

"Almost. Her water broke. I just need to make sure the foal is presenting properly then let Penny do the work."

After another examination, he patted the mare then stepped back. "Looks good," he told Caroline. "You might want to get your camera."

A smile lit her face, and Jack's heart bounced unexpectedly. It was fun to see someone get caught up in the excitement of the event. He'd done this solo or turned it over to Roger the last several times. For a moment, he remembered Amy's first time. The mare had had a difficult time of it, and he'd been afraid either the mare or the foal wouldn't live. He'd been reluctant to let his daughter observe after that, but she'd handled it well, and had developed both compassion and passion for the animals.

As they watched, the birth unfolded. Caroline viewed most of it from behind the camera. Every couple of minutes she gasped or made a soothing sound. Jack tried to stay out of her way at the same time he stood ready to help Penny. Finally, the foal dropped, and then the afterbirth.

"Oh, my gosh," Caroline squealed. "She did it!"

A few minutes later, Penny licked the foal then stood and began nudging the baby to do the same.

"The poor thing. Can you imagine trying to stand immediately on those spindly little legs? Come on, baby," she cooed.

She turned to Jack. "Do you have a name picked out?"

"No. Thought I'd wait and let my grandson choose one."

Her eyes widened. "That's a great idea. Very sentimental of you, Jack."

"Guess I have my moments."

She gave a light laugh. "Good to know."

They continued to observe, and thirty minutes later, the foal struggled to her feet, slipped, then tried again. After a few more attempts and a little rest, she righted herself and snuggled against her momma.

"Oh, Jack, look at that." Grinning, she placed a hand on his thigh—and he involuntarily flinched.

His head snapped around to look at *her*, not the new foal. He stared at her, but she didn't seem to notice his reaction. It'd been a long time since he'd felt the spontaneous touch of a woman.

Finally, he offered a slow smile. "She looks healthy. I'll let Doc Webster know, and he can stop by in the next couple of days."

Caroline raised her camera again and snapped about a hundred shots of the new foal. "She's adorable. What an amazing thing. I'm so glad I got to be here for it."

To himself, Jack admitted having Caroline at the barn made the birth more of a special event. He began cleaning up while she continued to fuss over the newborn.

When she gathered her things and began walking

toward the barn doors, he hovered behind her.

At the entrance, she turned back.

"Oh, my." She waved him forward. "Come look at this, Jack. I don't often see this time of day, but it's beautiful."

He took a few steps forward and glanced at the eastern sky. And agreed. The sun just peeked over the horizon, washing the fields in soft pink light. "It's pretty."

"It's almost magical the way the dew glistens in the light. I haven't pulled an all-nighter in years," she told him. "That was fun. Thanks for letting me stay."

His eyes met hers, and he caught his breath. He had the craziest thought to pull her close and wrap his arms around her. He'd enjoyed sharing the experience with her. Felt somehow connected. He swallowed hard. "Thanks for keeping me company," was all he could manage.

In the awkward silence neither of them moved.

"I…uh, guess I'd better get cleaned up," he added, his voice a little strained. "Day's gonna get started here soon."

"It's already off to a good start." She took his arm, and faster than he could process it, she stood on her toes and pressed her lips to his cheek. "See you later," she whispered.

Electricity surged through him, and shock rooted him to the floor. He let her take two steps before he came to his senses. "Caroline?"

She turned back, a questioning smile on her face.

He closed the gap between them and placed his hands on her shoulders. Hardly breathing, he looked into her eyes, then he brushed a thumb across her cheek. "I—" He had no idea what he wanted to say. Instead, as if an invisible force took over, he slowly lowered his lips to hers.

When she let out a soft sound, he slid an arm to her back and deepened the kiss. Her lips moved against his, and a longing he hadn't felt in years stirred deep inside him.

The whinny of a horse impatient for fresh oats interrupted the moment, and Jack pulled back. "Well," he said.

Caroline put a hand to her chest, and he wondered if she was as surprised as he was. Did she feel something for him, or had they gotten caught up in the moment? He needed to step back. To think. This was not—

"I'll see you later," she said softly.

He didn't move until she pulled her car onto the roadway. Then his knees nearly gave out, and he sagged against the door frame.

Chapter Nine

She'd kissed Jack Armstrong.

Well, he kissed her. But she kissed him back.

Caroline's cabin sat only a few minutes from the barn. The short drive didn't provide nearly enough time to unscramble her thoughts. She climbed out of the car still in a daze.

She pushed open the cabin door and went inside then slumped back against it. *Whew*. That was unexpected. She could only plead insanity.

She dropped her bag and camera on the sofa and rubbed her temples, remembering the feel of his lips on hers—warm and tingly and….and intoxicating? If she didn't know better, she'd think she had a hangover. She debated whether to have coffee and a shower to wash it away or crawl into bed and sleep it off.

Obviously, the mare and foal bonding had made them both mushy. Or the early hour had clouded their brains. Maybe a little of both. Anyway, it was just a kiss. It didn't have to mean anything. It wasn't as if she'd pledged the rest of her life to a stuck-in-his-ways rancher in the middle-of-nowhere Texas who had no intention of ever stepping foot farther than the county line.

With a little laugh, she shook her head. Didn't matter. Being on friendly terms with the man would make her stay more pleasant, for sure, and could be a nice diversion. She didn't mind some male company, but this friendship, relationship, whatever-it-might-be, came with an expiration date.

Caroline allowed herself a three-hour nap. It was nearly noon by the time she got a snack and settled in front of the computer. She opened her laptop and began downloading the pictures she'd taken of the foal's birth.

When she opened the photo files, she squealed with delight. The foal was so darn cute. She flipped through several frames then her hand stilled, and she caught her breath. Several frames included Jack.

She zoomed in and felt an unexpected flutter in her chest. His face had softened. His smile held genuine pleasure in the frames where he looked at the horses— and in others where he looked straight at *her*.

He'd been gentle with the mare. Calm and confident and patient. She remembered his quiet strength and his solid muscles under her touch. She took a long sip of iced tea and also remembered the feel of his arms around her. Strong and sturdy, warm. A shiver vibrated through her. She had no doubt Jack Armstrong would be a fierce protector of anyone he loved. And he did have a nice smile when he chose to turn on the charm. Wait, Jack and charm in the same thought? Talk about a turn of events.

He really was a handsome man. And apparently had a softer layer underneath that rough-around-the-edges cowboy exterior. Together, a rather nice package. The early-morning beard growth added to his rugged appeal.

Following that line of thought, Caroline opened a new folder on the computer and began moving photos of Jack into it. One stopped her—the one she'd taken the night he'd ridden by the cabin on his way home after the cow had been found sick. Again, she zoomed in. If she were writing a book about cowboys, this would be the cover shot. He and his horse were outlined in a faint glow from the last bit of sunlight before dark. Almost a silhouette, the photo had a dramatic pull. Horse and rider as one after a long day on the ranch, a faint cloud of dust diffusing the image.

When her phone rang, she started, her heart racing as if she were a teenager caught parking in her boyfriend's car. With a light laugh, she turned from her computer to her phone and saw her daughter's face light the screen.

"Hi, sweetie." She spoke into the phone then pushed back from the table and wandered outside. She'd been working inside and hadn't realized the day was so beautiful. A pleasant breeze floated across her skin, and the sun shone in a crisp blue sky interspersed with puffy white clouds.

"Hey, Mom. How's it going?"

"Good. I'm sorting photos. Getting some nice shots."

"Yeah? Of what?"

The direct question had her tongue-tied for a moment. Probably best not to let Lauren know the subject matter Caroline had been viewing. The questions would be relentless.

"Some pictures from last night." Not a lie in the least. "The coolest thing happened. I got to watch the birth of a foal."

"Oh, that's awesome. You were at the barn at night?"

Caroline rolled her eyes. "Yes, the barn isn't far

from my cabin. I'll send you a picture. The little foal is so darn cute."

"You're not riding at night, are you? That sounds—"

"Lauren." She used her best mom voice.

"Well, you said you were taking pictures of sunsets."

"Yes, from the front of the cabin. Give me a little credit here."

"Do they have my number as an emergency contact? What if something happened, Mom?"

"Yes, honey. I filled out a bunch of forms, and one of them included an emergency contact. You can relax, okay?"

"Fine," she said in a huffy tone. "How long did it take?"

"What?"

"The birth of the baby horse."

"Oh, gosh, all night. I needed a long nap this morning."

"You were at the barn all night? Who else was there?"

"Jack, the owner, oversaw the whole thing. He knew exactly what to do."

When her comment was met with silence, Caroline added, "I mostly watched and took pictures." And they'd made a connection. They'd talked. Jack had opened up a little, told her about his granddaughter. The sad—

"Mo-oom."

A confusing hint of surprise laced Lauren's words, and Caroline frowned. "What?"

"That sounds…like you spent the night with a

man."

Caroline sputtered a laugh. Well, technically she had spent the night with a man, but not in the usual sense. No, it had been most unusual. She was still wondering about that kiss. And the consequences of it. "In an uncomfortable barn."

"Is this guy married?"

"No."

"Wait, is this the guy Gabby told me about? That wreck…"

"It is. He's been through a lot."

"Do you like him?"

Caroline sucked in her breath. How to put this? "Yes, he's an interesting man. He's—"

"Oh, my gosh. This is so funny. You didn't like the idea of online dating, and now you meet this guy. Wouldn't it be crazy if you—"

"Take a breath, honey." Her daughter's voice held way too much excitement. "I barely know him. Anyway, I take it back. He is married. He's married to this ranch. Hardly ever leaves it."

"Hmm. Maybe he just needs someone to get out of there with. How old is he? Is he nice-looking?"

Caroline couldn't help laughing, but her heart gave a funny bump. "Lauren, really. Yes, he's nice-looking. He's good with animals, and he's old enough to be stuck in his ways."

"Well, keep an open mind. It's okay, you know. You're a single, adult woman after all."

"I realize that."

"Dad's been gone a long time," Lauren added softly. "And you deserve to have…someone."

Lauren's tone turned serious, and Caroline

swallowed hard as thoughts pummeled inside. She and Lauren often spoke of memories of Andrew, but rarely about Caroline's personal life. Was her daughter concerned she'd end up her mother's sole caretaker? If Caroline had a companion, would it ease Lauren's tendency to worry about her? Jack Armstrong was certainly not the answer to that. Retirement would come soon enough, even if not this year, and she didn't intend to be stuck in one place.

"Anyway," she said briskly, "we watched a foal being born. Not exactly romantic. What are you up to?"

"Oh, subtle change of topics, Mom."

Caroline could practically see her daughter's eyes roll. "I think we can be done with that conversation," she responded, aware that her voice sounded ridiculously prim. She lifted her hair from her neck in hopes of a cooling breeze.

"I'm working on a presentation for a client in Denver, a boutique hotel. I hope I get to go out there sometime this summer."

"Sounds great. Maybe I'll stow away in your suitcase. By the way, I went to town yesterday. It's teeny-tiny. Think pinprick on a map. Probably not a good Mother's Day spot."

"Okay, we can figure out something else."

"All right." Caroline shaded her eyes and scanned the sky. "Oh, wow, the clouds are amazing today, like rows of cotton balls. Listen, sweetie, I'm going to let you go so I can get some pictures."

"Of clouds? I thought you were taking pictures of wildlife."

"And anything else that's interesting." Again, the photos of Jack came to mind. They definitely qualified.

She wasn't sure if they'd end up making sense in the book, but— Oh, wait. She had permission to take photos of the ranch but hadn't asked about people shots. If she included any, he'd have to sign a model release. With the phone nestled between her ear and shoulder, she stepped back inside and picked up her camera.

She'd told Jack she'd see him later. Did he take it literally? Was he expecting her to contact him? Show up at the barn or pool? She hadn't been invited to the house.

"Okay, have fun. Talk to you later," Lauren said.

Caroline signed off with a soft "Bye, honey." And wondered if there was any chance Jack would agree to sign a release. Would he feel used? Want to edit her work? She was almost afraid to ask.

****

Jack spent the afternoon scanning the banks of the creek for poisonous hemlock. At the sound of a horse's hooves, his pulse quickened. He stood and looked toward the road. Roger on Cheyenne headed toward him. And Jack felt a ridiculous disappointment that it wasn't Caroline.

He took a few steps away from the creek. If there was hemlock in the area, he probably couldn't have spotted it anyway. He'd have to look more thoroughly tomorrow. He was too distracted. He'd begun to feel the effects of a sleepless night—along with the effects of kissing Caroline. His mind was a muddle of thoughts and questions. He didn't regret the kiss, but now what?

Work was normally a refuge for him. Out in the fields, he could come up with any number of tasks and projects to occupy his time, to keep him from dwelling on his losses.

"You been to the barn?" he asked when Roger stopped his horse a few feet away.

"Sure have. Mom and baby look good. Doc checked 'em out."

Jack nodded. "The foal seemed pretty strong this morning. Given her age, I imagine that'll be Penny's last."

"How's it going here?" Roger gestured toward the creek. "Find anything?"

"Nothing so far." Jack lifted his hat and wiped his sleeve across his brow.

"Well, horses are fed and watered. Looks like our guest didn't go riding today. You might as well knock off a little early, seeing's you had a late night."

Jack squinted, not sure whether to read anything into Roger's words. He couldn't have known that Caroline joined him for the overnight birth, could he? Jack didn't see how. And he also couldn't help wondering what *their guest* had done with herself today—other than mess with his mind. "Yeah, think I'm about ready to wrap up here."

He glanced back at Roger and was surprised by the intensity of his stare. "Something on your mind?"

Roger shifted on the horse. "Maybe. Had several phone calls at the house last night."

"Yeah?" Jack waited a moment in the silence. Roger usually cut right to the chase. "About what?"

"Our guest. She went to town yesterday and apparently caused quite a stir."

"What does that mean?"

Roger put a hand on his hip and met Jack's eyes. "Look, we've been friends a long time, and I don't want to get in your business."

"Uh-huh. What business?" Roger's slow nod and slower pace to the point were about to get on Jack's nerves.

"You start something with this Caroline gal?"

Jack rubbed a hand over the back of his neck. This was unexpected. "You can simply call her Caroline." He looked past Roger for a moment then glanced around. Finally, he sucked in a deep breath. "What if I have?"

Roger swung down from the horse. "She seems like a nice lady."

"Seems to be."

"You're due for something good to happen."

Meaning he thought Caroline was something good? For Jack? "What's this got to do with your phone calls?"

"Just want you to be aware that folks are talking, that's all."

"God almighty, Roger. I'm standing here getting old. *What* are they talking about?"

"You and Caroline. Seems at least one someone was under the impression she is specifically your guest. Staying at your place."

Of course. That was a far juicier story.

"As opposed to a cabin on your ranch," Roger clarified.

"Yeah, I get the drift," Jack told him, derision in his voice. He should've expected that when she told him she'd been to town. It's why he rarely went—the simplest drop of a comment could swell into an ocean of gossip. He pulled a stalk of grass and leaned against the fence then looked across the fields. He didn't care what anyone said or thought. It didn't matter. Talk didn't last long. And probably neither would this infatuation or whatever it was. Caroline would be on to her next adventure soon enough. Maybe she'd settle back down in Nashville, but right now, she was a rolling stone. Had places to go, pictures to take, wine to drink.

He flicked a glance at Roger. "I like her."

Roger gave a slow smile. "Thought you might. Why don't you take some time off? Take her to Abilene for a night out. Have a nice dinner. Town dance is coming up. Nora's been talking about it. Maybe Caroline would like that."

"You two going?"

Roger shrugged. "Always do."

Yeah, Jack and Rosalyn had always gone, too. She and Nora helped organize it many times. Always made a big fuss about what to wear to the spring dance. Wanted something fresh. Sometimes they made a shopping day of it in Dallas. More than anything, he remembered the laughter. People were happy, feeling good, celebrating another summer. Rosalyn's smile shone a thousand watts all night. Those were good times.

He turned and braced his arms on the fence railing. "Still feels like cheating." He absorbed the silence, grateful for his friend's mindfulness and brevity.

"It's been a while," was all Roger said.

Jack's throat constricted, and his glance landed on the ring Rosalyn had placed there three and a half decades ago. Seemed like an eternity.

"Maybe I'm just too old for this." But even as he said the words, he admitted to looking forward to seeing Caroline again. He was drawn to her soft hazel eyes that seemed to look deep inside him. Those same eyes that could tease and laugh—or admonish with a steely stare.

"That's bull," Roger said.

"Well, thanks for the heads-up. Tell Nora I'm sorry about all the interruptions." He couldn't help a smile as he imagined her well-spoken, well-delivered responses to the callers.

"She's got your back, you know."

"Yep." He cringed to think he'd asked her whether she'd set him up. "Hey, the kids are coming tomorrow. Tell her to take the weekend off. I know they'd love to see you both, but no cooking for her. We'll grill out."

"I'll tell her."

Jack watched Roger and Cheyenne head up the road and debated whether to call it a day. He could always check fences along the way back to the house. The real question was whether to stop by the cabin. He'd have to go up and around the back pastures to avoid going past it. That would take him close to the ledge—best sunset-watching spot on the ranch. But he didn't think he could handle the memories that would dredge up right now.

He shook his head and swung onto Charlie's back. Maybe he should let Caroline know Reed was coming and suggest a different horse for the weekend. Jack let Charlie meander down the road toward the cabin at a leisurely pace.

As they turned the bend, Jack squinted against the late afternoon sun just beginning its descent. What the heck was that? Looked like something had been dumped along the side of the road. He glanced toward the entrance. Had someone come in? Another visitor—

wait. Oh, holy hell. That looked like a person.

His pulse pounded. At Jack's command, Charlie moved into action and galloped down the road. Moments later, Jack recognized the figure lying near the road when she raised her head. His heart jumped to his throat. *Oh, no.*

Nearing her, Jack brought the horse to a stop and leapt to the ground. "Caroline? Caroline!"

She pushed up to a sitting position, and Jack crouched beside her.

"Are you all right? What happened?"

She wrinkled her brow. "What's the matter?"

Jack took her arm, searching her face. "Are you hurt?"

"What?" She gave a short laugh. "I'm fine. Move back a little."

She held up the camera Jack had failed to notice in his panic.

"I'm trying to— Rats. There goes my butterfly."

"What?"

"I had the coolest shot. Look at those cloud formations. Aren't they spectacular? From this angle, I can get the butterfly and grasses in the foreground with the blue sky and clouds—"

"Clouds?" Jack echoed. He looked at the sky where a trail of white clouds billowed amid an intense blue background.

Clouds. His chest heaved as he blew out a breath. "You're kidding me. You're lying here in the dirt to take a picture of the clouds? You can't do that standing up?"

"I'm looking for the most interesting angle. For my book, the photos have to be dramatic."

"For crying out loud," he nearly shouted. "I thought you were hurt or something."

Her eyes met his, and a soft smile crossed her face before she lifted her hand to his thigh. "And you were worried?"

Her soft touch rippled through Jack. "Yeah," he muttered. "It's not every day I find people collapsed on the side of the road on my ranch."

He stood and offered a hand to help her to her feet. "You scared the hell out of me."

"Thank you, Jack. That's very sweet. I'm sorry I gave you a scare."

As his heart bounced, the conversation he'd just had with Roger came roaring back. "I, uh…" His throat clogged, and he reached for Charlie's reins. "Carry on, then, I guess. Sorry I messed up your shot."

She waved a hand as if to shoo away his words. "It's fine. Hey, have you seen the new foal today? I mean, since this morning?"

"Nope. I'll stop by when I put Charlie away. Roger says Doc was here and everything looks good, though. I'm heading that way, if you want to come along."

She dusted her hands on her jeans and looked up the road. "Uh, sure, if you think Charlie will be okay carrying both of us."

The blood rushed to his lap. That wasn't exactly what he meant, but now he imagined her riding behind him, arms circling his waist to hold on, and he thought he might black out. Obviously, the sleep deprivation was affecting him.

"Oh, never mind." She waved a hand. "You were going to put Charlie in his stall, and I don't want you to have to come back up here to drop me off. I'll meet you down there in my car."

"I do have a truck and a jeep," he reminded her. "Either vehicle can make the short trip back up. Charlie is fine."

He swung down from the horse and took the camera from her. "Let me have this, and you hop on." She could ride in front of him and hang onto the saddle. He'd have to put his arms around her to gather the reins, but he'd have more control over that. He helped her into the saddle, then handed her the camera and pushed himself up behind her. If she noticed him breathing hard, maybe she'd assume it was the physical exertion.

He settled in behind her. As he reached for the reins, the gentle herbal scent of her hair teased his senses, and he felt the warmth of her legs against his thighs. He sucked in a deep breath, and motioned Charlie to move. It was the longest short ride to the barn ever.

Inside, he stopped Charlie and helped Caroline down. "Why don't you check on the little one while I take care of this guy?"

"Sure."

He and Charlie both needed a cooldown.

A few minutes later, Jack joined Caroline outside Penny's stall.

Caroline turned to him, smiling, and almost bouncing up and down. "Jack, come look at this."

He moved forward expecting to see the mare and foal, but Caroline raised her camera in front of him. Her eyes sparkled. "Look. I got it!"

"Got what?" He stepped closer and peered at the back screen of the camera. Then let out a soft whistle.

With a shake of his head, he met her eyes and grinned. "That's amazing." Perfectly focused in the frame, the yellow butterfly perched on a stalk of grass with the blue sky and clouds behind. It was a spectacular composition. Impressive.

He couldn't help himself. He slipped an arm around her shoulders. "Nice work."

"Thanks. Thought you'd like to know you didn't mess it up."

He put a hand to his chest. "I'm greatly relieved," he deadpanned.

Caroline laughed. "I'm sure." She gestured toward the stall. "Looks like everything is great in here, too. They're so sweet."

The foal stood huddled against its mother and stared at them with an awareness that had been missing early this morning. The thought reminded Jack how long he, himself, had been up. He shoved a hand in his pocket and leaned against the door.

Caroline turned to him and cocked her head. "Did you get any sleep today? You look tired."

Jack sent her a wry smile. At the same time, he registered the warm concern in her eyes. It'd been a long time since he'd seen or felt that. Well, he occasionally caught Nora giving him a look, but that wasn't the same. "It shows, huh? No nap. You know, I thought I might invite you to dinner, maybe throw a couple of steaks on the grill. But…"

"But you're exhausted. What's funny is, I thought I might invite you for dinner at the cabin. Rain check?"

"Rain check," he agreed.

"Let's get one of those vehicles and you can run me back. I think an early night is a great idea."

He nodded and debated the timing. Maybe he should ask about the dance before he lost his nerve. Before he could reconsider. He cleared his throat as they exited the barn. "Something I want to ask you."

She turned with a quizzical expression. "Yes?"

"The town has a spring dance coming up, and I wondered if you'd like to go."

A smile spread across her face. "I saw a poster about that when I was in town. It sounds like fun. I'd love to go."

He mulled over the conversation. Had he made it clear that he was asking her to be his date? He was more than a little rusty at this. "With me," he clarified. "Would you like to go with me?"

Her smile widened and lit her eyes. "I'd love to go with you, Jack. Thanks for the invitation."

As they climbed into the jeep, she cocked her head. "Do you know the details about the dance?"

"Uh, like what?" He knew nothing. Hadn't been in years.

"Never mind. I'll chat with Nora. She'd know, right?"

"She would." Relief surged through him. "Good idea."

A few minutes later, Jack pulled the jeep in front of the cabin. He started to open the door, but she stopped him with a hand on his arm. "Don't get out. I can make it the five steps to the door."

"I'm sure you can, but I'll walk you up."

He followed behind and waited while she fiddled with the lock then pushed the door open.

She turned and smiled. "Thanks. Hope you sleep well."

He nodded and caught her hand. "I know it's only five o'clock, but may I kiss you goodnight?"

She squeezed his hand and leaned against the door frame—farther from him—rather than leaning into him.

Their eyes met and held. "You may," she whispered. "But…"

He took a step closer. "But?"

"Jack, I'll only be here a few—"

He pressed his lips to hers. He didn't need to hear what he already knew.

Chapter Ten

The next morning, Caroline took another gulp of coffee then set down her mug and pulled her boots over her socks. After the previous all-nighter and daytime nap, her internal clock was out of whack. She hadn't slept well. It had taken forever to fall asleep, and now she was getting a late start.

The forecast called for clouds with cooler temps, and she hoped a brisk ride in the open fields would prove refreshing—help clear her mind. She had no doubt Jack Armstrong accounted for some of her sleep troubles. As a surprising variable in the ranch-nature-photo equation, he'd thrown her off-kilter.

She added snacks and drinks to her backpack then picked up her camera and headed for the barn. After a quick peek at the new baby, she made fast work of saddling Star. As they left the barn, Caroline glanced toward the main house and wondered if Jack was already out and about.

If a horse or vehicle had passed by the cabin, she hadn't heard it.

On the road, she let Star canter to the closest path through one of the pastures. Then she leaned forward. "All right, Ms. Star, let's let loose a little." The cool breeze whipped through Caroline's hair, and her cheeks tingled. And, of course, her thoughts returned to Jack.

It was fun to see the ice thaw, to see deeper inside.

Was she helping to bring him back to life? The thought sent warm vibes up her spine. But what did he see in her? She was past her prime. Okay, not bad for her age. She kept active, maintained a healthy lifestyle, and had enough energy to do things. She let out a long sigh. Doing things was a big problem since Jack did nothing but ranch work as far as she could tell.

She'd been on her own a long time now and had become used to it. But sometimes it was lonely. Sometimes she'd like to curl up with someone in front of the TV, share a bottle of wine, warm up the sheets at night. But if she had a relationship with someone, she'd want companionship outside of the house, too. Someone to travel with, explore, try new things. Could Jack be a companion? She didn't see how, if he wouldn't leave the ranch.

On the other hand, he seemed like a solid, dependable man she could count on. Reliable, trustworthy. *Solid.* The word took her thoughts another direction—she thought of his kiss last night, and her face heated. His chest under her hands felt firm and muscular. No flabby beer belly or softness to Jack Armstrong. She'd come so close to leaning into him but had the presence of mind to stop herself. Part of her wondered how those arms would feel wrapped around her, holding her close. But it was too soon.

Maybe she should cash in that rain check for dinner? Smiling, she pulled her cell phone from the pocket of her backpack. She took a deep breath and texted Jack.

—Care to use that rain check for dinner tonight?—

If the skies cleared, they'd have another nice sunset. She hadn't planned to entertain when she'd bought supplies for the cabin, but she could throw together something.

****

She brought Star to a stop then swung down and walked along the road, holding on to the halter. The sky was a purplish color with possible thunderheads in the distance. She framed Star against the background and snapped some shots then moved farther down the road. Her phone buzzed, and she reached for it, expecting to see Jack's number appear. Instead, Joe's face smiled on the screen.

"Hey, Joe. What are you up to?"

"Caro, dear, I've got a proposition for you."

"Really? Do tell."

Suddenly, Star's saddle blanket flapped in the wind. Caroline glanced at the sky and found the clouds getting thicker and darker. Might be time to head back to the barn. She tightened her grip and turned the horse around.

"Have you ever been to the Outer Banks?" Joe asked.

"Once. It's been a long time, though. I'm considering the area as one of the locations for my book."

"Yeah? Well, how about you join me and a few students out at Hatteras? I was thinking it might be a good place for you."

"That sounds fabulous. I'd love to." She couldn't help grinning. Going with someone who knew the area could make for smoother travels, and she always enjoyed Joe's company. Being around students would be fun, too. They often had a perspective that shed new light on any situation. It was a sweet gesture on Joe's part. He knew she missed her students.

"We're heading out next week. If you can get to Jacksonville or New Bern, we'll pick you up. I'm renting a couple of vehicles."

Caroline's stomach dropped. "Next week?"

"I know it's short notice. Wilson's group had a trip planned but had to cancel and they can't get their money back, so we have a house to use out there."

Next week. Was she ready to leave the ranch? Could she go do the Outer Banks trip then come back?

"How long are you staying?"

"Got the place for ten days but might not stay that long."

Hmm. She toyed with Star's halter, thinking. The logistics of getting there and getting back would be complicated. And expensive to book tickets at the last minute. Her heart flip-flopped. What about Jack? If she left now, she might squelch whatever spark of something they had going. She needed time to figure out if there was even something worth exploring. She groaned inside. And she'd just agreed to go to the street dance with him.

A splatter of rain dropped on her head. Dang, the forecast said cloudy, not rainy.

"Hey, Joe, I'm starting to get rained on, and I've got one of the ranch horses out in a field. Let me get going, and I'll think about this. Can I let you know tomorrow?"

"Of course. No rush here. The invitation is open. You be safe out there."

"Thanks."

Caroline ended the call then swung onto Star's back as light rain began to fall. "Sorry, girl." She patted the horse. "I got bad intel." And, of course, with no sun, she hadn't worn a hat. Grumbling under her breath, she signaled Star to canter toward the main road.

By the time they got to the barn, the rain had stopped, but it left Caroline damp and chilled. Her phone had buzzed on the way back, but she hadn't taken time to look. Now, she pulled it from her pocket.

—Plan on dinner at the house tonight. My family will be here.—

The breath whooshed from her lungs. *Oh.* So no cozy night for two. She'd envisioned spending a quiet evening getting to know Jack better and exploring this bud of attraction blossoming between them.

She read the words again. Pretty matter-of-fact. A big announcement with little information. Well, meeting the fam could be fun. It'd be interesting to watch the family dynamics, anyway. That could tell her a lot about the man. She wished she'd had more warning, though. Or time to talk to Jack. Was his family in for a shock if she showed up? Her guess was he'd told them nothing about her. She smiled to herself. In fact, if she read him correctly, he probably figured it was no one else's business.

She hooked Star to the ties then yanked a towel from the rack inside the washroom. She blotted her face then brushed rain from her arms. At least she'd have time to clean up and change clothes before dinner. First, she tapped a response to Jack.

—Sounds great.—

With a towel from the tack room, she began drying Star. Then she brushed the horse's mane and started on her coat.

"Star!" A voice echoed through the barn.

Caroline stilled the brush in her hand and peeked around Star's head. She smiled at the boy who stood a few feet away. Looked like the family had arrived.

The boy's quizzical bright-blue eyes stared at her.

"Hello there, young man. I'm guessing you must be Dylan." And what a cutie.

Grinning, he nodded. "Yeah. And this is Star."

"I know. I've been riding her. I hope you don't mind. She's such a nice horse."

"I can ride her, too."

"That's what I hear." When he moved closer, a scar peeked from under his longish hair on one side, and Caroline wondered what other lasting effects the boy had from the accident. She turned as voices and footsteps sounded at the barn entrance. A younger version of Jack strolled inside holding hands with an attractive woman who Caroline guessed to be about six months pregnant. Reed and his wife, of course.

Caroline set down the brush and tore a hand wipe from the container on a nearby bench then took a few steps forward.

The couple stopped, and surprise showed on their faces. The woman's gaze slid past Caroline to the horse behind her.

Caroline reached out a hand. "Hello, I'm Caroline. I'm staying at one of the cabins for a few weeks. I was just brushing Star."

"I'm Kristen. Great to meet you." Kristen extended her hand then slipped past Caroline and crooned at the horse waiting, still hooked to the cross ties. "Star, baby, you look great."

Jack's son stepped closer. "Hi, I'm Reed. Jack, my dad, owns the ranch."

Caroline would have recognized him immediately even without seeing the newspaper articles or knowing the family was coming. The resemblance between father and son was strong. Both men were tall and fit with a tanned complexion and confident stance. And both Reed and Dylan had inherited the Armstrong blue eyes, though a darker shade than Jack's.

"Good to meet you, Reed. What a wonderful place this is. I'm enjoying it immensely. How nice that you're close enough to bring Dylan out regularly."

His brow crinkled a bit.

Oh. Now he was probably wondering how she knew that. He probably didn't expect a guest to know about him or his family.

"Yes, we—"

Kristen joined them again. "Sorry, just had to say hi to my sweet four-legged friend over there."

"Of course."

"She belonged to Kristen before Grandpa," Dylan offered.

"Oh, my. She is well-loved then."

When boots sounded on the concrete, they all swiveled toward the barn doors.

Jack stepped inside. "What've we got here?"

"Hey, Dad," Reed said.

"Grandpa!" Dylan dashed toward Jack and wrapped his arms around his grandfather's waist.

Jack ruffled the boy's hair. "Would you look at that? You get taller every time I see you."

When Dylan pulled back, Jack shook Reed's hand then moved in and kissed Kristen on the cheek.

Caroline smiled at the affectionate exchange. Wouldn't surprise her if the accident had brought them closer together. A tragedy could sometimes do that. She hoped so.

He turned to her. "I guess you've met my son and daughter-in-law." He patted Dylan's shoulder. "And my grandson."

"I did."

His gaze rested on her. "You get caught in the rain?"

Ugh, she'd forgotten about that. She probably looked a little on the bedraggled side. "Yes, for a few minutes. I was just drying Star." She tilted her head toward Penny's stall in the next section of the barn. "Um, about that thing that happened…I wasn't sure if it was a surprise."

"Oh, hey." Jack clapped his hands together. "Big news. Penny had her baby."

With excitement in their voices, they all took off for Penny's stall.

Caroline hung back. She'd love to see Dylan's reaction, but she wouldn't insert herself into this family moment. Her throat clogged as she watched the four move as if a single unit, and she was reminded of how small her own family circle had become. Her only sibling, a brother seven years older, lived in St. Louis with his partner and no children. When Mom was still alive, they got together for Christmas, but that hadn't happened for several years. Maybe Caroline would reach out to Thomas this year.

With a soft sigh, she turned to Star still waiting to be put in her stall. "I think you're all set," she told the horse.

From the corner of her eye, she saw Jack peek back around. "Caroline, you coming? You might want a

127

picture of this."

"I'll be right there." Smiling inside and out, she led Star into the stall then picked up her camera and hurried to the other side.

Dylan was already inside the stall with Penny and the new foal. And his smile was a mile wide.

Caroline raised her camera and took several shots.

"Caroline is a nature photographer," Jack announced.

"Amateur," Caroline added. "I'm actually a biologist, but I love photographing nature."

"A biologist?" Dylan piped up. "I'm going to be a marine biologist."

"Are you, now?" Caroline lowered the camera. "That's exciting. Have you explored the creek here on the ranch?"

Dylan let out a hoot. "There aren't any sharks in the creek." He said the words with confidence but glanced at Reed as if to be sure.

She smiled. "Ah, so you're interested in sharks and the ocean. Well, you're right about that, but there are lots of other things in the creek. I saw a frog, some really cool dragonflies, and lots of minnows. But you have to be careful, and never go alone," she added. "There could be snakes in there, too."

"Wait until you see the picture she got of a rattler," Jack said to Reed. "Nearly gave me a heart attack."

"I guess I startled the snake and your dad," Caroline said with a laugh.

Kristen and Reed exchanged a look, and Caroline would've chalked it up to concerns over snakes on the property except for the open fascination in their eyes when they looked back at her. Caroline's face warmed.

They confirmed her hunch that Jack had never been particularly friendly with any other visitors to the cabins. She'd love to know their thoughts about her. They seemed friendly enough, but she sensed a guarded curiosity in Reed's eyes. Did it matter? Did she want them to like her, accept her? Accept her as what? She gave herself a mental shake. Those questions couldn't be answered right now.

"So, guess who gets to name this little darling?" She pointed to the foal and looked at Jack.

He gestured toward his grandson. "What do you think, Dylan? Got any ideas?"

Dylan looked like a deer caught in the headlights. His mouth dropped open, and he whirled around and looked at Kristen.

Apparently, Kristen was the horse expert in the family.

"Let's see. Sometimes people use a horse's color or personality in their name. That might be a place to start."

The new baby was golden tan with a light mane. She looked even cuter today with her coat dry and clean.

Dylan studied the horse. "She's gold. Goldie? Wait, what about Dusty, like the dirt on the road? Or—" His eyes widened. "What about Sandy?"

"Those are all great choices," Reed said. He looked around the group. "Any objections?"

Jack shrugged. "Fine by me."

"Which do you like best?" Kristen asked Dylan.

He flung his arms around the foal. "I think she looks like a Sandy."

Caroline crouched and raised the camera again to

capture Dylan hugging the newborn. *So darned cute.* She guessed she knew who Dylan's new favorite horse would be. She glanced up at Jack and caught her breath. The man wore a genuine smile that transformed his face. He was…he almost looked…endearing.

His eyes met hers and held for a moment. A wave of heat rushed through her. If they were alone, she'd probably move in closer…

Whew. Might be time to retreat to her cabin and have a nice, cold beverage and reset.

"She's adorable," Kristen said. "Dylan, do you want to stay here with Sandy while we unload the car?" She looked at Jack. "We brought a lot of groceries."

Kristen smiled at Caroline. "It's the unwritten rule of the ranch. Anytime someone comes out from the city, they have to bring a cooler full of groceries."

"I appreciate that," Jack said. "Thought we might grill out tonight." He looked at Caroline. "You're in, right?"

"Um, sure." She felt the stares again. "Sounds lovely. What time?"

Jack shrugged. "Anytime. Maybe an hour or so? Have a drink on the porch first. I think Nora and Roger are joining us, too."

Oh, good. A group dinner with friends would be less awkward. This felt a little too much like bringing home a surprise date for Christmas. She hoped Jack's family would be pleased that he might be on the verge of coming up for air and engaging with the world again, but they obviously didn't have any warning. They might need some time to adjust.

Her phone buzzed in her pocket. As the group meandered toward the barn doors, she glanced at the phone. A message from Joe.

—Hey, no pressure. But Lisa says she might tag along to Hatteras if you're in.—

Caroline's stomach clenched. *Oh, no.* That just complicated her dilemma. She'd love to see Joe's wife and do some fun girl stuff on the beach. Why, oh why, did this have to happen at the same time?

Chapter Eleven

"So...is this a dinner party?" Reed asked.

He cornered Jack on the porch where he'd been enjoying an early-evening drink. Jack rattled the ice cubes in his glass and flicked a glance at his son. "It's dinner with friends."

Reed's eyes narrowed. "Caroline is a friend? How do you know her?"

Jack sucked in a deep breath and drummed his fingers against the table. The rest of the guests should be arriving for dinner any minute. He knew Reed would be curious and ask questions but didn't expect them so soon. The "party" hadn't even started. "She's staying in cabin one."

"Right, but did you know her before?"

"No. Just met her last week."

"What's she doing here?"

"Taking nature pictures. If you want to know more, you can ask her when she gets here." He glanced toward the road and wondered what was taking so long. He didn't want to sound testy, but he'd prefer Reed get to know Caroline through spending time with her and having a natural conversation. Not playing a Q-and-A game. The whole situation was awkward enough already. He'd never invited another woman into the family circle for dinner.

Reed held up a palm. "Got it. Wasn't sure if there

was anything I should know first."

Jack wasn't sure, either. This was a new situation for him. He wasn't about to speak for Caroline, declare her his girlfriend or ask his son's permission to...*date,* if that word was even used these days. Couldn't they simply have dinner?

He forced down his shoulders and moved to the grill to at least pretend to start getting ready. He wouldn't start it until everyone arrived, but he needed to do something to keep from fidgeting and watching the road.

Only moments later, Caroline's car came into sight, and his heart lurched. He gave himself a mental scolding. *Stop acting like a lovesick kid.* He wasn't even sure he wanted to pursue anything at this point. If those few kisses led to more, was he ready to go there? And could he ever convince her to stay on the ranch? Even if she had intentions of maintaining some kind of relationship, he could imagine her losing interest over time. The logistics would be complicated.

Caroline stepped out of the car. She tucked her loose hair behind an ear and looked toward the porch with a smile.

Returning the smile, Jack moved past Reed and met her at the top of the stairs.

"Evening," he said. He gestured toward the bottle of wine in her hand. "You can save that. We've got wine. Let me pour you a glass." He'd noticed her preference the night he had dinner with her at the cabin and already had a nice sauvignon blanc on ice.

Her smile widened. "That'd be great, thanks. Hi, Reed." She tossed a sweater over the back of a chair. "Turned out to be a nice day, after all."

"According to the forecast, you guys might be in for some storms next week," Reed told her.

Jack handed a glass of wine to Caroline.

"Thanks." Her brow wrinkled. "That won't cause a problem with the treatment for the hemlock, will it? Would you have to re-apply?"

"Don't think so," Jack told her. "Pretty sure forty-eight hours is enough."

"You find any more?" Reed asked.

"No. I think we got it nipped," Jack said. He avoided his son's eyes, aware that Reed would find it odd that Caroline knew anything about ranch business. He hadn't gone into a lot of detail when he mentioned the problem to Reed.

With impeccable timing, Kristen and Dylan joined them on the porch.

"Okay, the veggies and potatoes are cut and seasoned," Kristen said. "So, they're ready for roasting whenever you start the steaks, Jack."

Caroline set her glass on one of the tables. "Let me help," she said. "What else needs to be done?"

Kristen waved her off. "Not a thing. Just relax. I'd love to hear more about your photo project."

Relief whooshed through Jack, and he smiled inside. The gathering seemed natural. Caroline pitched right in as if she were part of the group, not a guest. No hesitation. No awkwardness. Felt like a normal family get-together.

"Not a lot to tell yet," Caroline said. "I'm just getting started, but I've already got some great shots. The ranch has been an amazing place to explore."

"You went exploring?" Dylan looked up from the book he'd brought out.

"Yes. That's what I came for. My book will be about exploring nature."

"Kristen writes books," Jack said.

Caroline swiveled to Kristen. "Really? What do you write?"

"Children's picture books."

"They're really good," Dylan piped up.

"Dylan was a dream fan when he was younger," Kristen said.

"How fun. What—"

"I write under my maiden name, Kristen Hanover."

"Oh, my gosh. I've heard of you." Caroline's eyes went wide. "There's a cute independent bookstore near my house. I go there a lot, and I think they've had displays of your books."

"She's won some awards," Jack added with pride in his voice.

"Wow. I can't believe I'm in the company of a celebrity. Very cool. It'll be so fun to read them to your own child one of these days." She glanced at Jack.

He hadn't mentioned Kristen's occupation before. Didn't want to seem as if he were name-dropping or one-upping Caroline on the business of being an author. He admitted he was pleased to see her make a connection with his daughter-in-law.

"That porch swing is calling my name," Caroline said. She picked up her glass and moved to the swing, closer to Jack.

He held his breath as she brushed past him. If they were alone, it'd be so easy to reach out to her. She did have an effect on him.

"This swing is so cute. It's like something out of a magazine."

"Nora ordered new pillows for it this year," Jack said. "Have a seat."

She plopped down and started rocking. "My grandmother had one at her farmhouse when I was growing up, and it was my favorite place to perch."

"It's all yours," Jack told her.

"Thanks." She took a sip of wine, closed her eyes, and let her head fall back. "This is the life. I could sit out here and read for hours."

Jack smiled. Could she? Could she be that content with such a simple pleasure? He wished he could enjoy the moment without wondering when she'd leave or what would happen next.

****

Car doors slammed shut, and Caroline jerked upright. She peeked around Jack to see Nora and Roger walking toward the house. She stood but held back while they greeted all the family members. When Nora's gaze landed on her, her eyes widened.

Caroline smiled and waved. Apparently, Nora didn't expect a cabin guest to be here.

"Caroline!"

"Hi, Nora. Nice to see you."

Nora glanced from Caroline to Jack and back again. "Nice to see you, too." Her tone was a little singsong and perhaps falsely bright, but she gave a cheery wave. "How fun you could join us."

Caroline didn't sense any slight or idea that she might not be welcome. She chalked it up to surprise. Nora had been so friendly.

Dylan moved in beside Nora and tapped the bag in her hands. "What'd you bring?"

Nora grinned. "I bet you're thinking there's some

kind of treat in here, aren't you?" She slid a round, plastic container onto the table. "Fresh strawberry pie. I swear, I've got strawberries coming out my ears." She turned and cocked her head. "Dylan, could you check that for me?"

In a clunky sleight of hand, she slipped something to Dylan behind her back.

Grinning, he took a step closer and pretended to look inside Nora's ear. "Yep. Great big one!"

She leaned closer and cupped a hand behind her ear. "What's that you say? I can't hear you."

Dylan pulled back his arm in an exaggerated gesture and held up a large, red strawberry.

As they gave each other a high-five, Caroline laughed. Seemed maybe these two had done this routine before. Sweet of Dylan to indulge the grownups and continue to play along. She turned for a quick look at Jack and found his eyes resting on her. She'd love to know his thoughts. Was he watching her interactions? Watching the reactions of his friends and family members? Wondering about her family gatherings? She and Lauren usually spent holidays with close friends. Caroline occasionally met a cousin for lunch, but they had few gatherings.

"Jack, are you keeping up with your berries?" Nora asked.

From his place at the grill, he glanced toward the netted garden that sat between the house and barn and shook his head. "Guessing I'm a little behind."

"We can take care of that tomorrow," Kristen said. "Can't we, Dylan?"

The boy gave a half-hearted shrug that suggested he'd go along, but it wasn't at the top of his list of things to do at the ranch.

"What else do you have planned for the weekend?" Caroline asked.

"Nothing, really," Kristen told her. "Normally, we'd go riding." She patted her abdomen. "But with this little bean, my riding days are over for a while. We'll probably do a lot of hanging out."

That would be great for Kristen, who probably needed some downtime, but Caroline figured Dylan would be bored and go stir-crazy. She glanced at Jack. "I bet Dylan would enjoy going to the creek and poking around a little."

"Yeah, Grandpa. Can we?" The kid's eyes lit up.

It belatedly occurred to her Jack might not want her making suggestions on how he should spend his time. For a moment, she envied him his grandson. An eager learner was always a joy to be with.

Jack gestured toward Caroline. "She'd be the one to take you. She's an expert."

Caroline couldn't help laughing. He'd pushed her suggestion right back at her. "I see what you did there," she told Jack.

He grinned at her. "Maybe we can work out something."

"I also did some research on Abilene when I was looking around online," Caroline said. "Have you ever been to the zoo there?" She spoke to Dylan but glanced at Jack and wondered if he ventured off the ranch for his grandson's benefit.

"It's been a couple of years since we've been over there," Kristen said. "That's an idea." She grabbed Dylan's hand. "You think about what you'd like to do."

Jack clapped his hands. "Hey, pool's open, too."

Oh, jeez. Caroline almost rolled her eyes. Of course, Jack wanted the pool open for Dylan. But it was another activity that guaranteed they wouldn't have to leave the ranch. What was the deal? Nora's words rang in her ears. *"I have to make my own fun around here."* But why? Was it just a way of life that everyone got used to? She couldn't imagine the cattle needing constant attention. Didn't Jack trust his staff? Maybe the man had trust issues.

Reed cocked his head at Caroline. "So you like animals as subjects."

She smiled at the opportunity to engage Jack's son in conversation. "I do. I enjoy taking pictures of animals in the wild, but I like zoos and aquariums, too. Most people don't have the opportunity to see a lot of animals in their natural habitats."

"Speaking of pictures, did you bring your camera?" Jack asked. He gestured around the table. "They might like to see your photos."

As his hand moved, the gold wedding band he wore caught the sun and gleamed around his finger. She sucked in a deep breath and watched him. When he put his hand on his hip, her eyes were drawn there. He nicely filled those jeans. Her pulse hummed a little, and she admitted she was intrigued by the man. But how could she start something with someone still in love with his wife? She absolutely could not have a relationship with Jack with the ghost of his wife lingering around them. In this situation, three was definitely a crowd.

She might have to try and find a moment to talk to him alone before she gave Joe an answer. As corny as it sounded, it might be time to ask Jack his intentions.

Darlene Deluca

"Oh, rats. I left it at the cabin." She gave a little laugh. "I doubt they'd want to look through a hundred frames of dragonflies, anyway." Caroline moved to the table. Much as she enjoyed the swing, she didn't want to appear anti-social.

"Caroline, how do you like your steak?" Jack asked on his way to the door.

She'd swear a hush descended on the group, and all eyes turned toward her. Was that a trick question? Was there a right and wrong answer? Well, for her there was only one way, and that was fully cooked.

"This might be considered a character flaw," she said. "But I prefer well-done meat of any kind."

Groans and laughter erupted around the table.

"Uh-oh, Jack. Now, what?" Roger goaded him.

"Dad's been known to refuse to serve steak turned into, and I quote, 'bricks of charcoal,' " Reed added.

She looked at Jack and laughed. "Guilty as charged."

"Had a feeling that would be the case," he told her. "Don't worry, I'll butterfly a filet, and that should do the trick." He shot his son a quelling look.

"Well, don't go to any extra trouble," Caroline said. But there was no way she could eat steak that was bloody inside. If it came to that, she'd have veggies for supper. She'd withstood peer pressure and snooty waiters for decades.

"Everyone gets what they like," Jack said, his eyes on Caroline.

She flashed him a smile that reached deep inside as she understood he'd just told the entire group he'd make an exception for her. Her heart thumped quickly. For a moment, she felt special. She hadn't been someone's special person for a long time. Sometimes she missed those moments when a silent message had passed between her and Andrew—a simple touch or a knowing look shared between the two of them. She missed that sort of intimate connection, a couple's telepathy. That she might share that kind of bond with Jack sent shockwaves thundering through her.

The sound of Kristen's chair scraping against the porch floor pulled Caroline from her reverie.

"I better start the veggies," Kristen said as Jack returned to the porch bearing a tray full of meat.

Nora stopped Kristen from getting up. "You sit and relax. I've got this."

"I'll help." Caroline followed Nora into the house and couldn't help glancing around. To her left was a bright, updated kitchen with clean white cabinets and a large center island that looked brand new. She swallowed hard and wondered how long Jack's wife had been able to enjoy the beautiful space.

To her right, Caroline took in the large, wooden table with ten cushioned chairs. The size of the table hinted at dinner parties and family gatherings. Beyond the table was a sitting area with sleek brushed-brass lamps and a large television over a stone fireplace. A long buffet that sat against one wall held a stunning blown-glass bowl and several family photos. She hadn't spent a lot of time thinking about the big house, but she was pleasantly surprised by the decor. No hunting trophies or cowboy paraphernalia. Rosalyn Armstrong had had good taste.

Caroline would've liked to peer closer at the pictures, but Nora was already busy at the refrigerator.

"Did Jack give you the grand tour?" Nora asked.

"No, this is my first time in the house. Except for down by the pool."

Nora's head popped up. "Oh, really?"

Heat washed over Caroline's face. That "oh" held surprise. Did Nora think she'd been hanging out at the house? Spending the night?

"I think we can roast the veggies and pan-fry the potatoes." Nora closed the fridge door with her foot and placed trays of food on the island. Then she pulled a cast iron skillet from a cupboard and looked at Caroline. "So, tell me. How did all this happen?"

Caroline cocked her head. "Umm. All what?"

"Dinner with the family. Jack invited you?"

Caroline sucked in her breath. Nora smiled, and her tone was pleasant, but Caroline couldn't shake the feeling that Nora didn't one-hundred percent approve.

"Yes. It turns out the man doesn't mind a little company for dinner occasionally." She infused her voice with humor, hoping to remind Nora of their earlier conversation at the cabin when Caroline suggested inviting Jack to dinner. If she remembered correctly, Nora almost encouraged it.

Caroline took the skillet full of potatoes and butter to the stove and turned so that she faced Nora. "You're surprised."

Nora shook her head. "Not really. Jack doesn't easily warm up to people, but I can tell he likes you. And I know you helped out with the poison-weed trouble and have proven yourself smart and useful."

"He also invited me to the street dance in town."

Nora's mouth opened then closed, and she stared at Caroline. "He did?"

"Yes, I'm supposed to get the details from you.

What to wear, that sort of thing."

"Oh, my. That's news." She let out a deep sigh and twisted the towel in her hands. Her gaze moved past Caroline.

Caroline waited, sensing Nora had more to say.

Finally, she leaned against the counter and met Caroline's eyes. "You know, it's funny. I've often wished for Jack to meet someone and have a life again. Don't get me wrong. I want that for him. And you…" She smiled. "You're lovely. It's just that…" Her voice thickened, and she dabbed at her eyes. "I'm sorry. It brings up so many memories and makes me miss my friend."

"Of course, it does. I understand," Caroline said softly. "No one can replace her. But change happens, and sometimes we have to start over. Adapt to new circumstances."

Nora eyed her with a thoughtful expression. "You've been there."

"I *am* there. I'm a widow of ten years, I'm considering retirement, and my only child is all grown up. It's time for me to reinvent myself. And…and I'm not entirely sure what that looks like."

"Right. You're searching for something, too. I get that. I just don't want to see Jack hurt again. He's been through so much."

Caroline flinched. She shouldn't take Nora's words personally, but they stung a little. "Nora, I promise you, I'm not out to hurt Jack. I understand you care for him and worry about him. I don't want to offend you, but Jack is a grown man."

"I know. But how much can one person take?" She splayed her hands on the island and pinned her gaze on

Caroline. "I mean, do you think there's some future between you two?"

Caroline stirred the potatoes, giving herself a moment to think before responding to Nora. She watched the sliced spuds turn golden brown while she contemplated her feelings. In her head, she'd accepted the challenge of bringing the man back to life. But she had to admit that her heart was involved, too. His slow smile and easy cowboy gait made her tingle inside. Jack had a quiet strength about him. He had an obvious love of the land and wasn't afraid of hard work. He was fit and... Her face warmed, and in that moment, she knew she wasn't ready to leave.

"I can't tell you where this is going yet, Nora. These are deep waters for me, too. If nothing else, maybe this will help him decide whether he really wants another relationship." Privately, she wondered if Jack needed a little tough love, a nudge back into the real world. Maybe he'd been protected long enough. No one gets through life without some hardship, without facing some serious questions and difficult decisions.

"You know, my heart's on the line, too. I haven't had a serious relationship with anyone since my husband died. I don't want to get hurt any more than I want to hurt Jack." She had a life back in Nashville, and getting involved with Jack could upend that. She had travel plans and a daughter to spend time with and a project to finish. She couldn't give herself an answer any more than she could give one to Nora. The only thing she knew for sure was that something had ignited between her and Jack.

She offered a smile. "We might have to wait and see how things play out." Even if it meant risking a little heartache.

Chapter Twelve

On Saturday morning, Caroline sipped her tea at her computer rather than on the front porch. The monitor glowed with an unwieldy number of tabs open as she switched back and forth, comparing airline ticket prices and flight schedules.

She'd chosen tea over coffee for the task—easier on her stomach. She'd enjoyed a lovely evening last night with Jack and his family and friends, but awoke feeling a little unsettled, her emotions ping-ponging from content to confused and everything in between. The collision of her past, present, and future was so unexpected. Each pulled her in different directions.

If only there were two weeks' difference in either Joe's trip or the Stockton dance. She blew out her breath. *Schedule.* Wasn't that exactly what she'd been trying to avoid when she left home? Not being tied to a calendar or someone else's timetable?

Too bad she had to make a quick stop in Nashville to pick up different clothes and water shoes. Another complication, but she wasn't going to buy all-new gear. Joe's latest text gave her the opportunity to fly out of Nashville with the group, but it meant moving her departure up. She'd have to leave first thing Monday morning.

She ran the mouse over the most promising options, double-checking dates. She could make this flight work if she wanted to. She hated the idea of letting down Joe's wife. If Lisa was pinning her decision about going to Hatteras on Caroline, she should go for Lisa's sake. Or she could stay put on the ranch for Jack's sake and continue to explore what simmered between them. Jack probably wouldn't care as long as she was back in time for the dance. Or would he take it as a sign she wasn't interested? She shook her head to clear it. "Enough," she muttered. "I'm doing all of it for my own sake."

Splitting her time would be expensive and probably an exhausting undertaking, but thinking about the spontaneity of going to the coast gave her a little boost of adrenaline. Besides, she wanted to stay active and enjoy her time off. Renewal was part of the purpose of a sabbatical. And that meant being flexible and open to opportunities.

When her phone rattled against the table, the noise startled her back to the present.

—Dylan chose the creek. You good with that?—

Her heart bounced at Jack's text. That answered the question of how Caroline would spend her Saturday.

—Of course.—

She wondered if the whole crew would be coming along, or if the rest of the family was happy to have someone new to keep an energetic, curious kid entertained. She didn't yet know whether he demanded a lot of attention or could be content on his own for good chunks of time. Some bright kids could get lost in their own world.

She got up and retrieved her credit card. Better take care of the travel plans before anything changed or sold out. She didn't want to piece that puzzle together again.

A moment later, the phone rang, and she picked up with a smile. "Hey, Jack. I'm looking forward to an outing with Dylan. Who else is in?"

"Looks like I'll be the only one tagging along."

She gave a light laugh. "You're not the tagalong. I am. Sounds fun. Are we riding or driving?"

"We better take a jeep. I'll get a cooler ready with some drinks and swing by to pick you up."

"Great. I've got snacks."

"How's ten o'clock sound?"

"Works for me. I'll be ready."

She ended the call and poured a fresh cup of tea. She still had plenty of time to enjoy a more leisurely cup on the patio before getting ready. Outside, cool air brushed over her skin, but the sun promised a warm day. A faint breeze wafted by as she sank into a chair and raised her face to the sky.

The ranch was a beautiful place. Vast, yet comfortable. Caroline had expected a quiet place where she could relax and think and reflect. It delivered that. She just hadn't expected to have so much on which to think and reflect. The possibility of a romantic relationship was way more than what she came for. Meeting Jack's family was another surprise. The vibes of kinship and familiarity—shared stories and jokes—took her back in time.

Though the gatherings were years in the past, she remembered fondly the rowdy group holidays at her grandmother's house as a child herself and when Lauren was young. Those were good times. But the family had fractured when her grandmother died, and kids got busy with their own schedules.

She honestly didn't know if her daughter missed

the larger family events or how she might react to being part of another family's celebrations if Caroline ever got that close to someone. More likely, Lauren would be the one to find a new family and pull Caroline into their gatherings. Someday, perhaps there would be in-laws and grandchildren. That would change everything.

She admitted to being a little nervous about spending the day with Jack, curious about his take on meet-the-family night. But she thoroughly looked forward to hanging out with Dylan and exploring the ranch through his eyes. She enjoyed teaching and interacting with college students, but younger kids were a lot of fun, too. She often volunteered for community science events and helped with summer nature camps. She liked to think she might inspire a kid or two down a path to a scientific career. Or at least, to view the world through a wider lens.

Maybe while the boy inspected the stream and ponds, she and Jack could have a quick heart-to-heart. The underlying currents from last night would work themselves out as long as she and Jack were on the same page.

An hour later, the crunch of gravel outside signaled their arrival. She snapped the lid on her to-go cup then swung her camera over her shoulder. At the door, she lifted her backpack then stepped outside to greet Jack and Dylan.

"Good morning, you two." She tossed her things into the back seat then climbed into the front seat Dylan had vacated.

"Hi, Miss…" Dylan looked at Jack. "What do I call her?"

"She's Miz Tate to you."

Caroline laughed. "Oh heck, that's too formal. What about Miz Caroline?" She, too, looked at Jack for his approval.

He agreed with a short nod.

"Grandpa, is she your girlfriend?"

Oh jeez. Kids came with no filters. She held her breath and shot Jack a sideways glance. The question had been directed at him, not her.

"I believe we decided she's Miz Caroline." His voice was gruff, and Dylan mercifully didn't pursue it further.

Caroline hid a smile behind her hand. Thankfully, Dylan's question required no response from her.

A moment later, they turned off the main road and arrived at the first gate. As soon as the car stopped, Dylan scrambled out.

"I can help." Caroline started to get out, but Jack's hand on her arm stopped her.

"He can do it."

"That gate's pretty heavy." Her eyes met Jack's.

"I've been criticized for expecting too much and not being sensitive, and I'm trying to get better. But he can do this."

Caroline looked from Jack to Dylan.

The boy fiddled with the latch. The metal gate was solid, but most boys his age could probably handle it. She didn't know if Dylan had physical impairments from the accident that weren't visible. Because of his injuries, people probably treated him more timidly than they would any other kid his age. To her, he seemed normal in size and stature, maybe a little thin. His hair didn't completely cover the scar on his face, but it wasn't disfiguring. She hoped it wouldn't define him or get him bullied.

Caroline glanced back at Jack and wondered who had criticized him. Obviously, someone whose opinion mattered.

"Lots of opinions when it comes to parenting, and grandparenting, I suppose."

He nodded. "And times change."

"True. You know, when my daughter was young, I hoped for her to be curious more than anything. I encouraged her to ask questions and take her time looking at nature and the things around her. It used to drive my husband crazy because it meant Lauren asked, why, why, why and dawdled around." She smiled as memories crashed in. There were so many. They'd practically been on a first-name basis with all the keepers at the Nashville Zoo. "A trip to a park or zoo could take hours. But you know what? I believe it gave her the ability to think critically and to ask what-if? And those are great skills for a successful career."

Jack swiveled her direction. "I didn't spend much time analyzing that kind of thing when the kids were young. Left most of it to my wife. That's the way it went in my family."

"Well, like you said, things change. Kudos to you for realizing that and making an effort." She gently touched his sleeve. "You're right to consider his abilities and help build skills."

"Doing things like this will give him confidence. I'm all for book smarts, but kids need to learn how to do stuff, too."

The gate swung open, and Jack moved the jeep forward through the opening, then they waited while Dylan secured the latch again.

He hopped into the car grinning.

He got a chin-bob from Jack, but Caroline held up her hand for a high-five. "Great job, Dylan. Thanks for doing that."

They jostled up the road a mile or so, and then Jack pulled to the side. "Easy access to the creek from here," he said.

Only minutes later, they set up chairs along the bank of the creek and peered into the murky water.

"Are there really snakes around here?" Dylan asked.

"I saw a snake, but not around the water," Caroline told him. "There's only one kind of venomous water snake in Texas. That's the western cottonmouth. So be aware, but don't worry."

Jack's brows rose. "Is that something you already knew, or did you research it before you came to the ranch?"

She warmed under the appreciation in his eyes. "A little of both. I try to be prepared when I'm out in nature."

"Look!" Dylan shouted.

Caroline crouched, and her eyes followed Dylan's finger. "Oh, it's a toad. Good eye, Dylan. Nice job. Too bad I don't have a field guide with me. We could look up what kind."

"I've got a couple at the house," Jack told him. "You can take one home if you want."

Dylan grinned. "Yeah, cool."

Jack sank into a chair and gestured toward Caroline. "Have a seat."

She met his eyes. Something in his voice told her it wasn't a casual suggestion. She grabbed her drink and plopped down beside him.

"What are Reed and Kristen up to today?" she asked. Seemed like a good icebreaker. Probably wasn't the right time or place to tell him her plans had changed in case that became a broader conversation.

"I believe Reed was going for a ride, and Kristen wanted to sleep in and then sit at the pool." Jack glanced over. "Hopefully, we're helping make that agenda happen."

"Right. I imagine she could use some R and R." Whether Jack wanted time alone with her, or his grandson, or was making himself scarce for Kristen's benefit, Caroline appreciated his thoughtfulness.

"She keeps pretty busy. I admit we got off to a shaky start when Reed first brought her to the ranch. But she turned out to be exactly what he needed." His voice trailed off, and he plucked a blade of grass from the field. "She helped them pick up the pieces. Took to Dylan and has been a terrific stepmom to him."

"That's wonderful. They seem happy, and now a new baby." The world keeps spinning. Life begins again. The pieces of the puzzle are rearranged. "Lots of happy times ahead."

"I hope so."

Whew, that got serious in a hurry. She nudged Jack's arm. "Tell me, was there any conversation after I left last night?"

Jack glanced at her then out at the land beyond them. When he looked back, a smile flickered across his face. "About you?"

Caroline fiddled with the lid of her cup but didn't look away. "Yeah, about me."

His smile widened. "You like direct

communication."

"I do."

"There was."

"Are you going to make me pry it out of you?"

He chuckled. "No, ma'am. Apparently, it's an amazing thing that such an intelligent, talented, personable, charming, *unattached* woman would happen upon the ranch and might not mind my company."

Caroline burst into laughter. "I see."

"Is it true?"

She sucked in her breath. "You know, I can only speak to a few of those items."

"You going to make me pry it out of you?"

Okaaaaay, direct communication. *Walk the talk.* "Well, according to a few documents hanging on the wall of my office, I'm reasonably intelligent."

"Uh-huh." He studied his hands.

"And I am unattached."

"Uh-huh."

She waited until he looked her direction then sent him a soft smile. "And I do enjoy your company."

"Good." He nodded. "That's good."

"Does your family agree?" She glanced at the creek where Dylan walked up and down the bank. She loved the serious intensity on his face—how searching for signs of wildlife absorbed his attention.

"Agree with what?" Jack asked.

"That it's good."

His eyes widened slightly. "I have no reason to think otherwise. Do you?"

"No, but I'd be the last to know. They're wonderful people, Jack. I enjoyed getting to know them. But when someone new joins the group, the dynamics can shift. Sometimes that's uncomfortable."

His face darkened. "No one's going to tell me my business."

She couldn't help laughing. "No, I suppose that would—"

"Grandpa, check this out."

When Jack hesitated, Caroline waved him forward. "Go ahead," she said softly.

She watched his retreating figure. His confident gait matched his words. The man exuded a king-of-his-castle, lord-of-his-lands aura. Jack may believe he didn't answer to anyone else, but she guessed his son would have something to say on the subject no matter how much Reed found her charming or smart or good for his dad.

She picked up her camera and stepped toward the creek, but the sound of hooves stopped her. She swung around and found Reed on one of the larger horses trotting along the road. *Um, that was weird.* Hopefully he couldn't read her thoughts. She pasted on a smile and waved.

"Hi, Reed. Come join us."

Reed swung down from the horse and looped the lead line around the fence post.

"Hey, Caroline. Good timing. Thunder has been wanting to graze for the last fifteen minutes." He clapped the horse. "Go for it, bud."

"Did you have a nice ride?" The horse's coat shone with perspiration, as did some wayward locks underneath Reed's hat.

"Sure did. Thunder doesn't mind a good workout occasionally. Fun to get out in the open and pick up some speed."

Caroline gestured toward the cooler on the ground. "We've got cold drinks if you'd like something."

"I would." He made his way to the cooler and pulled out a bottle of water. "Thanks. Guess I wasn't as prepared."

"It's warmer than usual from what I understand."

"Little bit. Probably warmer than Nashville."

"Definitely."

"It's what you were looking for?"

His voice was pleasant, but she wondered if there was a double meaning to the question. Stalling, she took a sip of her drink. *Don't read anything into it.* "Well, I didn't come for the weather specifically. But I have to say, it's been nice to get a jump on spring."

"Yeah, it's—"

"Hey, Dad! Come look at this."

Reed turned toward the creek but stayed put. "What've you got?"

"Some kind of fish. And some minnows."

"No sharks?"

Dylan rolled his eyes. "Yeah, huge one. Just about bit my arm off."

Reed laughed and turned back to Caroline. "Hope this isn't keeping you from your own work."

"Not at all. It's fun to see someone else energized by nature. I guess it's part of why I stuck with teaching for so long."

"Dad said you've got some great photos. Could I take a look? Love to see that snake he was talking about."

"Oh, sure." She removed the camera from around her neck, found the beginning frames, and set it for playback. Then she handed it to Reed. "Just push this button to flip through."

"Got it."

She left him with the camera and joined Jack and Dylan. "How's it going over here?"

"I think we have a biologist in the making," Jack told her. His voice held a note of pride, and she wondered if he had visions of Dylan becoming a veterinarian or taking over the ranch someday. Dylan had a fascination with sea life, but the kid was nine. His interests could change a hundred times.

"Excellent." She knelt beside Dylan. "Finding some cool stuff?"

"Yeah, something just buzzed by. Maybe a dragonfly."

"Maybe. I got some pictures of a cool blue one the other—"

Oh, no. She bolted upright. She shaded her eyes and looked across the field at Reed. Still absorbed in studying her photos. She groaned inside. That wasn't all she had pictures of. She'd organized her files on her computer and put all the photos of Jack in a separate folder. But not so on her camera. The raw images were still on the disk. Every single one of them.

She should've stayed there and taken the camera after Reed saw the rattlesnake. Without a doubt, he'd think she had a thing for his dad—if not stalking him. Obviously, he already knew she and Jack had started some sort of relationship, but some of the photos were so…personal. Close shots of Jack's expressions, smiles for her. *How embarrassing*.

"Dylan, you about ready for a break?" Jack asked. "Then we could move to a different place, maybe one of the ponds."

"Okay."

She fell into step beside Jack and Dylan. "I think the snacks are still in the jeep."

"I'll get 'em," Jack told her.

Caroline approached Reed but avoided his eyes. *Give me the camera, already.* She reached for it. "Did you see the rattlesnake?"

"I did. Great shot. Can't say I'm excited that it's here on the ranch, though."

"Yeah, but I suppose it's good to know."

"You got some nice shots of Dad." His voice lowered.

It was a simple statement, but full of observation. Caroline could feel his stare. In the awkward silence, she wanted to sink into the ground. But she pulled herself together. She sucked in her breath and met his eyes. "Thanks. Turns out he and his horse are quite photogenic." She gave a little laugh and hoped her face wasn't as red as it felt.

With the camera securely around her neck again, she wiped her clammy hands across her jeans. She wouldn't be making that mistake again.

When Jack returned with the snack bag, Reed stood. They'd only brought three chairs.

"You coming to the pond with us?" Jack asked.

"Nah, I think I'll put Thunder in his stall then head back to the house."

Jack gestured toward Caroline. "Did you see her pictures?"

"I did. Amazing. Never knew the ranch had so many photo ops."

She willed him to shut up about the pictures, then

an idea sparked. "I should get a picture of the three of you. It'll just take a minute. How about there by the fence?"

"That'd be great," Jack told her.

He and Reed stood side by side, and each placed a hand on Dylan's shoulder in front of them. "Oh, this is cute," Caroline said. Hard to believe Dylan wasn't Reed's son. They obviously shared the same DNA.

Reed leaned against the fence then pulled Dylan's hat down over his eyes.

"Hey!" The move got him a playful punch from Dylan. "Dad, look out! Snake!"

Reed swiveled, and Dylan doubled over, cackling.

"You two knock it off," Jack said, but his smile held amusement.

Caroline laughed. It was nice to see that despite the tragedy they'd endured, the family was healing and moving forward. The easy playfulness between Reed and Dylan showed in their smiles and actions. She peered into the viewfinder again, and her throat clogged. She remembered being silly with Lauren at that age.

She hadn't had this much exposure to a family unit in years. And for the first time in years, she felt as though she were missing out. Her heart somersaulted, and she let her thoughts drift. *What if?*

Chapter Thirteen

Jack hated to renege on the dinner invitation he'd extended to Caroline. But in this instance, he figured the women knew best. They agreed that Kristen needed a stress-free, low-key evening. He'd discovered his daughter-in-law hadn't felt well all day when he and Dylan returned from their pond adventure.

From the sitting area adjacent to the kitchen, Kristen gave Jack a wan smile. "Sorry to be such a party-pooper. I was looking forward to spending more time with Caroline. She seems like a great gal."

Jack handed her a glass of water. "She said the same thing about you. It's not a problem. Besides, she's traveling alone. Says she enjoys a book and her own company." Under other circumstances, he'd say they'd do it another time. But he had no idea if that opportunity would present itself. He appreciated that Kristen was open to including Caroline, and he could reassure her on that score.

"Dylan thought it was cool to hang out with a real scientist today," Kristen added. "It was sweet of her to do that. Right, Dylan?"

Dylan looked up from his electronic game. "Yeah, she's nice."

"She's a popular professor," Reed said from his perch beside Kristen.

Jack frowned. "How would you know that?"

Reed popped the top from a bottle of beer and shrugged. "I Googled her, Dad. Haven't you?"

Jack crossed his arms and stared at his son. "No. I haven't gone snooping around into her personal business." Was that the way things worked these days?

"It's not snooping. It's public information. Don't you guys do checks on the people who rent the cabins?"

"Nora handles that. There's a form they have to fill out, and it goes to a company she's hired. Not exactly a background check but a scan for red flags."

"Good."

He didn't like the idea of checking up on Caroline. Felt nosy, as if he didn't trust her. But now he couldn't help wondering what Reed had seen.

"Jack, why don't you go ahead and preheat the oven," Kristen said. "I won't eat much, but you might as well bake both pizzas. That'll give you easy leftovers."

"Fine by me." Normally, he appreciated leftovers with little demand on his time or cooking skills. But…a new reality jolted his system. Truth was, sitting at the table or in front of the TV alone sounded lame…lonely. He'd been doing just that for years. He had to admit, dinner with Caroline sounded much more appealing.

But inviting someone to dinner for leftovers was lame also. Invite her over and ask her to cook? Another no. He let out a deep sigh, and Roger's words rang in his ears, "*take her to Abilene for dinner out.*" She'd probably like that. Get him off the ranch. But did he want to? What was that children's book Rosalyn used to read…*If You Give a Mouse a Cookie*…? What if he took a woman to Abilene? Then what? A weekend in Dallas? And then…? Would he have to keep one-upping himself? He didn't know what the expectations were anymore. Was he complicating his life? Wasting his time?

Another idea came to mind. He could put together a simple charcuterie selection and grab a bottle of wine then take her up to Sunset Ledge. Could he? The collar tightened around Jack's neck. The ledge was a special place, a romantic place. For him and Rosalyn, a night at the ledge often ended with lovemaking.

Blood whooshed in his ears. That train of thought was like shooting electricity into his veins. Did he have those same longings for Caroline? He pushed off from the island and strode to the oven. But the idea had taken root, and he mentally prepared a list of supplies for going up to the ledge. He'd need to round up the flashlights and make sure they had fresh batteries. Make sure the folding chairs still functioned.

Kristen rose from the sofa. "I think I'll go on upstairs." She stopped and picked up the box of crackers on the table. "Don't forget there's strawberry shortcake, too. Berries are already sliced in the fridge."

Dylan looked up again. "Yum!"

"Thank you, Kristen." Jack patted her arm. "You get some rest."

He glanced around the kitchen and spied the baking dish covered with a cloth. He smiled to himself. No reason leftover strawberry shortcake couldn't be served to a guest. Later, away from prying eyes, he'd send Caroline a text. He glanced at Reed—and he might spend a few minutes at the computer.

****

Jack tried not to check his watch. He didn't necessarily want to cut short his time with his grandson, but the night dragged on, and he'd long-since lost interest in the movie. At nine forty-five, Jack peeked at the watch again—and Dylan caught him.

"Grandpa, you don't have to stay up with me. I'm not a baby."

"I know that, young man." He reached out and ruffled the kid's hair. "I enjoy your company."

"It's almost over anyway."

"When it is, how about you play your games quietly in your room until you're ready to fall asleep?"

"Okay."

Jack took Dylan's attitude as permission to ignore the remainder of the movie. He picked up his phone and began a text to Caroline.

—Evening, Caroline. The family will probably leave after lunch tomorrow. Would you like to have a simple dinner and watch the sunset with me? I know the perfect place.—

The quick ding of the phone let him know she was still up.

—Hey Jack, that sounds lovely. How's Kristen feeling?—

A whisper of pride flowed through him. Caroline was a thoughtful woman. She was quick to ask about Kristen.

—Turned in early. Hoping she gets a good night's sleep.—

—Me, too. Enjoy your visit with them, and let me know what I can bring for sunset dinner.—

—Not a thing. I hope you don't mind leftover strawberry shortcake.—

—Are you kidding? Sounds amazing.—

—Goodnight. Sleep well.—

163

He waited until Dylan gathered all his things and went upstairs, then Jack turned off the television and headed to the office. He hoped he didn't need any special programs installed. He used his computer for accounting and placing supply orders. Not for *social media*. Not for spying on people.

When the monitor sprang to life, he took a deep breath and settled into the chair. "Here goes," he muttered.

A long list of results populated the screen. The first was Caroline's professional page from Vanderbilt. He clicked on the link, and her smiling face appeared. It was a pretty picture that captured her personality. Even in serious career attire, a gold suit with matching blouse, she looked friendly, approachable.

He looked closer and grinned. A gold and diamond dragonfly glittered from the chain she wore with that power suit. How appropriate. The page had been updated to label her on sabbatical, but still included a bio and list of accomplishments. She'd been with the university for twenty-five years and co-authored a whole host of papers. After her bio was a personal statement. One line jumped out at him—

"...to teach and deliver critical information to a new generation of students, but also to inspire and engage them in the natural world around us." He could almost hear the confidence in her voice.

The next page featured some photos of her in both classroom and field settings. Her intensity and enthusiasm shone on her face. He returned to the search results and found one of the professor rating sites.

"Made a boring subject interesting."

"Took this class because I had to get a science

credit. Ended up changing my major."

"My favorite professor."

Very impressive. Jack scrolled through more praise for Caroline, and the truth punched him in the gut. He didn't think it could ever happen, but he was attracted to another woman. Wanted to be with another woman. With this woman.

His glance dropped to the gold band on his finger. He twisted the ring around. He'd become more aware of it recently—aware that it had become a memento, a treasure from another time. He'd clung to it like a life preserver as he drowned in deep waves of grief. But he saw now, in order to breathe again, to come up for air and live again, he was going to have to take it off.

He sat in silence for a few moments, then pushed back from the desk and turned out the lights. Quietly, he headed for the storage room. He opened the supply closet and found a rag and cleaning spray. Then he located the lantern and flashlights. He switched them all on and off and examined the batteries. One seemed fine. One cast only a dim flicker. The other was corroded.

In his head, he checked off a list of things to do as he prepared for a climb up to the ledge. Thankfully, Caroline had come to the ranch properly prepared. That in itself shocked him. How this beautiful, smart, lovely woman had stumbled across his ranch was a mystery. Seemed barely short of a miracle. He didn't actually believe it, but had fate intervened on his behalf?

A tremor of adrenaline vibrated through him, and he couldn't help smiling. He ripped open a package of D-cell batteries. Somehow even the fresh batteries seemed like a good omen. He was looking forward to the outing with Caroline—and anticipation was something he didn't feel much of these days. Not for himself, anyway.

Of course, he welcomed the soon-to-be-grandchild, and hoped for happy days ahead for his son and the family. He couldn't help thinking it'd be nice to have someone to share the news with. He remembered Caroline's delight in the new foal, how she'd named the baby calf. No doubt she'd turn to mush over a new baby.

Whistling, he pulled one of the folding chairs from its bag and examined it. A little dusty, but still functional. He sprayed the cleaner on the aluminum frame and dusted the seatback. Then he stilled his hands and laughed at himself. Whistling. He did a lot of mundane tasks to keep himself busy, his mind occupied. But when was the last time he'd caught himself whistling?

****

Between the two of them, Jack and Reed finished off the pot of coffee in record time Sunday morning. Jack chalked it up to nervous energy.

"We're gonna go ahead and hit the road," Reed said after brunch. "I don't like being this far away from a hospital or Kristen's doctor. It'll probably be our last visit before the baby comes."

Jack didn't protest. Abilene had a hospital but certainly not a neo-natal unit that could handle a premature birth or major problem. He figured Kristen would know if there was a serious issue, but he couldn't fault Reed for having pre-birth jitters.

"Best to be cautious," he said.

"You could come to Dallas anytime, you know."

"I know." He had a standing invitation.

"Yeah, Grandpa. You could come for my school Fun Day. We do races and stuff and there's a carnival with a bouncy house and cake walk. I won a big chocolate cake last year."

Jack groaned inside. All great activities for a nine-year-old. "Sounds like fun," Jack told him. But there wasn't a chance he'd leave Roger to pick up the slack on the ranch for something like that. He turned to Reed. "You have a plan for where Dylan will be when the baby comes?"

"Yep. All set. He'll stay with Kristen's friend Jana. She was maid-of-honor at our wedding and Dylan's kindergarten teacher."

"I remember her. Good deal." Jack stood and patted Dylan's shoulder. He didn't mean to rush them out, but he had a task he needed to take care of on his own. He wouldn't do it while Reed was there. His son might need a little more time to adjust to the idea of Jack seeing someone.

Jack helped load the car while Reed got Kristen settled into the passenger seat. "You take care," Jack told her.

"Bye, Grandpa." Dylan waved the old pocket field guide Jack had found among his reference materials. "Don't forget. I'm going to give you a pop quiz."

"I'll be ready."

Jack watched the dust billow behind the car for a long time—until the car was no longer visible. Then he turned slowly back to the house. He climbed the stairs and entered the kitchen. Silence wrapped around him. The house was quiet. Still. Empty. His footsteps echoed on the hardwood floors as he made his way to the library.

He paused for a moment with both regret and hopefulness in his heart. Pulse pounding, he turned the handle and pushed open the door. *It was time.*

He didn't know what kind of relationship Caroline might be looking for, but he couldn't imagine she'd want to move forward while he still wore another woman's ring. And it wouldn't be fair to her.

He sank into Rosalyn's chair and picked up the framed photo from the desk. It was one of his favorite pictures of the two of them—a candid that Roger had shot. Rosalyn sitting on a fence with Jack standing beside her, and they were looking at each other. He remembered looking at his wife that day and had never been happier. And he'd seen the same love shining back at him.

Rosalyn had always been generous with her love. Taught their kids to be, too. "Here's the cool thing about love," she used to say. "You can give it away all day every day and never run out." In his heart, he knew she wouldn't want him to live without love.

"I miss you so much, babe, and I always will," he whispered. "I know you know that, Ros. So, I'm…" His throat tightened, and he could hardly get the words out. "I'm going to do this thing." He twisted the ring. "It's something I have to do."

The ring was tighter than it used to be, and it resisted the first tug. But another couple of twists, and it shimmied off his finger. He replaced the photo, and with the ring in his fist, walked quietly from the room. In their bedroom, he gently placed the ring inside a small box that held his father's old watch and a few coins from his mother's purse.

Jack knew getting involved with Caroline Tate could bring more loss, more heartache. He wouldn't pin any hopes on keeping her at the ranch. But he'd learned how unpredictable life could be. And he wasn't a coward.

****

Caroline breathed a sigh of relief. She'd called Nora to make sure she could hold the cabin for her and get permission to leave a few items behind. And the conversation had transitioned easily to the dance. No difficult questions or discussion of her relationship with Jack.

"I'm sure whatever you wear will be perfect, but the unofficial dress code is a denim skirt and a fancy blouse and boots," Nora said.

"Sounds great. I'll pick those up when I stop at home." She wouldn't have time to shop so something in her closet would have to do. A shimmery turquoise top with low back came to mind. That might work. "Really looking forward to my first small-town street dance."

Nora chuckled. "Fair warning, you'll be the talk of the town. You take care, and we'll see you when you get back."

Caroline ended the call, but Nora's words echoed. *Talk of the town.* Because she was a curiosity—Jack Armstrong's date. Well, surely she could hold her own and not do anything embarrassing. It'd be interesting to see Jack mingling with the town folks. She had the feeling that even though he'd become something of a recluse, he was held in high regard.

She glanced out the window. Clouds were moving in. Hopefully they'd blow on past and not cause problems for sunset watching. A few high clouds could

169

Darlene Deluca

add interest to a sunset, but heavy cover would make it a bust. Either way, she hoped they'd still get together so she could tell Jack her plan in person.

She blew out a breath and reached for her jacket. Time for a break. Outside, the air felt heavy, but the skies were mostly clear. Maybe she'd go for a quick ride before she met up with Jack later. She went back inside to collect her things and went out the front door. She stopped short. *Oh, my.*

To the west, heavy, threatening clouds had formed in the distance. She pulled her phone from her bag. There'd been no mention of rain in the forecast this morning. It took a moment for the weather app to load. When it did, an alert flashed on the screen. Tornado watch. Caroline shook her head. That came out of nowhere. So maybe no ride.

She chewed her lip, wondering what kind of plan the ranch had set up for severe weather. Nora hadn't mentioned anything. There might be something on the website. She'd better go to the barn anyway. Stormy weather sometimes made horses agitated. She went back inside and grabbed the bag of peppermint candies, then drove the short distance to the barn.

Caroline had only been inside a few minutes when she heard footsteps. She turned to see Jack striding toward her.

"Thought I might find you here," he said.

The warmth in his voice told her he'd *hoped* to find her. "Hi. Is the gang on the road now?"

"Probably home by now. Sorry they had to rush off."

"No worries. Hope Kristen is feeling better."

"Seems to be. Did you have a nice evening?"

"Very pleasant." She gestured toward the doors. "I was looking forward to watching the sunset tonight, but I'm afraid we might have to scrap our plan."

"We'll see. We can always do it another night."

"Of course." Sunset Ledge wasn't going anywhere, and—

A sharp clap of thunder shook the barn.

"Yikes. That sounded close," Caroline said. "What's the storm protocol around here? Is there a place to hunker down?"

"We've got a storm shelter at the house."

"Oh, is that—"

"That's where you'll go if necessary."

She cringed as unpleasant images of dark, creepy, musty holes in the ground came to mind. "Is it attached? Like a basement or one of those outside—"

"It's not as bad as you might think." He sent her a cocky grin. "It's combined with the wine cellar."

Relief rushed through her, and she let out a nervous laugh. "That doesn't sound too bad at all. In fact—"

Jack's phone pealed, and he pulled it from his pocket.

"Hey, Nora." He paused a moment then glanced at Caroline. "Yes. I heard that. No problem. She's right here."

Caroline couldn't hear the other side of the conversation, but obviously it was about her.

"No worries. I'll make sure she gets there. I'll touch base with Roger in a bit. You stay safe."

He ended the call and smiled. "Nora checking up on you. Bad for business if we don't keep our guests safe, you know."

"Right." She returned his teasing tone. "I know

how important it is to get a good review of the storm shelter."

Neighing from the other side of the barn interrupted them.

"I better check on Penny and Sandy," Jack told her. "Be right back."

"Hey, Jack, what do you do with the horses if there's a tornado? Leave them inside or turn them out in the pastures?"

He turned back to her. "Roger prefers to keep them inside. Thinks they're better protected."

"Okay. I'm going to hang out with Star for a while and try to keep her from getting jittery." She swiveled around to the horse and murmured as she patted her neck. "Don't you worry."

A few moments later, she tripped over her own bag, and her brush clattered to the floor. When she stooped to pick it up, she came face-to-face with a striped bark scorpion peeking from behind a straw bale.

She let out a shriek and jumped back. And immediately heard Jack's boots dance across the concrete toward her.

"Caroline?"

"Hey, Jack." She smoothed her hair.

"What's wrong?"

She waved a hand. "Oh, nothing."

"Nothing?" he echoed.

"Not a thing." She glanced toward the offending critter, which had scurried back under the bale of straw after making Caroline look a fool. *Thanks a lot.*

Jack frowned and crossed his arms, staring at her. "You screamed about nothing?"

"Really. It's okay. I saw a scorpion, and it

surprised me. That's all." The thing was non-venomous, but still a creepy crawler.

He took a step forward and touched her arm.

She jumped as if he'd pinched her.

And Jack burst out laughing. "Wait a minute. Let me get this straight. The woman who stares down rattlers, gets on her hands and knees in a pasture with poisonous weeds, and lies in the road to get a picture is afraid of a little scorpion?"

"Of course not." As her face warmed, she glared at him. "Like I said, it surprised me." She attempted to nudge the man out of the way. "I need to get Star's bucket."

He didn't budge. "Roger can do that. You don't need to take care of the horses." Chuckling, he propelled her against him and kissed the top of her head. "And you don't need to be embarrassed. Believe me, no one would ever mistake you for a damsel in distress."

She couldn't help it. Laugher bubbled to the surface. "I should hope not." She raised her chin. And time suspended.

His blue eyes sparkled with amusement and…and something else.

Her breath caught, and in the next instant, his warm lips met hers.

Caroline closed her eyes and breathed in the scents of the cool air, the hay and straw, all the outdoorsy scents of Jack Armstrong.

When he broke off the kiss, he pulled her closer and rested his chin against her forehead. "You're driving me crazy. You know that?"

She let out something between a gasp and a laugh

and stepped back to meet his eyes. "I'm not sure how to take that."

He brushed a calloused thumb across her cheek. "Neither am I."

She pulled back and rested her palms on his chest. "But it's a good thing, right?

He let out a slow, ragged breath.

She could almost feel indecision in his thoughts, the tension in his stance.

"I might need a little time to get used to that idea," he told her hoarsely.

She nodded, and her glance dropped. And she gasped. His gold wedding band was missing from his hand. "Jack!"

"What?"

She swallowed hard and fought to regain her composure. *Don't read anything into it*, she scolded herself. He probably took it off to work and forgot to put it back on.

But it was too late. He'd seen the direction of her gaze. And could probably guess her train of thought. She moved back. "Listen, we might be in for a storm. We should probably—"

He grabbed hold of her hand. "Caroline."

His deep voice sent warm vibrations through her veins.

"I took it off."

The blood pounded in her ears, and she put a hand to her chest.

His gaze locked onto hers and held.

"That...that's a hard thing to do," she said softly.

A current of energy passed between them, and she dropped her hand to his, to the circle of un-tanned skin around his finger. She understood it had been a deliberate act. An emotional one, no doubt. The day she'd removed her beautiful diamond wedding ring was seared in her memory forever.

He gave her hand a gentle squeeze. "It was time."

Chapter Fourteen

A wind gust rattled the barn rafters. Caroline gave Star another pat then hurried to the entrance for a first-hand look at the weather situation. She ran her hands up and down her arms as she scanned the skies. The sun had disappeared, and the temperature had dropped several degrees.

She wasn't a meteorologist, but if she read the signs correctly, hail was also possible. What a clatter that would make on the barn roof. The noise would shake the horses for sure. She glanced around the exterior to make sure there were no loose hoses or buckets ready to become projectiles. Everything looked secure but...Oh, *the garden*. Maybe she should check to see if Dylan and Kristen had picked everything that was ready yesterday. Hail or tornado would wreak havoc on the garden.

She could hear Jack still on the phone with Roger, so she retrieved a feed bucket from the supply closet and headed for the garden. She walked the rows and found that most of the crop was actually underground, so not in any serious danger. Still too early for most vegetables. Crouching in the strawberry patch, she plucked a few ripe berries that Kristen and Dylan had left.

The task gave her hands something to do while her brain switched back and forth between the impending storm and the significance of Jack's missing ring. *It was time,* he'd said.

Was he testing the waters? Tiptoeing in to see if he was ready? What if they got involved and then she left? How would that affect Jack? She didn't want to be another source of pain. Another in the list of hurts. She didn't want that on her conscience.

But he was a grown man. It wasn't as if she'd come on to him. He had initiated the kisses every time. She'd be lying if she said she hadn't enjoyed them or that she wasn't attracted to him. Her heart thumped as she remembered the feel of his arms around her. At the same time, a voice cautioned her. What would be the consequence of helping to bring Jack Armstrong back to life?

She pushed back her hair and leaned against the bucket, closing her eyes. Truth was, she rather liked the idea of being the one to do that. They didn't have to make a long-term commitment. Maybe just an icebreaker to get him to see life through a new lens. And to realize there was a whole world out there to explore.

She plopped the last berry into the bucket then moved to the cucumbers. The first raindrop splattered against her head. The cukes were still small, but she yanked them from the vines anyway.

A moment later, small pebbles of hail pelted her. And Jack's voice carried through the air.

"Caroline? Caroline!"

She picked up the bucket and left the garden plot, securing the gate behind her. Maybe it would hold. Jack's voice carried alarm, and she hurried toward the barn. The hail pieces were small but still stung against her skin.

"Caroline!"

Jack rushed toward her and took her arm then swung her around the opposite direction.

"Wait, Jack. The horses—"

"The horses will be fine. Let's get inside."

She turned and looked at the darkening sky. A menacing wall of clouds loomed in the distance. Didn't look good. Wait…were they churning? Her pulse jumped. Was that—

Jack tugged on her arm again. "Let's go."

They ran toward the house. Halfway there, the nuggets of hail hit faster, harder, and Jack pulled her under the shelter of the eaves to the freestanding garage that stored the ranch vehicles.

Caroline flattened against the doors until Jack entered a code into the small control panel, and the doors lifted. Inside, they huddled together and watched the ground turn white as hail scattered across the open yard.

"We better stay put for a minute, but as soon as this clears, we need to get to the house," Jack said.

Horses whinnied from the barn. The noise inside the garage was deafening. "I feel bad for the horses," she told Jack. "This will upset them so much."

"Nothing we can do but wait it out." He nudged the bucket at their feet and raised his brows. "You went to the garden?"

"Yes. Wanted to salvage whatever I could. This hail will do some damage."

Though he shook his head, his face broke into a grin. "You're amazing."

She laughed, but his words were like warm honey

to her insides. That was pretty tall praise from a guy who didn't often show emotion. "Because I picked a few fruits and veggies?"

"Because you thought to do it. You thought about the horses. You're cool under pressure and take action. Most people would run for cover." He took hold of her arm. "And that's what we should do as soon as this stops. We'll head for the back door."

"We don't need the cellar just for hail," Caroline told him. She hated small spaces, especially anything that resembled a cellar. Her grandmother's farm had had one. Caroline hunkered down in it twice as a child when tornadoes threatened. It had creeped her out, and she still remembered the heavy darkness and dank smell.

Jack's brow furrowed. "Could be more than hail. That's the safest place to be in a tornado."

She blew out a breath. "Let's wait a couple of minutes and see what happens."

Jack's eyes stared into hers. He cleared his throat. "Caroline. You're not uncomfortable about being down there with me, are you?"

"Of course not." She shook her head. "I know it seems silly, but I don't like small spaces with no fresh air or windows."

"We don't do big basements in Texas," he told her. "Anyway, I doubt we'll be down there long."

A moment later, the hail stopped as suddenly as it'd started.

"Come on." Jack took her arm.

Caroline grabbed the bucket, and together, they raced toward the house.

Inside, Jack pushed open a door she hadn't been

through before and switched on lights.

Holding the handrail, Caroline started down the wooden steps. She glanced around. The room was dimly lit, but with clean, white walls, it didn't feel damp or closed-in. A small sofa sat against one wall. Another wall supported a row of tall storage cabinets. A bank of diagonal cubbies held dozens of bottles of wine.

She completed her assessment, and her eyes were drawn to the sofa again. It was a cozy place for two.

****

Jack surveyed the room. Only the sofa for seating. When the kids were young and they had to shelter down here, they used to drag their beanbag chairs with them. "Have a seat," Jack told Caroline. "We might as well open a bottle of wine since we're here. And probably missing out on wine with a sunset." That thought hit with a heavy thud inside his stomach. So much for all his prep and planning. And *anticipation*.

"You don't think it'll clear when this storm passes?"

He shook his head. "There's a good chance it'll still be cloudy. Everything will be wet, which means the rocks will be slippery. And I'll have to ride the ranch and check for damage." That was life on a ranch. He swallowed his disappointment and gestured toward the bottles. "Want to pick something out?"

"Any white will be fine." She moved toward him. "So, you have the room stocked with glasses and opener just in case?"

A trace of humor softened her voice, and Jack smiled. "Can't control the weather, so it's best to be prepared."

"I'll say."

He reached for a bottle. Aware of her standing beside him, it took a couple of tries to get it opened. He filled two glasses then handed one to her.

"Thanks." She took a sip of wine. "I'm bummed about missing the sunset. I hope we can go to Sunset Ledge when I get back."

His thoughts stuttered, and he nearly dropped his glass. "When you get back?" he echoed.

She put a hand to her chest. "Oh, Jack, I'm sorry. With so much going on, I haven't had a chance to tell you. I'm leaving in the morning to meet up with Joe and some students for a week at the Outer Banks."

The matter-of-fact tone of her voice confused him. Her words were like shards of glass against his skin, but her body language was calm, relaxed, as if nothing were wrong. She was leaving? But coming back? "Oh. I…um. Fill me in." He took a drink to stop the stammering.

"I'll head out tomorrow and be back next Thursday, so plenty of time for sunset and the street dance." She flashed a bright smile.

"Let me get this straight. You're going to the Outer Banks and then coming all the way back here? For a dance?" He couldn't control the skepticism in his voice. That sounded a little far-fetched. Surely, she knew he wouldn't be taken for a fool.

"That's the plan. I've got it all arranged with Nora."

"I see."

"It's a great opportunity," she added. "I'm stopping in Nashville to change out clothes and have dinner with my daughter, then the group heads to North Carolina on

Tuesday. Lots of opportunities for photos and essays for my book. People encounter a lot of wildlife along the coast."

Jack did his best to act natural even though unwanted thoughts tumbled through his head. Would she want to come back once she returned to the real world? Out among other people? Her friends, her daughter? A beach on the Atlantic Ocean was so far removed from the ranch, it might as well be the moon.

He cleared his throat and shoved his free hand into a pocket, hoping for a nonchalant stance. "Sounds like a good place to find the kind of photos you're looking for."

"Oh, definitely. It'll be great to go with someone who knows the area. I won't have to waste time figuring out the logistics."

"Sounds good."

"Hey, can you get a Wi-Fi signal down here? How will we even know when it's safe to come out?"

Jack leaned against the cabinet. "If we get high winds or a tornado, we'll hear it. I'd say we give it thirty minutes, then I'll run up and check. Might be able to get a signal."

"What about the livestock?"

"Same as the horses, except most of the cows are in the fields. We'll check for any injuries after. Could be some flying debris."

"I hope there's no damage."

Jack offered a slight smile. "We'll deal with it."

She touched his sleeve. "How's little Lola doing?"

He looked into the soft hazel eyes gazing up at him and thought how easily they could hypnotize him. And couldn't help a genuine smile. "She's doing well.

Starting to gain some weight."

"Oh, good." Caroline crossed the small space and curled up on the sofa. She shook back her hair and patted the seat. "Might as well settle in."

Jack followed. He wondered what she would do if he sat close and stretched an arm across the back. Instead, he sat not quite at the opposite end, but slightly turned to face her.

"How often does this happen?" she asked. "Tornadoes? Sheltering down here?"

"Hmm, maybe once every couple of years." He glanced around. "We've got cards down here somewhere. And a couple of blankets. Used to keep board games for the kids. You want anything?"

Her eyes brightened. "Sure. A card game might keep our minds occupied for a little while."

Maybe. But would playing cards keep his mind from obsessing over her impending departure? He got up and opened one of the cupboards that held a series of drawers inside. "They used to be in here." He couldn't remember when they'd last been used. But he found them easily enough. Three decks. He chose the ones with the Texas bluebonnets design—a subtle reminder of the assets of Texas.

"Here we go." He placed the cards on the sofa.

Caroline lifted the box. "These are pretty. I confess I don't know many card games. How about some plain old gin rummy?"

He grinned. "Works for me. You know, sometimes it's better to be master of a few than jack of all trades."

She shot him a look full of suspicion, her eyes slanted. "Are you telling me you're a rummy master?"

He chuckled. "Lucky for you, I haven't played in

years. Maybe it'll come back to me. Deal me in."

With a flourish, she shuffled the cards. "Here goes."

Jack watched her hands deftly shuffle and deal the cards and couldn't help noticing that she kept her nails medium length, trim and nicely shaped, but without polish. They seemed a reflection of her overall personality. She had a simple elegance about her.

When he glanced at her a few moments later, she raised her brows. "Tough decision?"

"Hmm?"

"It's your turn."

"Ah." Hoping his face didn't flush, Jack made his play but had no idea whether it made any sense for his hand.

"How long will it take to ride the ranch and check for damage?" she asked.

Jack blew out his breath. *Too long.* "A few hours at least. I have more property than what you've seen. Over the years, I've bought more land than I need for my own herd to protect it from outside investment companies. You get too much of that, and it changes the community. Puts the independent owner out of business."

He had more of his assets tied up in land than he'd like. But he would do everything he could to make sure the people doing the work of ranching were the ones who owned and profited from the land.

"Oh. Sounds like it could be a sore subject."

Her voice and brows lifted as if asking a question rather than making a statement.

"It's something I feel strongly about. No one should lose their business over a little bad luck or a rough year here and there, especially long-time landowners with deep roots in the area."

"Sure. I'm sorry it adds to your workload. What all do you have to check?"

"Fences mostly. Don't want strays wandering in or out. And all the buildings."

"Right." Her gaze moved to the stairs. "I don't hear anything, do you?"

"No. But I haven't been paying much attention." He looked at his watch. "Let's finish this game, then I'll go up and take a peek."

She put a hand on his arm. "You sure that's a good idea? We can wait a little while longer."

With a nod, he turned his attention back to his cards. Nothing made sense in the hodge-podge collection of cards. Still, he lifted one from the deck in a pretense of playing the game.

He cleared his throat. "So how many more locations will you need to finish the book?"

She kept her eyes on her cards. "Mmm, probably three or four. I'm not trying to cover every region of the country, just a smattering of interesting places."

"And it has to be done by the end of the year?"

"Not necessarily, but I want to have a good rough draft by then." She smiled. "Even though the sabbatical means time off from campus—"

Something clattered against the house, and Caroline let out a short scream and ducked. "Oh, my gosh."

Wide eyes stared at Jack.

"Sounds like something's going on out there." *Captain Obvious.* She let out a groan and shook her head. "I sure hope everything's okay."

"Try not to worry."

The wind howled above them.

But there was nothing he could do except try to calm Caroline's nerves. "You were telling me about the sabbatical."

"Right. I'm supposed to get renewal time, but I'm also expected to produce a viable project."

"Even if you decide to retire?"

"Yeah." Her voice carried a low, thoughtful tone, and she ran her fingers back and forth across the strand of pearls. Then her eyes met his. "And I want to go out with a nice accomplishment either way."

"Ah. That makes sense." Admiration rushed through him. She'd proven more than once she had a strong work ethic. And integrity.

"I've been wondering about something," he told her.

Her brows lifted. "Yeah? What's that?"

"Those pearls. Pearls with blue jeans and boots out on a dusty ranch? A special gift?"

Holding her cards close, she crossed her arms and regarded him. "Let me guess. All this time you've been thinking I look ridiculous, like a silly city girl."

His face warmed, and he sent her a sheepish smile. "At first maybe, but now they look right on you."

She gave him a soft smile. "They belonged to my grandmother. They were a gift to her from my grandpa on their first anniversary. They helped her through the unglamorous tasks of life on a farm. That woman spent her days cooking and canning, washing dishes and cleaning house, mucking stalls, cleaning up after chickens and a family. She wore the pearls on inside days when she was sewing or doing lighter work that wouldn't hurt the necklace. She loved these pearls—said they made her feel pretty even doing all those mundane tasks. And if she waited for a special occasion, they'd almost always be shut away in a box. She wore them for sixty-some years."

"And you feel the same way."

"Absolutely. I love carrying on her tradition. And it's fun to have a reminder of her. She used to tell me, 'Enjoy your things, and love your people.' "

Jack processed the words, how they tugged at his heartstrings and drew him into Caroline's life. "I like that," he said.

"Me, too."

"You were close?"

Caroline's gaze went distant for a moment. "Yeah. My mom couldn't wait to get off the farm, and didn't want to go back often, but I used to spend summers there. I loved visiting. Well—" She gave a little laugh. "—except for that musty cellar. That was downright spooky."

Jack laughed at the description, understanding her reluctance to come to the shelter.

She put a card on the pile and leaned forward. "Gin."

Jack shook his head and dropped his cards. "Nice work." He'd forgotten about the card game.

"Thanks. I have a feeling you weren't on top of your game."

"Sorry about that."

She reached out and touched his hand.

He caught his breath as her fingers brushed over the bare spot on his ring finger.

"I've been wondering about this. You said it was

187

time. Does that mean you're ready to start dating?" she asked softly.

Dating. Jack let the word roll around in his head a moment. It sounded like something from a foreign language. "Dating?" he echoed finally.

Caroline cocked her head and held his gaze. "Yeah, going out, seeing women?"

Jack thought of the few single women he knew, mostly widows of men he'd known. And felt zero interest. Couldn't imagine there ever being a spark. No, the spark was for the woman in front of him. Why her? Why now? He had no idea. But the feelings were real. And exclusive.

He cleared his throat. "I…I thought I was seeing you."

Her smile widened, but her glance shifted behind him.

He lifted a strand of her hair. "I'd like to. I know you have plans. I know you're leaving, but—"

She looked at him again. "Are we officially calling the dance a date?"

His heart bounced, and relief rushed through him—along with anticipation. An "official" date. Who could have guessed? And who would ever have thought he'd feel so happy about it? He took her hand and gently pulled her up from the sofa. With only inches between them, he tipped up her chin. "I'm good with that."

His phone buzzed in his pocket. He looked at the screen. "Roger's calling. Stay right here. I'm going to run up and check it out."

At the top of the stairs, he closed the door and answered Roger's call.

"What are you seeing?" Jack scanned the sky.

Purple clouds still rumbled overhead, but they'd lost the intensity of earlier.

"Seems the worst has passed," Roger told him. "I got a little tree damage out in the yard. You want to ride out?"

"I'll bring the truck and meet you at the storage building," Jack said. He hurried back to the cellar. "All clear," he hollered as he thumped down the stairs.

"Great. How does it look?" Caroline met him at the bottom step.

"So far so good. Roger's seen some tree limbs down. I gotta get to work."

"Of course. I'll go check on the horses."

Jack nodded. "That would be helpful. Thank you."

He shifted, unsure, and she put a hand on his arm. That was enough invitation for him. He bent and placed a kiss on her lips.

"We'll see the sunset next time," Caroline whispered.

"Yes. I'll see you when you get back." He'd have to take her at her word…and hope that she would, in fact, return.

Chapter Fifteen

Caroline stepped over a puddle in the driveway and opened the car door but hesitated as she scanned the fields. No sign of Jack. He'd probably been out at dawn this morning to finish riding the property and checking fences.

A wave of guilt washed over her. She felt as if she were bailing out when things got messy. But Jack had assured her there was nothing she could do. The storm had clipped the southeast corner of the ranch. According to the news meteorologists, as many as five small tornadoes had touched down briefly. As of last night, Jack and his crew had found a few shingles ripped off various buildings and light damage to fences. Some mess, but no loss of life. They'd been lucky.

With a heavy sigh, she climbed into the car. One message the storm sent loud and clear was that on a ranch, there's always something to deal with.

As she started the car, she considered making a stop at the barn to check on the horses. But that was just wasting time. They were fine. She'd made sure of that last night. The storm spooked them, but they'd settled down when the rain finally stopped. The smart thing would be to get on the road and make sure she had plenty of time to get to the airport, return the rental car, and slog through Security before her flight to Nashville.

She drove slowly past the turnoff, and the car

rattled past the big house toward the iron gates. At the exit, she looked in the rearview mirror. The morning light gave the still-damp fields a misty, ethereal glow. She sucked in her breath. It was beautiful. For a moment, she regretted the direction she was headed.

With a laugh, she shook off the odd sense of melancholy. "Good grief, you'll be back next week." Besides that, she was having dinner with her daughter and had a fun week ahead. No time to brood about the ranch—or its owner. Or her own unusually spontaneous, possibly erratic, behavior.

****

At three thirty, Caroline hoisted her bag from the airport carousel and hurried outside to meet her daughter.

Lauren emerged from her car waving and wearing a smile.

The sight of her daughter's cheery grin and familiar curls always put a smile on Caroline's face. People often said the two of them looked alike, but her daughter's hair came from Andrew's side for sure. She let go of her bag and drew Lauren into a tight hug. "Hey, sweetheart. Thanks for playing chauffeur." She tossed her suitcase into the car then climbed into the passenger's seat. "So, what's new?"

Lauren pulled the car away from the curb and glanced over with raised brows. "Nothing new here. You're the one with all the adventures."

Adventures. Caroline liked the sound of that. It'd been a long time since she'd done anything she could call an adventure.

"I'm glad you're getting out and doing things," Lauren told her. "You're too young to be stuck in

Nashville the rest of your life."

"As are you, love. What's next on your plate? Tell me about this Tommy guy. You've been out a few times now, right?" Her daughter dated regularly, but so far, no one had captured her heart.

As Lauren spoke, Caroline couldn't help drawing comparisons and thinking about Jack. But she held her tongue. She absolutely could not trade dating stories with her daughter. That felt too weird.

"He…um…he's thinking about trying to go to Denver this summer when I do. If we're still together then."

Caroline turned. "Aaah. That's a new development. So, I guess I shouldn't start planning a trip to Denver." She made sure to infuse humor into her voice. She would gladly step aside on that one.

"Well, it's probably not a great place for your pictures anyway, right?"

"True." The city wouldn't have what she wanted, but she had visions of capturing photos of elk and deer and hummingbirds. Nothing she couldn't do on her own. Maybe in another part of Colorado. "No idea where I'll need to be then," she said. "I'm enjoying choosing my places according to the seasons. Have to say, it'll be nice to not worry about getting to campus in the cold and if it snows this year."

"No doubt," Lauren agreed.

"I'm glad you found someone you enjoy spending time with." She never wanted her daughter to aspire to marriage as her primary measure of success. "I'd like to meet him. Maybe when I get back, we could all meet for dinner?"

"Maybe." Lauren pulled the car into the driveway.

"Home, sweet home." Caroline surveyed with a critical eye the house she'd lived in for more than twenty years. She and Andrew had considered it their forever place. An older house, it was full of character and charm with mature landscaping and beautiful stone features. The house had been a stretch financially in the beginning, but they'd both fallen in love with it.

Sadly, it had always been too big. They'd expected to have another child or two. Instead, they filled it with offices, a guest room, and a rarely-used music room. A memory squeezed her heart—Andrew standing outside looking up at a huge maple tree in the yard and planning a treehouse for the kids. He'd pulled her close and gestured his plan in the air—placement of the stairs and door, the pitch of the roof. But he'd gotten busy, and the tree had to be cut back, and the treehouse never happened.

The house and lawn remained trim and tidy. But somehow, even with the welcoming wreath on the teal-colored door, it looked lonely. Maybe it had missed her. Had she missed it? She'd been so busy—

"Mom?"

Caroline swiveled. "Hmmm?"

"Want me to stick around and go to the restaurant from here?"

She checked her watch. "Up to you. I need to toss a load of clothes in the washer and start packing to leave again tomorrow. Our reservation is for six thirty. We could meet there, or I can swing by and pick you up." If she had time, she might send a quick text to Jack. He hadn't indicated that he expected updates, but…

"Okay, why don't you pick me up?" Lauren said. "I'll see you about six fifteen."

"Perfect."

Caroline stepped inside the house and turned off the alarm. For a few moments, she wandered the rooms, soaking up the comfortable familiarity. The bright blue and yellow pillows and throw blanket on the sofa made her smile. Her favorite place to curl up with a cup of tea and a book. When she tried and failed to imagine Jack visiting, she laughed out loud.

Her house screamed cozy, and the neighbors were visible from most windows. Certainly not the vast expanses of uninterrupted vistas he was used to on the ranch. Even if he wasn't against traveling, he'd be so out of his element.

"Not that it wouldn't be good for him," she muttered. Would she ever see him in anything but jeans and cowboy boots? Both times he'd been at the pool, he'd been fully dressed. Surely the man owned a suit for weddings and funerals. She pictured him in a tux and had to admit, the image was intriguing.

She shook the bowl of potpourri on the side table and inhaled the faint vanilla and rose scent. It was tempting to sink into the cushions and ease back into her life, but there wasn't time.

In the laundry room, she opened her suitcase and shoved clothes into the washing machine. As she passed the window toward her bedroom, she did a double take, surprised to see her pink flowering dogwood and the neighbor's house instead of the green fields of a Texas ranch. How quickly she'd gotten used to that scenery.

She'd only been away from home a few weeks. And out of her office a few months. Already she felt like something of a nomad. She blew out a heavy breath. There had to be some trade-off for the flexibility and freedom, right? Change always demanded its price of transition.

She lifted her suitcase to the bed and began the process of unpacking the items that didn't need to be washed. She'd need to repack with more layering for the coast. Maybe some hoodies for sea breezes. And dresses? College kids couldn't afford much, but she knew Joe liked to splurge occasionally. They might manage a nice dinner.

Nora's words about a fancy top echoed in Caroline's mind, and she turned her attention to the shimmery turquoise top with rhinestone buttons on one shoulder hanging in her closet. It was one of her favorites, but she'd never paired it with boots and denim skirt before. The way it sat on her shoulders made it hard to wear a jacket. Hopefully, the weather in Texas would cooperate, and they'd get a warm evening. Her thoughts stuttered, and she laughed at herself as her cheeks flushed.

Surely, she wouldn't need a jacket. She'd be dancing. With a man who…who might be inclined to keep her warm. She imagined Jack sliding a lazy arm across her shoulders. Would he? Curiosity tugged at her, and she wondered whether the man ever engaged in public displays of affection. And remembered Nora's warning. They—or Caroline—would be the talk of the town. She'd bet whether Jack realized that or not, he wouldn't let others dictate his actions.

Speaking of actions, she'd better stop daydreaming and get a move on. So much to do and so little time. But first… She pulled her cell phone from her pocket, sucked in a deep breath, and punched Jack's number in her message app.

—*Just checking in. Made it home. Dashing off to dinner with my daughter soon. Hope things are in good shape there.*—

One nice thing about a text, no sign-off was required.

Seemed as though she blinked, and it was time to pick up Lauren for dinner. Caroline pulled her car into the lot of Lauren's townhome and texted her. Moments later, she appeared, carrying a large gift bag brimming with tissue paper.

"What is that?" Caroline asked when Lauren climbed into the passenger seat.

"A Mother's Day gift." Her voice carried a hint of surprise.

Caroline winced. "Oh. That's sweet, honey. Sorry, I guess when I changed plans, I forgot about that."

Jeez, all this spontaneity was making her look like a scatterbrain. She couldn't help wondering if everyone else saw the same image.

****

Jack climbed down from the ladder and pulled off his work gloves.

"Looks good," Roger said.

"Should hold until I can get the new shingles up, anyway." Jack shook his head, thinking of the near-empty shelf in the storage building. There weren't enough shingles. He'd planned to order more after the last storm but had completely forgotten about it. Now, he'd have to send one of the guys over to Abilene to pick some up and hope they weren't sold out.

His phone buzzed inside his pocket. He rarely got messages or calls during the day, and sometimes he didn't bother to carry the phone. But with the storm… He pulled the phone from his pocket to find a text from Caroline.

Smiling, he read the message. She was checking in. That was something. He was on her mind at least. Then again, she'd been gone less than a day. Hadn't joined her group on the coast yet. No sunny beaches or academic colleagues to distract her—yet. It had crossed his mind more than once that the company at the ranch might not be as intellectually stimulating as she liked or was used to.

Checking in. Did she want idle chat? A simple thumbs-up? He had nothing new to report but didn't want to ignore her message. He tapped out a simple response.

—*Good deal. Glad to hear you made it safely. Enjoy the time with your daughter.*—

Dinner with her daughter. He wondered if Caroline had mentioned him and what the response had been. Or would be. He thought of Reed's guarded reaction to Caroline. He'd been friendly, and often encouraged Jack to get out more. But Jack had a feeling that when a parent started seeing someone new, even adult kids were wary about adding a stranger to the dynamics. Maybe her daughter had already "Googled" him. Wouldn't find much of interest.

He was headed for the entrance to the building when inspiration struck. Just on the other side of the fence was a group of mothers and calves, Lola being one of them. Even without looking at the tags, she was easy to identify. She had a white splotch around one eye. He pulled his phone from his pocket again. Then he stepped closer and leaned over the railing.

"What in the Sam Hill are you doing?"

Jack started at the sound of Roger's voice behind him. As heat crawled up his neck, Jack turned and scowled. "Taking a picture. Do you mind?"

"Of what?"

Jack gestured toward the cows standing nearby on the other side of the fence. "Can you not see these here cows?"

"Yeah...so?"

"So that's Lola, the little runt that—"

"Say what?" Roger stared at him.

Jack instantly knew his mistake, and he cringed inside. They did not name their calves on the ranch. He tried to laugh it off. "It's a silly thing, okay? Caroline named the calf when it got lost that day. Got sentimental—"

Roger burst into laughter. "You gotta be kidding me."

"Do I look like I'm kidding?"

"No, but your face is red." He wisely took a step back. "What are you taking a picture for?"

"To show the calf is doing well and growing." Wasn't that obvious?

"Show who?"

"To show Caroline, you idiot. Stop being dense."

"Well, I'll be." Roger shook his head and laughed some more. "You got it bad, buddy."

"And you're about to get a boot up your arse. I'm gonna go call Smitty's and get those shingles ordered. Tell Denny I'll need him to go over with the truck tomorrow and pick 'em up."

Roger tipped his hat. "Yes, Boss. Will do." Still chuckling, he turned and left Jack to his task.

Feeling a fool, Jack snapped a few more pictures then tucked the phone away. He'd send her one later.

****

Almost as soon as Caroline and Lauren were seated inside their favorite Italian restaurant, a server brought water and a basket of bread.

Caroline nodded and reached for a piece of bread. "Didn't realize how much I've missed this."

Lauren let out a short laugh. "Missed what? Bread?"

"Ha! No, believe me, I ate plenty of carbs on the ranch. But I had to cook most of them myself. I didn't have anyone waiting on me. I rather enjoy it."

"Yeah, what's not to like?"

They ordered dinner then Lauren pushed the gift bag toward Caroline.

"Glad we could fit in a dinner date. I thought about waiting until the following weekend, but I want you to have these before your next trip."

"I won't be here the following weekend anyway."

"Oh, wow." Lauren's eyes widened. "I didn't realize you already had another trip planned. Where to next?"

Caroline took a sip of wine and brushed a few crumbs from the tablecloth, aiming for a nonchalant appearance. "Back to Texas."

"Wait. What? You're going back to the ranch?" Her brows pulled together. "You didn't get enough pictures of horses and dragonflies?"

Caroline let out a nervous laugh. Stalling, she plucked a piece of tissue paper from the bag and peeked inside. "I'll take my camera for sure, but I'm really going back for the street dance they're having in the little town there." She glanced over to see Lauren's hand stopped halfway to her mouth.

"You're going back for a dance?"

"Yeah, I made some friends there. Gabby's Aunt Nora is delightful. She and her husband are going. I think it'll be fun. I've never done that kind of small-town event." She reached into the bag and withdrew a bright red leather journal. "Oh, honey, this is fabulous."

"I know you still like real paper even though you have your tablet."

Caroline smiled. "I do, indeed. Feels more personal." She reached into the bag again and pulled out something wrapped in tissue paper. "Ooooh, how exquisite." A long, soft scarf in shades of teal and turquoise with a pop of coral. "Sweetheart, this is too much. But you know what? I think it'll go with the top I'm planning to wear for the dance. That's amazing."

"Serendipity. I love it." Lauren gestured toward the bag. "There's one more thing."

Caroline took out a sleek white travel mug. As she turned it, she couldn't contain a laugh. With a quick glance around, she leaned closer to her daughter. "Haha! I love it. You know me well." The lettering on the mug read, "Miss, Mrs. Ms." with a line drawn through the words followed by: " It's Doctor, actually."

"Thought it would be good for your trip." Lauren grinned.

"Joe will get a kick out of it for sure." She wondered what Jack would think of the message. Would he think it was braggy? She didn't usually advertise her title, but wasn't about to keep it a secret, either. Anyone who put in the work to achieve a PhD deserved to use it.

"Okay, Mom, what about this dance? I can't believe you're going all the way back to Texas for a small-town dance. It must—"

Caroline knew the instant Lauren put two and two together.

Her eyes widened. "Oh, my gosh," she nearly shrieked. "Are you going with the ranch guy?"

Caroline blew out her breath. Might as well 'fess up. "Yes, with Jack. He's the owner."

"Well, this is interesting."

"Don't get carried away. It's just a dance."

"Uh-huh, with a single man. Sounds like a date to me. Any chance you have a picture of this dude?"

"Maybe." On impulse, she'd uploaded a few to her phone library. She pulled the phone from her purse. "Oh!" She had a couple of texts waiting.

"What?"

"Looks like I missed a message from him." She clicked on the message and grinned. "Awww." He hadn't just acknowledged her earlier text, he'd sent an adorable photo of Lola. She turned the phone to Lauren. "Look at this. It's the little calf whose mom was poisoned. Isn't she cute? He just wanted me to see how she's doing. That was sweet."

Lauren leaned forward. "Mom, I'm picking up some vibes. You like this guy?"

Her face warmed, and she lifted her glass. "Well, I—"

"Oh, my gosh. You're blushing."

Caroline took a sip of wine. "I do like him. He's a little rough around the edges, but he's a good person. Kind of a character."

"Uh-huh. In what way?"

201

She couldn't help laughing. How to sum up Jack Armstrong? "The man is an honest-to-goodness cowboy. And he takes his ranching very seriously."

"Pictures?"

"Oh, right." She flicked through her files and found the three she'd sent to herself. "Here you go." She watched her daughter's face, looking for her reaction as she studied the images of Jack.

A light danced in Lauren's eyes when she finally met Caroline's again.

"Well, well. Maybe you won't have to resort to online dating after all. He's handsome."

"Yes."

"And what else? Smart? Is he educated? Generous? A gentleman?"

Caroline held up a hand. "Slow down. I'm still peeling back the layers."

"But you want to know more. And are willing to go all the way back to Texas to do it."

Caroline's heart flip-flopped. Her daughter's words were presented as statement, but Caroline heard the questions as well. The same questions she'd asked herself. Was still asking. As much as she looked forward to the trip to the Outer Banks, she already pictured herself back in Texas and dancing in Jack's arms.

Finally, she sent Lauren a soft smile. "Yes, I want to know more."

Chapter Sixteen

Caroline looked up from her camera and shot Lisa an apologetic smile. "You can go ahead if you want. I don't think I have a good composition with her yet." Three days into the trip, she'd spotted the small fox in the grasslands adjacent to the beach. She'd tracked it for several minutes, but the critter was fast, darting in and out of sight.

Lisa laughed. "No worries. I knew what to expect when I signed on. She's a cutie."

Caroline crept closer, snapping photos as fast as possible. She wanted a nice shot of that adorable furry face for her book. Most people knew about the wild horses on the islands and the birds and sea life all around the area, but some might not be aware of the small mammals that also made their home there.

This part of the beach was teeming with activity. There was so much to see. She could hear the awe and pure excitement in the voices of the young kids who ran up and down the beach.

She and Joe's wife had left the rest of the group examining some kind of sea kelp. After a few more frames, Caroline straightened and stepped back. "Okay, I guess I've harassed the poor thing long enough."

Too bad she couldn't snap a pic with her cell phone. Jack might enjoy seeing it, but it would never be sharp enough. She hadn't spoken to him since arriving at the Banks except for a couple of brief text exchanges. The first two days of their excursion had proven productive but exhausting. The logistics of getting to the islands with so many people had been cumbersome. Maybe after dinner she could sneak in some alone time and give him a call. She figured he'd be hesitant to call her in case she was working or with the group. *Assuming he had the inclination.*

Shading her eyes, she turned toward the ocean. "Want to head closer to the water?" she asked Lisa.

"Absolutely. Let's go."

Caroline couldn't ask for a better beach day. The sun shone in a mostly clear blue sky with only a slight breeze in the air. They meandered toward the wet sand. Close enough to get their feet wet but not be knocked over by a wave—or get her camera wet. When the water lapped at her ankles, she gasped. "Yikes! That's cold." She scurried back to the dry sand. Then nearly stumbled as she hopped around to avoid a small crab making its way along the beach.

"Hey, little guy." She crouched to get a better look. "This one's really dark. Pops against the light sand." She removed her cell phone from her pocket and snapped a few photos.

"Why are you taking pictures with your camera *and* your phone?" Lisa asked.

Caroline's face warmed. She certainly wouldn't confess that she wanted to send them to Jack from her phone. She knew how that would play out. Lisa would tell Joe, and Caroline would never hear the end of it. "The phone files are so much smaller, they're easier to show people."

Sending photos to Jack was a small way to stay

connected, to show him a glimpse of her world. Would he enjoy seeing her in another setting? Did he like to experience other parts of the world through photos, if not in person?

"You're going to have a bazillion pictures." Lisa stooped and picked up a seashell. "Ooh, here's a pretty one."

Caroline's laughter bubbled to the surface. She knew for a fact that Lisa had already filled one plastic bag with seashells. "And you're going to need to buy another suitcase for your bazillion shells."

Lisa chuckled. "I just might. Don't tell Joe, okay?"

"What, he doesn't enjoy playing pack mule?" Caroline smiled and realized with a jolt that she'd missed this over the past few months—this easy bantering and sharing laughter with friends. With her withdrawal from the daily university grind then starting the new project, she'd isolated herself from social gatherings. Had withdrawn into a cocoon of her own thoughts and company.

The downtime had given her much-needed rest and time to pause and think—maybe it had restored her balance and now she could enjoy spending time around people again. With a pang to her chest, she thought of Jack and his solitary life. He never said he was lonely, but he did admit to enjoying her company. It'd be interesting to see him interact with his friends and the townspeople at the dance.

Would she be ready to go back to the quiet atmosphere of the ranch in a few days? At least they had a social event to attend. Maybe she could strike a balance. But could Jack? She blew out a breath. Seemed as if every thought sent her right back to Jack

Armstrong. She chose the best frame of the black crab and sent it in a text.

—Found this little guy roaming the beach today. What an amazing place! Enjoying the wildlife and the sunshine.—

"Caroline!" Lisa grabbed her arm and pointed toward the ocean. "Look out there. Dolphins."

Caroline quickly hit Send without any kind of sign-off. She squinted at the shimmering waves. "Oh, that's awesome. Come on." She ran to the water's edge as she removed the lens cap from her camera. In the distance, a pod of dolphins danced and played in the water, bouncing up then disappearing again. A crowd began to gather along the shore. It took a moment to locate the dolphins in her viewfinder, but once she did, Caroline squealed with delight. Thanks to her zoom lens, the detail was pretty good. But another shot she couldn't capture on her cell-phone camera. She'd have to give Jack a slide show when she got back to the ranch.

The dolphins put on a show for about fifteen minutes then moved farther out to sea. "Well, that was fun," Caroline told Lisa. "Good eye spotting those. There's so much to look for, so much space. We could be missing all kinds of wildlife around us."

"The ocean is a big place," Lisa said. "Never know what could be lurking out there."

"I don't want to spend too much time looking for ocean life, anyway," Caroline said. "It's the beach area as habitat I want to focus on. I want to showcase what an ordinary person could see on a trip here and what the locals live with every day." From her backpack, she pulled the journal Lauren had given her. "I'd better make some quick notes. Wasn't it cool how so many people stopped whatever they were doing and came to watch the dolphins? It's fun to see people excited about nature."

Lisa patted her arm. "Joe's right. You have a gift for connecting the dots for people. I can't wait to see your book."

Smiling, Caroline jotted a few sentences that would help jog her memory when she sat down to write later. Then she glanced at her phone, expecting a reply from Jack. Nothing yet, but her message showed it had been delivered. She let out a soft sigh. Was he not checking his phone or getting a notification? Or was he simply not responding?

****

Jack stared at his cell phone. The two messages had his heart hammering. And not in a good way. He ran a hand over his jaw, unsure how to respond to either of them. Darla Schmidt wanted to run by and bring him a casserole? What in the world was that all about?

He'd only seen the woman a handful of times since her husband, LeRoy, died a few years ago. She'd stayed on the Schmidt ranch but had turned over the operation to others. He couldn't imagine what had prompted her desire to feed him. Everyone knew Nora cooked for him. And it wasn't as if he couldn't grill himself a steak. He shook his head. *Weird.*

The other message tangled his nerves. Another perky note and photo from Caroline. He knew he should take it at face value and not read anything more into it, but he couldn't shake his doubt. Couldn't help feeling as if she were testing—or pressuring—him. Having a great time without him. See what you're missing—hint, hint. Had she embarked on a campaign to get him interested in traveling? Even after he'd explicitly told her more than once he didn't have the time or the desire?

At least she was communicating with him. He should be grateful for that. He should trust her. He'd accepted that he had feelings for her. So why was it so hard to set aside his doubts? He swung down from Charlie's back and walked the horse to his stall. After taking care of the horse's lunch, Jack headed for the house and his own meal.

Nora's car sat near the back steps. He went inside the house feeling guilty that Roger's wife was at Jack's house and not theirs. And Roger was on his way home for lunch, too.

Nora closed the refrigerator door and met Jack with a smile. "Hey, that was good timing. I just put a meatloaf sandwich in there for you." She opened the door again and took out a covered plate. "I'll leave it on the counter. You might not need to reheat it."

"Thanks, Nora."

"Pot roast is in there, too. Ready for dinner tonight."

Jack nodded. "You're a saint."

She wiped her hands on a towel then picked up her purse from the table. "I better scoot."

"Yep. Roger's on his way home. Say, Nora." It occurred to Jack that she might know something about his odd text message.

She turned, brows raised. "Mmm-hmm?"

"I got the strangest text message from Darla Schmidt this morning. You have any idea why she would suddenly want to bring me food?"

"Bring you food?" Nora echoed. Her face went

blank. "I haven't the foggiest idea."

"I'm thinking she must have my number mixed up with someone else's. Did somebody die recently?"

Nora put a hand to her chest. "Not that I know of. How would she know your cell number?"

Jack shrugged. "I'm sure LeRoy had it. Probably has his contact list."

With a puzzled frown on her face, Nora waved a hand as if shooing a fly. "Don't worry about it. I'll call her and see what's up. I bet you're right. She probably didn't have her glasses on and hit the wrong button."

"Good deal. Thanks, Nora."

Nora's eyes suddenly went round, and her mouth formed an "O".

"What?"

"Wow. She didn't waste any time, did she?"

"Nora, what are you talking about?"

She put her hands on her hips. "Darla. I can guess what she's up to."

"Care to enlighten me?"

"Ugh, not really." She shook her head. "I'm guessing she heard you're bringing Caroline to the dance."

"So what?"

"Connect the dots here, Jack. You've been widowed a long time now. You're well-respected in the community. And maybe the word is out that you're dating. There are single women right here who would toss their name in the hat in a second, and I'd bet money Darla is one of them."

"That's ridiculous," Jack told her, his voice flat. "How would she know about Caroline, anyway?" He couldn't imagine women out there waiting for a chance to date him. That was absurd.

Nora let out a soft groan. "People talk. She's been to town. And I suppose it might be my fault."

Crossing his arms, he raised his brows and stared at Nora.

"Joyce Larson called me and asked if Roger and I wanted to get a table at the dance with them and the Martins. But the tables seat six, so I had to tell her we were already committed to a table with you and Caroline. I'm sorry."

Jack held up a hand. "Not your fault. Forget it."

"Let me see if I can put a lid on it." She turned and headed for the door.

Only a few steps away, she swiveled back around. "Hey, speaking of messages...have you heard from Caroline since she left? She make it to the coast all right?"

Jack braced a hand against the counter, not sure he wanted to have this conversation. Finally, he nodded. "Yep. Heard from her. Made it there just fine." He swiveled into the kitchen and lifted the foil from the plate Nora had set out.

"What's wrong?"

"Nothing. Sounds like she's having a grand time. Sent me some pictures." As soon as the words left his mouth, he knew they didn't sound as matter-of-fact as he'd hoped.

There was a moment of awkward silence until he looked up to see humor dancing in Nora's eyes. "What?"

She stared at him, hands on her hips. "Why, Jack Armstrong. Are you hoping she has a lousy time at the beach?"

He scowled. "Of course not. Why would I hope that?"

"Hmm, maybe because you want her to like the ranch better?"

"She's got lots of places to go besides here. This was just one stop."

Nora took a few steps toward him, her eyes studying his face. "You don't think she's coming back?"

He hitched his shoulders again. "It's certainly a possibility."

"Didn't she tell you she'd be back? I mean…what about the dance?"

"Yes, she told me she's coming back, but we'll have to wait until the car pulls through the gate to know for sure, won't we?"

Nora pursed her lips. "You're afraid she's going to stand you up? Wow, Jack, how about giving her the benefit of the doubt?"

Not meeting her eyes, Jack turned and pulled a carton of milk from the refrigerator. "I'm just saying it's possible she decides the dance isn't worth coming back for." He wouldn't give voice to the underlying thought—that she might decide *he* wasn't worth coming back for.

"Haven't you ever heard that absence makes the heart grow fonder?"

He snorted. "Yeah, and I've heard out of sight, out of mind, too."

Nora leaned across the countertop and rested a gentle hand on his arm. "Jack, she left some of her things in the cabin."

Her soft words made his heart lurch. His head

snapped up. "Did she?"

A smile spread across Nora's face. "Yeah. Several things, actually. Her boots, some books, and a couple of jackets. Things she wouldn't need at the beach, I guess."

Giddy relief swept through Jack, and he couldn't help cracking a smile. That was a positive sign. "Good to know."

"All right, I gotta get out of here. Stop worrying, will you?" She shot him a saucy grin. "It's not your style, Mister."

As soon as the door closed behind her, Jack sagged against the counter and gulped down the milk. He had to get a grip. Nora was right. All this over-thinking—not his style at all. While the news of the items left behind lifted his spirits, he was a realist. And he knew that the items left in the cabin could easily be boxed and shipped.

****

After a hot shower and change of clothes, Caroline headed to the front room in search of Joe.

"Hey, Caro," he called and beckoned her into the kitchen. "We're talking about dinner ideas."

"Music to my ears. I'm starving. What's the plan?"

"You look refreshed, as usual, but most of us are kind of wiped out. Long day in the wind and sun. What do you think about something easy like ordering in pizza?"

She cheered inside. A low-key night would allow her to give Jack a call and still turn in early. Joe had been kind enough to grant her a small, quiet bedroom of her own on the top floor of the expansive house, removed as much as possible from the noisy college students.

She had an early morning planned and needed a good night's sleep. Some marine biologists she'd met on the beach earlier had tipped her off—they'd spotted a bale of sea turtles heading this way. Once the turtles reached the beach, it would be the start of nesting season, and she couldn't wait to see that. "Pizza sounds perfect," she told Joe.

He patted the chair beside him. "Great. Have a seat and show me what you shot today."

"An invitation I can't refuse." She sat next to him and adjusted the camera for playback. "Look at the pinchers on this crab."

"Holy cow. Bet that boy could damage a finger or two." Joe swiveled to look at her. "Hey, that reminds me…I showed the picture you sent me of that lizard to Sherman and he went kind of crazy. Said it's endangered. Guess some folks have been trying to get a preserve set aside out there in Texas somewhere. I wonder if your buddy Jack would be interested in helping with that."

Caroline sucked in her breath and nearly choked. She stared at Joe while she processed his words. There was a lot to unpack in those comments. For now, she'd let the "her buddy Jack" description slide by. She'd captured a photo of an endangered species? *Oops*. She probably should've contacted Hank herself. Hank Sherman, the most tenured and revered professor in the earth sciences department, was a noted authority on reptiles.

Hopefully her lack of action wouldn't travel to the ears of Dean Why-Aren't-You-Doing-More. Last she knew, a couple of lizards were listed as "threatened" and several zoos were working to breed and re-introduce them.

"Hank was sure about the lizard?"

"The guy went nuts right there in the coffee shop." Joe flailed his hands for emphasis. "Had me forward the pic to him on the spot."

"Okay, cool. That one will go in the book for sure." She couldn't wait to tell Jack. Another reason to give him a call. She wondered if he'd ever seen one—or had any idea they were endangered. Surely the state kept landowners informed.

"I'm surprised Sherman hasn't contacted you," Joe said. "He probably will. This was just the other day when I ran into him."

"Well, I haven't been home, you know. And I doubt he has my cell number."

Joe laughed. "Caro, I'm guessing he could track you down. Just wait."

"I hope so. Maybe I'll shoot him an email. I saw only one of those lizards, but there would have to be more. I could show Hank where—" *Or not.* She broke off as she remembered her early encounters with Jack and his reluctance to have film crews or equipment on the ranch. She honestly didn't know how he'd feel about an endangered species or a sanctuary in the area. He was all about the cattle. She might have to tread carefully.

Joe's brows lifted. "What?"

"Nothing. I'm sure the wildlife-management people in Texas are keeping track of these guys. I feel stupid for not realizing what it was when I took the photo. Guess I'm not up on my Texas lizard varieties." She'd have to remedy that in a hurry. Possibly, she was spending too much time thinking about the Texas cowboy species.

At eight o'clock, Caroline heated a cup of tea and retreated to her room. Her longtime sense of discipline took charge, and she spent thirty minutes getting up to speed on endangered species of Texas before closing her laptop. With a fluff of the pillows, she curled up on the bed and reached for her phone.

Jack picked up on the third ring. "Hello there."

His voice was warm and deep. And Caroline's heart gave a funny lurch. She smiled softly into the phone. "Hi. Is this a good time to call?" Oh, jeez, her voice sounded high and breathy.

"Sure. How was your day?"

"Fabulous. Saw great wildlife. Had beautiful, sunny weather. Took a ton of pictures. Walked on the beach."

"Watched the sunset with a glass of wine in hand?"

She swallowed hard, his question taking some wind from her sails. Her thoughts stuttered. Why would he go there? Joe and Lisa had gone out as soon as they finished eating dinner, but Caroline hadn't been invited, and probably wouldn't have gone anyway. It was on her mind, though. She loved a walk on the beach in the evening, but doing that alone sounded lonely, and probably wasn't safe. Besides that, it was a…a *romantic* thing to do.

"Um, no, but that sounds like a great idea. Want to join me?" She gave a light laugh and held her breath. She could imagine the two of them strolling along the water's edge at sunset. But could Jack?

He cleared his throat and chuckled.

But the laugh sounded forced. She'd bet the idea

made him uncomfortable, and he wished he could take back the words.

"I know, I know," she said, letting him off the hook. "Too much work to do."

"Seems to always be."

Ugh, the conversation felt so stilted. Maybe Jack was one of those people who didn't do well with telephone conversations. Hard to believe this was the same man she'd kissed in the basement bunker during a tornado just a few days ago. "Well, I'm looking forward to Sunset Ledge. Crossing my fingers for a good one."

"Me, too. It'll be nice to have you back."

A tingle shimmied up her spine. All right, now they were getting somewhere. "You know, the ocean kind of reminded me of the ranch today."

"Really? How's that?" His tone perked up.

"Oh, gosh, the waves seem to go on forever. Looking out at the vastness, that endless view to the horizon, is a lot like looking out across the fields of the ranch. The land goes on and on until it touches the sky. Can you picture that?"

"When you put it like that, I can. I'll look forward to seeing your photos."

She rolled her eyes. Pictures were great, but you couldn't feel the ocean breeze or the light mist on your face looking at a picture. Why was he so reluctant to feel, to experience? She wondered if he could ever get past his grief and heartache. She gave herself a mental shake. *Baby steps.* If she went slowly, gradually, he might come around. She couldn't force him.

Instead, she changed the subject and told him about the impending arrival of the sea turtles. "These guys better show. I'm getting up before the crack of dawn for them."

"If nothing else, you'll see a pretty sunrise, right?"

"True. We'll spend the day exploring around here again then we want to get to a couple of the other islands."

"Sounds busy. But you're having fun?"

"I am. These college kids are a hoot. And I always enjoy spending time with Joe and his wife. It's all very low-key. Joe's got everything arranged, so I just go with the flow." Was he fishing for some indication that she missed him? Apparently, she did since he'd been on her brain all day. Should she mention it? "Hey, Jack do you have a video chat app on your phone?"

"Hmm. Not sure. I have something like that on my computer thanks to Dylan."

"Haha, you sound like me. Always asking the kids for tech support. I bet Dylan gets a kick out of helping Grandpa."

"Sure does. And likes to remind me how much I need his services, too."

This time, Jack's chuckle was low and genuine, and it warmed her insides. Too bad she couldn't see the smile that went with it.

"Of course. Okay, let's try to make the video thing work next time. I mean…do you want to? If you'd rather just wait until next week…"

"Caroline, I'd like that."

The blood whooshed in her ears as his words wrapped her in their warmth. There was no way she'd ruin the mood with talk of lizards, endangered or otherwise.

Smiling, she flopped back against the pillows. "Me, too."

Chapter Seventeen

Jack whistled as he climbed out of his truck. Thoughts of the nearing weekend buoyed each step up to the Stockton General Store. So far, all systems were go for a great sunset Thursday night. And the forecast for the entire weekend showed warm temperatures and sunny skies. He remembered a couple of not-so-perfect street dances over the years. Looked as if they would luck out this year.

Inside, he paused a moment to let his eyes adjust to the dimmer light.

"Well, would you look what the wind blew in."

He turned toward the familiar voice and moved to the counter to shake hands with owner Bill Thompson. "Hey, Bill. How are you?"

"Fine and dandy. How 'bout yourself?"

Before Jack could answer, Bill's wife swooped in with a wide grin. "Hey there, Jack. Sure is nice to see you."

Her effusive greeting sounded vaguely odd to him, but he smiled. "Good to see you, too, Arlene."

The woman stepped closer, an eager smile on her face. "What can we get you?"

"Need to pick up a few groceries." He reached for a small basket. He wanted to offer Caroline something a little nicer than a premade meal from his freezer. "Thinking some nice cheese and fresh produce.

Arlene's brows rose. "Sure, we've got all that. But listen here, you just come on over and have a seat, and let me get you a cup of coffee. Visit with us a spell." She waved a hand toward the counter area where several stools sat empty.

"You get any damage from those tornadoes last weekend?" Bill asked.

With that, Jack reluctantly was drawn into conversation. "Minor damage. Mostly some shingles. How 'bout you?"

"Darndest thing. Hardly got a breeze, but Jones just down the road lost a whole barn."

Arlene set a cup of coffee and some sugar packets on the counter in front of Jack.

He nodded and reached for the sugar. "Thank you."

"On the house. I've got snickerdoodles, too."

Jack's glance lingered on Arlene a moment. She seemed a little keyed up. Surely they weren't desperate for a customer. Then he remembered how Caroline had brought him snickerdoodles that night in the barn. He tried to remember if she'd liked them or another kind. Might be a nice reminder of the night they spent together. His chest tightened. That night something took root between them. "I'll take half a dozen of those, Arlene." He still had strawberry shortcake in the freezer, but they could take the cookies up to the ledge.

"Yes sir, I'll hold 'em back here until you're ready to check out. No rush." She turned her attention to her cell phone.

Jack took a sip of coffee then turned back to Bill. "No figuring out Mother Nature, that's for sure. Glad you didn't get any damage." His lips twitched. He would never wish harm on anyone or their property, but he hadn't minded the excuse to hole up inside with Caroline for a while.

"Hey, Jack, I hear you're coming to the dance Saturday night," Arlene said. "It's so nice to see you getting out again. You look great, by the way."

Surprise had him gaping at the woman. How would she know that? Had Caroline mentioned attending the dance to someone? Oh, yeah. Probably Nora. That's what happened when everybody knew everybody. "Thanks. I…um…yes, planning to be there." He wagged a finger in front of the couple. "You two going to make it this year?"

"Oh, we wouldn't miss it for—"

The chimes on the door sounded, and Jack glanced toward the entrance.

Beth Wilson, a veterinarian who lived in Abilene but also had clients around Stockton, headed toward the counter. She and Rosalyn had been friends. Divorced from what Ros referred to as a *deadbeat dad*, Beth had raised two kids on her own.

Arlene waved wildly. "Hey, Beth. What'll you have?"

Jack placed his mug on the counter and stood.

A moment later, Beth greeted him with a wide smile. "Jack, gosh, it's been a while. How are you?"

He leaned in and kissed her cheek. "Doing great. Good to see you."

"Here you go, Jack." Arlene filled his mug with fresh coffee.

"Thanks, Arlene, but I should—"

Beth took hold of his arm. "Can you stay a minute? Tell me about that grandson of yours. How old is he now? Arlene, I'd love a sweet tea."

221

Jack had the odd sensation he was being double-teamed. He didn't see how he could get away without appearing rude. With a sigh, he braced a hand against the stool but didn't sit. "Dylan's nine now—growing fast."

"Gosh, time gets away. Got any recent photos on you?"

Jack fished his cell phone from his pocket. "Might have a few. His stepmom is good about sharing."

"That's wonderful. I'm so glad Reed found a good one. You both have been through so much."

He opened his photo app and handed the phone to Beth. And it occurred to him that Caroline had snapped dozens of photos of Dylan and him, but he didn't have any of her. He could probably download the one from the university website, but he should try to remember to take one this weekend.

"Oh, what a cutie," Beth crooned. "He's…" Her gaze moved to Jack. "His injuries are all healed?"

Jack understood people were genuinely interested, concerned, but it wore him out to still answer questions about the accident and Dylan in nearly every conversation. He wished someone would ask about the boy's interests and personality. "Doing great. He's a bright kid. Fun to be around."

"Ah, no surprises there. I bet he loves coming to Grandpa's ranch."

"Seems to. Enjoys the horses. How are your two doing?" Much as he disliked this kind of small talk and wanted to get on with his errand, it'd be rude not to ask after her kids as well.

"Both are great. Ashley's expecting in July, so I'm finally going to be a nana."

"That's exciting. Congratulations."

"Thanks." She put a hand on his arm. "I hear you're starting to get out more. Going to the dance on Saturday. Good for you."

Heat spread like wildfire up Jack's neck. Had someone sent out a press release? That he was in the market for dates? Blood whooshed in his ears. Maybe Nora was right. Was that what Darla's strange offer to bring dinner was about? "Well, I—"

Beth picked up her tea and stood. "Listen, I've got to run." She placed a couple dollar bills on the counter. "Thanks for the tea, Arlene."

To his surprise, Beth leaned in close and lowered her voice.

"Next time you're in Abilene, give me a shout. We could meet up for a drink or dinner."

She flashed a smile and turned before he could respond. *Thankfully.* He, too, tossed down some bills, annoyance and shock mixing inside him.

"See you later, Beth," Arlene called out. She stepped toward Jack. "Isn't she a doll?"

"Not trying to set me up, are you, Arlene?"

"Pshaw." She swatted a hand his direction. "I know you don't need that sort of meddling. Nothing wrong with a little nudge, though, is there? We've got some lovely women here—"

Jack held up a hand to cut her off. "We do. Let's leave it at that, shall we?"

He wandered around the grocery aisles but couldn't get Arlene's *nudge* off his mind. What if Caroline didn't come back? Or what if she came for the dance and it was her last weekend at the ranch? Would he put his ring back on and return to a hermit lifestyle? Or had a seismic shift opened a chasm that couldn't be closed again?

Dating sounded exhausting. And he couldn't imagine ever being anything more than friendly to women who had been Rosalyn's friends. That felt weird. It was different with Caroline. Spending time with her felt natural—not like dating. He mulled that thought a moment. It seemed like a significant distinction.

****

On her last day at the banks, Caroline finally connected with Hank for a phone call about the lizard-conservation project. "So, do the landowners already know about the project?" Caroline asked Hank.

"Can't say for sure, but I would guess so. It's been talked about for years. Your photo is proof the lizards haven't disappeared completely. The feasibility study looks good. Not a huge expense. Minimal impact on landowners. This is a low-population area, and it's off the beaten path. That means the preserve will be for the flora and fauna, not tourists. Doubt it would need much in the way of roads and services."

"Right." That would probably make the project more appealing to people like Jack. "Do you know if they've had opposition?"

"There are always a few holdouts who have to be won over kicking and screaming."

Caroline's stomach clenched. She wished she knew if Jack was one of them.

"I'm guessing the next step is some kind of public hearing then the state would see about land acquisition. Actually, this one seems like a slam dunk."

"You think landowners will be willing to sell or

could this require eminent domain acquisitions?"

"Not sure. Probably some of both. You know, it's possible someone could contact you about using the photo in publicity materials. You good with that?"

"Of course." Personal considerations aside, she was a nature conservationist and a professional. She couldn't, in good conscience, not support the preserve.

"I'd be happy to keep you in the loop and let you know if I hear any news."

"I appreciate that, Hank." Caroline said goodbye and fiddled with her camera lens cap as she replayed in her head the conversation with Hank. Okay, the idea for a nature preserve near Stockton had been hatched several years ago. So even if Jack objected to it, he'd know she had nothing to do with the proposal.

A sudden wind gust blew her hair into her face. She glanced at the sky. A layer of clouds had developed, and the breeze carried a chill that wasn't there an hour ago. She zipped her jacket then headed back toward Joe and his group.

Still a few yards away, she stopped and snapped a few photos of Joe examining a plant and talking to the students. Despite the complicated logistics, she was glad she'd let him talk her into this trip. At this rate, she needed only a few more locations to have enough photos for a book—probably more than enough. She smiled to herself. Maybe she'd publish two volumes.

As she moved closer, Joe turned and beckoned to her.

He swung an arm across her shoulders. "Hey, Caro, check this out."

"What've you got?"

"Seabeach amaranth. A threatened species."

"Seriously? How cool. We are on a roll, my friend. Let me get a couple of pics." She shot several frames of the plant then gestured to Joe. "You get in there, too."

"Hey, speaking of threatened species, did Hank have any news for you?" Joe asked.

"Nothing too earth-shattering. He thinks there's a good chance a preserve for the lizards is going to happen."

"Nice. Sounds like a good project for you to get involved with." He leaned closer and lowered his voice. "If you leave Vandy, you could manage a nature preserve out there. A good next step." A light twinkled in his eyes. "Keep you close to that rancher of yours."

Caroline caught her breath. Was she that transparent?

"Hmmm," she went for a playful tone. "Decisions, decisions. Keeping my options open for now. But thanks for your keen powers of observation."

Joe gave a hearty laugh. "You'll figure it out."

"Eventually."

She shrugged off Joe's comment, but the idea lodged in her brain. Were new opportunities for a different life clicking into place? Could she be involved with the preserve? If this thing between her and Jack grew, Joe was right—it could give her something to do when she wasn't traveling. She could still use her skills and knowledge. Aside from the social aspect of life on a ranch, that was a big concern.

Stockton, Texas didn't have easy access to museums and libraries. The ranch provided plenty of nature and the horses, which she loved, but her mind needed stimulation, too. Working on a preserve would keep her toe in the field. She'd still be seen as a scientist.

Lisa sidled up next to Caroline and gestured toward Joe. "Ah, the botanist in his element."

"Yes, I snapped a few pics."

"Thanks, he'll like that. He loves to post new images on his website. To keep it fresh, he says. Doesn't want his page to look old or dated. I think *he's* afraid of looking dated."

Caroline laughed. "As if."

"He turns seventy this summer, you know."

"Yes. Hard to believe. Where does he get all that energy?"

"He loves what he does. It's that simple." She turned to Caroline with a grin. "Well, that and a serious FOMO complex."

Caroline raised her brows.

"You know, fear of missing out."

"Ah, of course."

"He won't even discuss retirement."

"You want him to retire?"

Lisa's face softened, and she glanced toward Joe with a smile. "Not really. Not as long as he can contribute, and I can tag along on these trips. At least this way, I get to see him." She blew out a long breath. "At the end, I don't want him to feel like he left anything on the table, missed any opportunities—and certainly not because I pressured him."

"Lisa, you're amazing. He's lucky to have you."

She waved a hand. "I just know pressuring someone eventually leads to resentment. And I don't want that. Besides, this way I still get to travel, *and* I get plenty of time to do my own things."

Caroline knew none of Lisa's words were a

criticism of her, and she shouldn't take them personally, but they hit home anyway. If she and Jack stayed together, she might very well fall into the position of pressuring him. Of course, she'd want him to explore with her. Would that, as Lisa suggested, lead to resentment? Would he end up feeling irritated and unhappy? She didn't want that, but what was the point of having a relationship that didn't include togetherness and companionship?

She needed to find out the answers to those questions. With more than six months left on sabbatical, she could explore her feelings as well as various habitats across the country. She'd have to take a day at a time. No pressure for her, either.

The other part of Lisa's comments needed further thought as well. Would leaving the university mean leaving something on the table or would it open new doors? "Well," she said finally. "I'm glad you came on this one. It's been a blast."

"So much fun, I—"

"Okay, everybody, listen up," Joe called out. "We need to gather our gear and head back to the house." He took a few steps toward Caroline and Lisa. "Clouding up. Good thing we're about done here. You ready to wrap things up, Caro?"

"Yes. It's been amazing, but I think I've got this location covered." The turtles this morning had been worth the entire trip. Only a few had made it to the beach, but seeing them had been an extraordinary experience.

"Excellent. Guess we better start the shut-down process. We've got an early morning ahead of us."

Those were not Caroline's favorite words. "How

early?" she asked.

"Got to be out of the house by five-thirty to get to the airport on time."

That would make for a long day with a lot of downtime at the airport. Her flight didn't get to Dallas until after four p.m. If there were any issues, she'd be cutting it close for sunset watching with Jack. Caroline replaced the cap on her camera, and Lisa fell in step beside her.

"Let's hope the weather cooperates," she said.

Caroline shrugged. "Should be fine."

"Haven't you seen the forecast?"

"Not recently." Caroline glanced at the sky. "Just a few clouds." Still, noting the resigned look on Lisa's face, Caroline whipped out her cell phone. "Last I checked, it was nice and sunny through the weekend."

Lisa let out a sharp laugh. "Well, you know what they say…if you checked more than an hour ago, that forecast is null and void."

She was right. Caroline blew out a heavy breath and groaned. When had this happened? Storms brewing all along the coast from Florida to Virginia—including Atlanta. Storms in Atlanta always affected air travel. *Ugh.*

"Lucky for us, forecasts are known to be wrong sometimes," she told Lisa.

The forecast hovered in her mind like an unwanted guest for the rest of the evening. At two a.m. the rain started—at least that's when it woke Caroline from a deep sleep. A loud crack of thunder sent a clear message—expect a turbulent day ahead.

Chapter Eighteen

—Jack. I'm so sorry, but I'm not going to make it tonight. Sigh. Too many weather backups.—

Jack read Caroline's text and let out a long groan. He sagged against the door of the supply shed. Like a fool, he'd checked the weather for Dallas and the ranch, but not for the coast. Like a fool, he'd gotten his hopes up, got everything ready. He looked forward to Caroline's arrival more than anything in recent memory. With anticipation coursing through him, he'd hardly slept last night.

He closed his eyes a moment and ran a hand across the back of his neck. *Calm down.* It's not her fault. It's just weather. Trouble was, he couldn't shake the feeling that if this relationship was meant to be, it should be easier than this. Was more than weather working against him? Clenching his jaw, he replied to her message.

—Sorry to hear that. You have somewhere to stay?—

—If I can squeeze onto the six-thirty flight, I'll stay overnight at an airport hotel then get a car in the morning. I'm on standby now.—

—Best to be safe. Keep me posted.—

—Will do, I'll call you later if I'm not on an airplane. Hey, Jack, the sun will set again tomorrow, right?—

He released his breath with a shake of his head. She dealt with adversity well. At least she didn't want to scrap the whole plan. They still had Friday night for sunset watching and Saturday for the dance. He couldn't help smiling into the phone.

—*Absolutely. We'll do it tomorrow.*—

He tucked the phone into his pocket. What to do with himself until then? The only thing he could do—shake off his nerves and get back to ranching.

He spent nearly two hours puttering around the barn, cleaning tack, and brushing the horses. More time working meant fewer hours to spend aimlessly inside the house. But he should eat dinner and be ready for Caroline's call if it came. He latched the door on Charlie's stall and switched off the bright overhead lights.

Outside the barn, he glanced toward the west and stopped short. His throat tightened. The sun still had an hour or so before setting, but it looked as if it would be spectacular. A few clouds crisscrossed the blue sky, and a yellow tint was just creeping in.

Hands on his hips, he gazed across the fields, thinking. After a quick bite to eat, he could take a picture for Caroline. Or they could do a video chat, and she could still share it with him if she was stuck inside the airport. He strode to the house. Everything he bought for tonight should still be fine tomorrow. He opened the freezer, retrieved a dish of Nora's beef stew, and placed it in the microwave.

A few minutes later, he let out a heavy sigh and dropped into a chair at the table. For years, he'd been eating supper alone. He ate meals out of force of habit. The routine was the only thing that kept him going.

Tonight, it was just the next thing on the agenda. He hadn't felt the suffocating boredom and loneliness this acutely since the first months after Rosalyn's death. But now they settled on his shoulders like a heavy, wet blanket.

He ate quicky, hardly tasting the food. Then he cleaned the dishes and headed back to the porch to wait for the perfect sunset moment.

****

Caroline stood in line at the gate counter. Again. She wanted to scream with frustration, but that would accomplish absolutely nothing. The full flights weren't the attendant's fault. Nor was the weather.

When it was finally her turn, Caroline handed the attendant her ticket and boarding pass. "Since I didn't get on this one, I'll need to be re-booked for tomorrow."

The woman, Lacey, nodded and began typing on her computer keypad. The rapid tap-tap-tap reminded Caroline of a movie, and she couldn't help but smile. She sucked in a deep, cleansing breath.

"What about my bag? It didn't get on that plane without me, did it?" She needed that suitcase. Her entire dance night outfit was packed inside.

Lacey grimaced. "I can't tell you for sure. Things are crazy. But if it did, it should be waiting for you in Dallas."

Fingers crossed. "I'll need a place to stay tonight, too."

"You'll have to check with customer service. But I wouldn't get your hopes up. By now, most places will be full."

Caroline groaned inside. Another line. She

probably should've skipped trying for standby and gone straight to a hotel. Of course, everything would be full by now. She'd wasted precious time.

When her phone pinged, alerting her to a new message, she shifted her bag and removed the phone. She let out a soft gasp. *Oooh.* Tonight's sunset on the Armstrong ranch was stunning. Deep pinks and oranges splashed across the sky like a Jackson Pollock painting.

Lacey held out new documents to Caroline. "I've got you booked—" She stopped and stared. "Are you okay? Are you scared to stay overnight?"

Caroline shook her head and tried to cover her frustration. "No, it's not that." She turned the phone so the woman could see. "This is what I'm missing tonight." But it wasn't just the beautiful scenery, she was missing a special moment with Jack.

"Oh, how pretty," the woman said. "I'm sorry. You're confirmed on the seven a.m. flight."

Caroline nodded. "Thank you," she murmured. Unable to face the customer-service line, she dropped into a nearby seat. She'd have to let Jack and Lauren know of her new itinerary. Instead of texting, she moved to a vacant area and punched Jack's number.

"Uh-oh," his voice came on the line. "I'm guessing this means you aren't on an airplane right now."

"No. The flight was full. What a crazy day this has been. Thanks for the picture. Wish I could be there. I'm so sorry to be missing that view. It's gorgeous."

"I'm sorry, too. It's pretty, but have to say, it loses some luster without you here to share it with me."

A warm glow spread through Caroline. "Jack, that was a very romantic thing to say." Her voice held a light teasing tone. But it was true.

"That was the idea," he told her. "Listen if you don't get on that plane tomorrow, I'm coming to…"

He broke off, and Caroline held her breath in the silence. Coming to get her?

"…I'm sending a car for you. Or I'll charter a private plane, how's that?"

She swallowed hard. He wanted her there but wouldn't leave the ranch to make it happen. Still, he was obviously disappointed. She gave a light laugh. "I'm holding you to that. But the airline says they'll get me to Dallas at ten. Planning to be at the ranch by one."

"I'm looking forward to that."

"Hey, Jack. I need to update Lauren. Let me text her then I'll call you back. You can keep me company while I navigate this mess."

"Be happy to."

****

Ten minutes later, Jack's phone rang. He quickly snatched it up, expecting the call from Caroline. Instead, Dylan's image appeared on the screen. Jack wasn't disappointed to hear from his grandson, but it wasn't the kid's best timing.

"Hello there, young man," Jack spoke into the phone.

"Hey, Grandpa. What are you doing?"

"Watching the sunset and waiting for your call."

"Huh-uh. You didn't know I was gonna call. Is that biology lady still there?"

Jack's heart tripped. "Caroline. No. She'll be here tomorrow, though."

"Okay, Dad and I can come Saturday. Mom has a baby thing with a bunch of friends, so we don't need to be here. We can come right after my soccer game."

"I see." Sounded as if they had it all planned out. But that wasn't going to happen. He'd already missed out on spending time with Caroline tonight. He wasn't inclined to share her the rest of the weekend. Or to be under watchful eyes. But how to tell Dylan he and Reed couldn't visit? Jack cleared his throat. "Well, buddy, I hate to tell you, but I'm kind of busy this weekend."

"That's okay, we won't bother you."

"Is your dad there?"

"Yeah. Just a minute."

Jack went inside, a dozen excuses playing in his head. But he knew not one would ring true to his son. He'd never told Reed he couldn't come to the ranch. *Couldn't come home.* Guilt washed over him. Why was this so complicated?

"Hey, Dad. What's up?" Reed's voice came on the line.

"Dylan says you guys were thinking about coming back out this weekend."

"Yeah, Kristen's got a spa day and baby shower. Since we had to cut last weekend short, Dylan wanted to spend more time with the new foal and maybe Caroline if she wouldn't mind."

"She was delayed getting back tonight, so won't get here until tomorrow. And I…well, we've got plans. There's the town dance on Saturday. What about next weekend?"

"The town dance?" Reed echoed.

Of course, he'd zero in on that. "Right."

"You're going to the dance? With Caroline?"

Heat crept around Jack's collar. For Pete's sake, he shouldn't have to think twice about it. "Right. Meeting up with Roger and Nora."

An awkward silence settled between them.

"So you don't want us to come?" Reed said after a full minute of nothing.

"Just saying it wouldn't be ideal."

"Okay, that's fine. We'll, uh, I'll see what our schedule looks like for next weekend. Will she...will Caroline still be around?"

"I honestly don't know."

"Well, are you two...I mean, are you in a relationship with her, Dad?"

Jack squeezed his eyes closed and let his head fall into his hand. "You know, Son, I can't tell you exactly where this is going, but I think we could say that."

"Wow. That's...that's great, Dad."

Jack heard the humor in Reed's voice, and he poked back. "I'm glad you approve. It's been a load."

Reed laughed out loud. "Have fun. I'll check in with you next week."

"Sounds good." Jack ended the call and went back to his home screen. Naturally, he'd missed Caroline's call. First, he poured himself a drink then settled onto the sofa. Ready to "keep her company," he tapped her number.

She picked up immediately.

"You all settled?" Jack asked.

She snorted. "Not even close. I'm standing in the customer-service line. My daughter pitched a fit when I said I might stay overnight at the airport, so I promised I'd at least try to get a room somewhere. It'll be such a short turnaround, though. I have to be back here at six a.m. Either way, I don't see how I'm getting much sleep tonight."

"For what it's worth, I agree with your daughter. If

you end up staying at the airport, I won't get any sleep, either. That doesn't sound safe."

"Uh-oh, are you a worrier, too? I'm a big girl, you know."

How easily the worry came these days. He didn't used to let circumstances beyond his control gnaw at him. But the accident had changed everything. You never knew when a split second could upend your life. Someone you love could disappear without a moment's notice. "Things happen," he said lightly. "I'd like to know you're somewhere secure before everything closes down for the night."

"Thank you, Jack. I actually agree. This is not the most appealing environment. A little too crowded with the human species for my tastes."

Jack laughed at her description. Sounded downright claustrophobic to him. He wondered what her reaction would be if he told her he'd never been inside an airport. Never had a need to. The only plane he'd ever flown in was a small, private twin engine from the strip at Stockton. That was simply to get a bird's eye view of the ranch and surrounding area.

Did that make him sheltered? A hermit? A bore? It had never mattered to him. Did it now? For Caroline, airplanes were a natural part of life, a routine way to travel. He admitted feeling a little lame.

"Hey, I'm inching toward the front of the line," Caroline interrupted Jack's thoughts. "I'll keep you posted."

"Good deal. I'll be waiting."

Two hours later, the ring of his phone finally broke the tense silence of the house.

"Caroline?"

"Whew. Guess where I am? Inside my room at a hotel twenty minutes from the airport. And I am wiped out."

"I'll bet. What an ordeal."

"I'm going to take a hot, steamy shower then call it a day."

As an image of Caroline in the shower came to mind, he fought to keep an even tone. "Perfect. I'll see you soon. Listen, when you get here, just come on up to the house."

"At one?" Her voice pitched up in surprise. "Will you be there?"

"I will. Working in the morning. Thought we could go for a ride, if you like. Or spend some time at the pool. Forecast says eighty-three and sunny. You still have your hat?"

"I do. In fact, I bought a new one. Both of those options sound lovely."

"And we probably have time for both."

"Can't wait. I'll see you then. Night, Jack."

"Goodnight, Caroline. Sleep well."

He placed the phone on its charger and blew out his breath. A grin stretched across his face. She was coming back. *Couldn't wait.*

At five minutes to one Friday afternoon, Jack stood in the front room and strained to see the driveway and gate even though he knew he wouldn't be able to see Caroline's car until it was well onto the dirt road.

Ten minutes later, he jumped when a silver car appeared through a haze of dust. He turned and nearly sprinted to the back steps.

Chapter Nineteen

By the time Caroline brought the car to a stop, Jack was halfway down the steps. Her heart bounced. He really was taking the afternoon off. She couldn't help the silly grin that prompted. She opened the door and nearly tumbled out, full of anticipation. Then her brain engaged. Now what? Fling herself into his arms? She stopped just short of doing so.

"Hey, Cowboy."

His smile widened as he stepped toward her. "Caroline."

She wasn't sure whether it was her legs that pushed her forward or whether Jack opened his arms. Anyway, in the next moment she met his chest, and his arms circled around her, pulling her close.

"I'm glad you came back," he murmured against her hair.

Something in his voice gave her pause, and she took a tiny step back so she could see his face. "Did you think I wouldn't?"

Jack's gaze shifted behind for a second, then he looked into her eyes and brushed a thumb across her cheek. "Was hoping you would."

When his glance dropped to her lips, she knew she was about to be kissed. Her eyes fluttered closed.

One of his hands pushed into her hair as his warm lips met hers.

She let out a soft sigh and twined her arms around his neck. The sound of her pulse pounded in her ears as Jack tightened his hold on her and deepened the kiss. Standing in his arms with the sun shining down on them, she felt deliciously warm and languid.

Minutes later, he rested his forehead against hers. Then he kissed her lightly and asked, "You need some time or are you ready for a ride?"

"I'll need to switch to my boots. Why don't I run to the cabin then meet you at the barn?"

"Sure thing. I'll grab a couple of bottles of water then see you over there."

Twenty minutes later, she pulled up to the barn at the same time Jack made his way to the entrance. "Good timing," she hollered. She waited a beat for him to catch up to her.

He opened the barn doors, and Caroline inhaled the heavy scent of fresh hay. She'd missed this. "Mmm, this never gets old. I swear, Jack, this is the tidiest, cleanest barn I've ever seen—or smelled."

He gave a light chuckle and squeezed her shoulder. "Glad to hear it."

Caroline stopped first to say hello to Star. "I have to check on little Sandy, too."

"She's growing fast," Jack said. "You go ahead. I'll get Star saddled and ready."

Caroline put out a hand to stop him. "Jack. That's not necessary. I'm perfectly capable of—"

Jack rested a hand on her arm. "Yes, I know you *can*, but why not let me help? It'll be faster, and you can spend more time fussing over Sandy."

She couldn't help a grin. "Okay, thanks." She left him to it and hurried to Sandy and Penny's stall. "Hey sweet girl," she crooned. "Look how adorable you are." The baby nuzzled Caroline's hand. She spent several minutes inside the stall with the mother and daughter, taking turns petting and brushing them both.

When she turned from the foal, she caught Jack watching her, a soft expression on his face. Their eyes met, and her nerve endings tingled. "All set?" she asked, aware that her voice sounded breathy and unnatural. Was the man *trying* to fluster her?

Jack braced against the stall door. "Almost. I... First, I..." He stopped as if waiting for her to finish the sentence.

She tilted her head. "You...?" She moved toward him, and when he opened the door, she slipped out of the stall.

Not meeting her eyes, he fiddled with the latch on the stall. Then, only inches away, he faced her and shoved his hands into his pockets. "I'd like to tell you about my week."

"Your week?" she echoed with a puzzled frown. "What do you mean? We've talked almost every day this past week."

"Yes, but I failed to mention a couple of things." He reached out and brushed a strand of hair from her face. "Like how much I looked forward to those talks. Or how much I wanted to hear your voice. I didn't tell you how often through the days I thought of you."

Caroline's throat clogged. His gaze held hers, and she felt as if his eyes looked deep into her soul.

"I've been stuck," Jack continued. "Stuck in the past. Just, I don't know, existing. I'm not doing a good job of explaining it. But you...you have an effect on me. I feel...I feel better, lighter.

"Oh, Jack, that's—"

"The thing is, I never thought this would happen again, but I've got feelings for you."

Tears spilled from her eyes. She took a step toward him, and he pulled her close.

"Jack." She said his name softly and melted against him, taking in the strength of his arms, the way he nestled her inside them. It was a nice fit.

He tightened his grip, rocking them both. "I was turning into a curmudgeon, and that's not who I want to be," he said against her hair.

"I'm so glad you're feeling again, Jack. Sometimes we have to reinvent ourselves." She didn't want to leave the circle of his arms, but she lifted her head. She placed a hand on the side of his face. "Hey, for the record, I have feelings for you, too," she whispered.

"That's excellent news." He brushed a hand through her hair, then with a low groan, he lowered his lips to hers.

A moment later, footsteps sounded on the concrete, and voices carried through the barn. Caroline pulled back and looked up at Jack. "Are Reed and company here?"

"No. We have a couple renting the other cabin for the weekend. Roger said they'd want to ride."

"Oh, okay. Do they need Star?"

"No. I already told Roger Star wouldn't be available." He leaned in close. "And I told Reed and Dylan they couldn't come this weekend."

Caroline gaped at him. "What? You did not."

Jack blew out a breath and nodded. "I did."

"Oh, Jack. Because of me?"

"Yeah. Because I want to spend my time with you

this weekend. No distractions."

She bit her lip, torn between agreeing with him and worrying about Reed's response. "Was…were they okay with that?"

"I'd say surprised."

"I would think so."

Jack slid an arm across his shoulder. "They'll get over it."

Caroline couldn't help laughing.

"Dylan wanted to know if you'd still be here."

"Oh no, maybe—"

"They can visit next weekend."

"Jack, I've already stayed longer than I intended. Nora might have the cabin rented."

He stopped walking and rested both hands on her shoulders. "Caroline, next time you come, you don't need a cabin. You'll stay at the house."

"Oh. Well…"

"I've got five unused bedrooms. No reason you can't stay in one of them."

Roger and the couple appeared in the hallway, relieving Caroline of the need to respond. *Good timing.* She'd need a minute or two to take in the implications of Jack's proposal. Actually, it wasn't even a proposal. It was a statement. Heat washed over her face. Though Jack had made huge strides in dismantling the wall around him, she couldn't help wondering if there was still a ghost in residence at the big house. Would she feel Rosalyn's presence there?

Jack dropped his arms and nodded to the group, and Roger made introductions.

"Enjoy your stay," Jack told them. Then he placed a hand on Caroline's back and ushered her to Star's stall. "Let's get out of here," he said. "I'll get Charlie and meet you out front."

Caroline led Star onto the road and glanced at the sky. Bright blue with a smattering of puffy clouds. Perfect conditions for a beautiful sunset. "I think we're going to get lucky tonight," she told Jack over the clip-clop of the horses' hooves. As soon as the words left her mouth, she cringed inside. Did she really say that? No doubt Jack would pick up on the double entendre. She couldn't look at him. "Should be a fabulous sunset," she finished brightly. "So, where we headed?"

Jack shot her a cocky grin but didn't mention her gaffe. "Thinking our new renters will stick to the main roads, so why don't we veer right and head west?"

"Good idea."

They rode side-by-side at a leisurely pace, the rhythm of the horses' hooves lulling them into comfortable silence, though Caroline's mind was anything but still. She couldn't shake where her thoughts had gone. It'd been a long time since she'd been intimate with a man. So long since she'd felt that kind of closeness and touch.

She glanced his direction. He sat straight and tall in the saddle, but at the same time he seemed perfectly relaxed and at ease. His handsome profile showed signs of age and hours in the elements, yet he looked healthy and fit. The hat completed the picture. *Such a cowboy.* She couldn't help smiling.

"Hey," he broke into her thoughts. "Want to pick up the pace a bit?"

She glanced at the open road ahead, and adrenaline shot through her. "Sure."

"At the next gate, let's move into the field and we

can let loose a little."

"The horses are okay with that?"

"Shouldn't be a problem," Jack said. "Sometimes I think they get bored with walking."

Inside the gate, Caroline tightened the strap from her hat under her chin. She grinned at Jack. "Ready." The open land beckoned.

Minutes later, the wind lifted her hair, and it whipped across her cheeks. Caroline couldn't help laughing as excitement surged inside her. The freedom was intoxicating.

Jack kept Charlie at pace beside Caroline and Star, cantering across the pasture.

When they slowed, Jack leaned toward her. "You good?"

"Oh, my gosh! That was fun!" She caught her breath then shook her hair and tucked loose strands behind her ears.

Jack extended his arm and squeezed her hand. "Your eyes are shining."

"Haven't had a good run like that in a long time. Whew, we should probably let the horses rest a minute then head back. I'll need to shower and clean up before sunset."

They turned back at a slower pace.

"How is it you started riding as a young girl?" Jack asked.

"My grandparents had a couple of horses on their farm. My grandpa got me started, then I begged my mother for lessons. It wasn't easy. All the riding stables were so far out from the city. I caught the bug, for sure."

"I'm familiar with that bug. My daughter—"

The rumble of a vehicle approaching moved them to the side of the road. Nora's jeep headed toward them then came to a stop.

"Well, hi there!" She shouted out of the window and waved. "Don't see you over this way too often. Were you looking for me or just out for a ride?"

"Out for a ride," Jack said.

"Hey, Caroline. Heard about those storms. Glad you made it back."

"Me, too! I didn't want to miss the dance."

Nora's glance shifted back and forth between Caroline and Jack. The initial surprise on her face was replaced by outright curiosity. Finally, she waved again and let the vehicle inch forward. "Okay, have fun. We'll see you tomorrow."

At the barn, Jack helped Caroline dismount, then he took the reins. "You go ahead. I'll take care of the horses."

"Thank you." She gave Star a pat. "Hope you enjoyed it, too, girl." Caroline turned to say goodbye to Jack and found herself drawn against him even though he still held the horses' reins. He dropped a quick kiss on her lips. "I'll pick you up around six."

"Pick me up? I can—"

"I'll come get you, so you aren't going back to the cabin alone after dark."

She smiled. "Sounds good." Walking to the car, she ran that scenario through her mind, and a little tingle shimmied up her spine. He'd be with her when she arrived back at the cabin.

****

At seven fifteen, Jack offered Caroline his hand, and they started up the incline to Sunset Ledge. He carried two folding chairs over his shoulder and a lantern in his other hand. Caroline carried a small bag with the wine, cookies, and a flashlight. She'd tied her sweater around her waist. He loved that she always seemed prepared and dressed appropriately for every situation.

"This is great," Caroline said. "I wasn't sure if we'd be hiking in grasses up to our knees."

"I cleared the path the other day. I try to keep it up. Reed and Kristen come up here sometimes." Not to mention he'd needed the time to prepare himself, to make sure he could bring Caroline. It'd been cathartic. As if each snip of the clippers had cleared the way for a new path forward, new memories. He'd been able to shed his worry and guilt, and went back down feeling peaceful, as if a weight had lifted from his shoulders.

When they reached the plateau of the rocky ledge, Jack set up the chairs. But Caroline stood with her hand shading her eyes and gawked at the three-hundred-and-sixty-degree vista.

"Oh, Jack. This is incredible."

"Highest point on the ranch."

"I feel like I can see the edge of the earth."

Jack smiled. "But Professor…"

Caroline nudged him. "Yeah, yeah, it's a figure of speech. Anyway, it's amazing."

"Just wait. It gets better." He handed her a wine tumbler then poured her a generous amount of sauvignon blanc.

"Thanks." She tapped her glass to his. "Better already."

"Cheers to a beautiful day with a beautiful companion."

Her gaze held his. "You know, you have a romantic streak, Jack Armstrong."

She shot him a smile that nearly buckled his knees. He took a quick sip of wine.

"It's nice," she added.

"Glad you approve."

He gestured toward the chairs. "Have a seat. The show will start soon."

"So, do you keep this a secret or does everyone on the ranch find their way up here?"

"This area is private."

"It's special," Caroline murmured.

"That it is." His voice came out low and husky.

She squeezed his hand. "I'm honored, sir."

His heart pounded, and his hands turned clammy around the wine glass. He understood she got the message that *she* was special. Only a handful of people were invited to the ledge.

"I remember one summer Roger and Nora were going through a rough patch. Rosalyn and I sent them up here while we watched their kids." He turned to Caroline with a grin. "Pretty sure it saved their marriage."

She rested a hand on his arm. "Wow. It's a magical place then. Hey, speaking of magical, you ready for cookies?"

"Whenever you are."

She rustled around in the bag she'd carried then produced two of the large snickerdoodles. "Here you go. Let's see how these pair with white wine."

He took the cookie. "You first."

With a flourish, she bit into her cookie then took a drink and moaned softly. "Oh yeah, that's tasty."

Jack laughed. "You might have a bit of a dramatic streak." The saucy grin on her face made him want to taste the wine and sugar on her lips.

She leaned toward him. "I'm sure you mean that in a good way, right?"

"Absolutely," he nearly croaked while trying to maintain some composure.

"Seriously, Arlene could sell these in shops if she were in Dallas. I'm looking forward to seeing her at the dance—and the other people I've met in town. I'm assuming everyone turns out for the dance?"

"It draws a pretty big crowd." Jack cringed inside thinking about his last encounter with Arlene. Hopefully the woman would put aside any matchmaking attempts when he showed up for the dance with Caroline. He didn't need *that* kind of drama.

"Oh, look." With a breathy squeal, Caroline gestured toward the sky. "The clouds are starting to glow."

Sure enough, the descending sun shone beneath the clouds, edging them in an electric yellow outline.

"And so it begins," Jack said. He finished his cookie then extended his arm and opened his hand toward Caroline. Liquid heat spread through him when her slim fingers intertwined with his.

Over the next several minutes he watched the sky turn from pink to orange and listened to Caroline's ooohs and ahhhs as the colors changed and deepened. He couldn't stop smiling.

"These colors are stunning," she said. "I'll have to bring my camera next time."

A number of thoughts hit his brain in rapid succession. She wanted to come again. She didn't have her camera—she wasn't working.

She looked over at him. "I just wanted to experience it this time."

His throat tightened, and all he could do was nod and squeeze her hand. And once again, he wondered how this lovely woman had stumbled into his life.

Caroline repositioned her arm to where it linked through his then took his hand again. "Look at those colors. Nature's artistry."

The blue sky darkened to a deep cobalt above the red-orange ball of the sun. It'd be over soon.

"Oh, my gosh!" She gestured with her wine glass in hand. "Look at that reflection. I didn't even see the pond before."

A mirror image of the sky twinkled on the water in the distance.

"Not quite the beach," Jack said.

"No. But just as gorgeous to look at."

Jack smiled in the dim light. Watching Caroline watch the sunset was every bit as captivating as the show itself.

When the last of the light slipped below the horizon, Caroline let out a soft sigh. "That was so amazing."

"We got us a good one." Jack held up the wine bottle. "Want to finish this off before we head down?" He was in no hurry to leave, but if they didn't, the only thing left to do was kiss her like crazy. Maybe if he leaned in… Yeah, and maybe he'd knock them both over and they'd tumble down the hill.

"I'd probably better not be tipsy on the way down," she answered his question. "How about we finish it at the cabin?"

Electricity surged through him, and he made an effort to breathe calmly. "That works for me." He handed her the bottle then lit the lantern and began folding up the chairs.

He took Caroline's arm and held the lantern in front of her as they carefully made their way back down the path. Good thing he'd been up and down that path hundreds of times because his focus was a long way from his footing.

****

Inside the cabin, Caroline shed her sweater and shook out her hair. She couldn't decide if it really was too warm in there or whether her internal thermometer was overheating due to the cowboy in her midst. She shot a glance at Jack. He'd gone straight to the kitchen and was already refilling their wine glasses. He appeared perfectly at ease.

She accepted the wine then leaned against the back of the sofa. Those intense blue eyes locked onto hers. She could hardly breathe in the heavy silence. The wine she sipped seared her dry throat. She forced a smile.

"Tell me more about this street dance. I don't want to embarrass myself." She gave a light laugh. "Are there certain steps I should know? Any line dances?"

Truth was, she hadn't danced with anyone in years. Embarrassment was a definite possibility. If she didn't step on his feet, she was certainly capable of tripping over her own.

Jack stopped his glass mid-drink, and a frown wrinkled his brow. "Umm…I have to tell you I have no idea. It's been a long time. I…we could ask Nora."

With a wave of her hand, Caroline pushed off from the sofa then pulled her phone from her purse. "You know what? I think we should practice. Let me open a playlist."

The speaker on her phone couldn't simulate the volume of a live band, but at least it helped fill the charged air. Maybe dancing would burn off some nervous energy.

Jack set his glass on the table then stepped toward her.

When he took her hand and slid his other arm around her waist, she thought her legs might give out. She tightened her grip on his shoulder.

In the next instant, he spun her around, and she laughed out loud.

"I was a ballet dancer for several years growing up," she said when she came back to face him.

"I can tell. You're light on your feet."

"I love to twirl."

He grinned. "That I can do." He spun her again, and she whirled under his arm then back to him. From behind, he held her against his chest, rocking in time with the music. He kissed her hair then twirled her to the front again.

"I think we'll be just fine." His low voice reverberated close to her ear.

Pressed against him, she wondered if he could feel her heart pounding. She looked up, and he stopped dancing. Heat washed over her as time stood still.

Jack cupped her face in his hands and lowered his lips to hers.

Caroline wound her arms around his neck, kissing him back, clutching him closer. A flame sprang to life, and her nerve endings tingled.

"Jack." She softly spoke his name.

Long moments later, he pulled back enough for her to catch her breath. "Jack," she said again. She placed her hands on his shoulders and met his eyes. Then she whispered, "You don't have to go back to the house tonight."

Chapter Twenty

Caroline tied the robe around her waist then, following the scent of freshly brewed coffee, stepped into the main room.

Jack stood against the counter already sipping from his mug and wearing a five o'clock shadow, jeans, and white T-shirt. Of course, she expected him to be there. Still, the view sent a little jolt through her system.

He looked up, and she sent him a soft smile. *An awkward grand entrance if ever there was one. Would he have any regrets?*

"Morning." His warm voice broke into the quiet room. He straightened and reached for another cup. "Coffee or tea?"

"Coffee is great, thanks." Watching his face, she entered the kitchen. His eyes flickered to hers but didn't linger. He was probably wondering the same thing about her.

"You're up early," she said. Meaning, *you got up without me.*

"Yeah, years of routine. I can't sleep in." He rested a hand on her arm and leaned in close. "But I loved waking up next to you."

She gave a shaky laugh as tingles shivered up her spine. "Same," she whispered. And she'd slept well. After so many years of a cold, empty space beside her, it'd been nice to roll over and find Jack's warmth there.

With a slow, easy smile, he handed her the cup of coffee and planted a quick kiss on her forehead. Then he opened the fridge. "A splash of cream, right?"

"Normally, yes, but I don't have anything fresh. Guess I forgot about stopping for groceries." *Way to look like an airhead.* She hadn't even given it a thought. But then, again, she hadn't decided how much longer she'd be staying.

A warm light sparked in his eyes. "Sounds like you were in a hurry to get here."

She couldn't help laughing as her face warmed. *Busted.* And now, when would she be going back? After last night…

The unspoken question hung in the air.

Jack cleared his throat. "Do you have any plans for the day?"

"Looks like I might have to hit the diner for lunch then pick up some groceries while I'm in town."

He shook his head. "I've got plenty of food for lunch. We could eat by the pool."

Caroline blinked. "You…you're not working today?"

"Thought I might take the day off."

Oh, my. That was unexpected. Maybe there wasn't always must-do work, but always something he could find to occupy his time. "Poolside lunch is a great idea." She inadvertently glanced at the closed bedroom door. She shot him a bright smile. "What time do we need to leave for the dance?"

"If I remember right, the band starts playing at five."

"Okay." Earlier than she thought. By the time she showered and got ready after some pool time, there wouldn't be much day left. "What's for supper tonight? Burgers?"

"There's usually a variety. Burgers and brisket for sure."

"All things beef, huh?"

"Pretty much."

"Sounds good."

A grin widened across his face. "You sound hungry. Should we go find you something to eat?"

With a laugh, she put a hand to her stomach. "I don't need a lot. Some toast would be fine."

"Why don't I go on up to the house? I need to check in with Roger. You can join me whenever you're ready."

"Good plan. I'll meet—"

Caroline's phone buzzed against the counter where it had been plugged in overnight. She took a couple of steps and looked at the screen. She barely kept from rolling her eyes.

A text from Hank.

—Hi, Caroline. Brody from the Texas Wildlife Commission wants to know the exact location where you took that picture. Can you give me an address? Landowner contact?—

Ugh. Did they really have to deal with this so soon after her arrival? She glanced sideways at Jack.

He raised his brows. "Something wrong?"

She bit her lip. Maybe this was a good time to get it all out on the table. "I hope not, but I need to tell you something. Hang on, I want to show you a picture." She flicked through her photos and found the lizard. Twisting toward Jack, she offered him the phone. "I took this the first week I was here. Have you ever seen one?"

He nodded and placed a hand at the small of her back.

The simple gesture felt so automatic. Natural—and a little possessive. She couldn't help wondering if she was about to blow it. She wiped a clammy hand against the terry robe.

"I don't see many of them," Jack said. "But they're around. I understand they like some plant that grows here." He shifted his stance. "Let me guess, you showed that to your friend Joe, and he wants to do a study or something."

Caroline gave a nervous laugh. "Not exactly, but you're close. This little guy is on the endangered species list, and I guess there's been a proposal to establish a sanctuary out here for several years. Joe showed the photo to one of the other professors, and he's been in contact with the state wildlife folks." She sucked in a deep breath. "They're asking me for more information. The location of the ranch and your contact info."

She searched Jack's face while he processed the request. He was doing a pretty good job of not reacting. "Would you be okay with that?"

Jack braced against the table and rubbed the back of his neck. Then he reached for her hand. "Why would they need that?"

"I don't know exactly." Heart pounding, she laced her fingers through his.

"They looking for land?"

"Jack, I don't know any details. I'll tell him no if you want me to."

He pulled her closer. "Hell no, Caroline. I'm not

using you to go between me and those people. Give them my number, and I'll handle it. They'll track me down eventually, anyway."

"So…but…are you opposed to a wildlife refuge?"

"In theory, no." He blew out a long breath. "You're right. They've talked about this before, but then it didn't go anywhere. I figured it was a money issue. I don't have a problem with them saving the creatures." He took a sip of coffee then shook his head. "I do care whether they'll pay fair market value for the land or try to force people to sell cheap. What about water? If they're diverting water that would otherwise go to my fields and ponds, I have a problem with that. What's the maintenance look like? Roads and traffic. Will it be a tourist destination—some kind of public park? Does it affect land values and taxes? Lots of things to consider."

"Yes, all valid concerns. They'd have to address all of those questions in public hearings, I would think."

He offered a wry smile. "Again, in theory."

"It's just that, well, I'm wondering if we'd be on opposite sides. As an ecologist, this is totally in my wheelhouse, Jack. It's the kind of thing I will always support. Plus…I might have a chance to be involved with this one."

His brows shot up again. "How so?"

"They'll need on-site management. If I don't go back to the university, and if I'm in the area regularly, it might be a way for me to stay active in the field. My professional life is a big part of who I am."

He was silent for a moment, then gently twisted a lock of her hair. "If that's what you want, you should try to make it happen. It's not going to be a problem."

He straightened and took a step closer, smiling. "And for the record, I one-hundred-percent approve of you being here regularly. *That* has my full support."

She gave a breathy laugh. "Good to know."

His lips met hers. "I'll see you in a little while."

"Give me an hour?" She could use a shower and a minute to regroup.

"Sure. Take your time."

Caroline watched his retreating figure until the door shut behind him. Then she flopped onto the sofa. *Whew*. The last twenty-four hours had been a whirlwind. And the next twenty-four showed no signs of slowing down.

She let her thoughts drift back to last night, and her insides warmed. Everything that happened seemed so right. In fact, she already anticipated a repeat after the dance. At one time, she'd been drawn to Jack, thinking he needed her—thinking she could bring him out of the past and open his broken heart again. Clearly, she'd done that. But in truth, he was doing the same for her. He made her feel desirable again, wanted and cared for.

"I have a love life," she said out loud to the universe as she waved her arms in the air with a flourish. That was how she'd refer to her relationship with Jack. She refused to call an accomplished sixty-year-old man who knew a lot about living a *boyfriend*.

The thought took her back to Sunset Ledge, and she let out a soft sigh. There was something special about holding hands with someone while looking out across vast fields or waves, to be a unified speck in time and place.

With a catch in her throat, Caroline picked up her phone and replied to Hank's text. She had some major decisions hanging over her head, but perhaps some gears were shifting into place. And she had a fun day ahead of her. She wouldn't let Hank and his lizard derail that.

****

Whistling, Jack sprinted up the steps to the house. Inside, he sagged against the door and shook his head, hardly able to believe last night. He glanced around the kitchen and seating area with a critical eye. Caroline would be here soon. He wanted her to feel welcome and at home—to see it as a place where she could be comfortable.

His gaze landed on the family photos scattered across the accent table. He slowly moved to the table. The surface was laden with memories. He picked up the frames one by one, remembering occasions, places, and the earlier days of his life. For a moment, he wondered if he should select a few and pare down the display. Would the photos of Rosalyn make Caroline uncomfortable?

Indecision gnawed at him. This was his life. Part of who he was. The photos could fade, diminish in importance, but the past was never going away. He had no desire to deny it. The close-up of his beautiful daughter laughing and hugging her two children always choked him up. He set it down and brushed a hand across the polished surface. There was plenty of room for new photos. New moments. Future memories.

At first, when Caroline came to the ranch and reached out to him, he'd thought she was toying with him, trying to get under his skin for fun. But he now realized she was too nice to play games like that no matter how obnoxious he was. He gave a short laugh.

She had feelings for him. He shook his head. Her touch, her smile made him feel as if he'd won the lottery. No, more like he'd found a rare and precious treasure.

He swallowed hard. They'd already begun to share photo-worthy memories. He'd have to remember to have someone take a picture of them at the dance tonight—their first official *date*.

Refocusing on the task at hand, he returned to the kitchen. He was about to open the refrigerator when his phone rang.

"Hey, Boss." Roger's voice came on the line. "What time do you want to get started today?"

Jack's thoughts stuttered. "Started?" he echoed.

"Finishing up the shots."

"You didn't wrap up that project yesterday?"

Roger let out deep sigh. "Nope. Thought Denny was going to let you know we didn't get done. You want to finish up today?"

Jack shoved a hand in his pocket. No, he did not. "What happened? Wasn't he supposed to help with that?"

"Sure, Boss, but he's green. Took a little longer."

"What's he doing today?"

"Haven't talked to him yet. Thought I'd check with you first. You want him on the clock?"

Jack heard the surprise in Roger's voice. Normally, Jack's Saturdays were wide-open for ranch work. "You saying I'll be expected to pay him overtime for weekend work even though he didn't get the job done on time?"

"I'd say you could probably expect that. It's not an exact science, you know."

"How much time are we looking at?"

"A few hours."

Jack groaned inside. If he did that, he'd have no time with Caroline until the dance. And she was still saying *if* she left the university, *if* she came back regularly. He couldn't help feeling that they needed to nail down some kind of plan or roadmap for the next few months anyway. That wouldn't happen if they weren't spending time together.

"Could it wait until Monday?" Jack asked.

"You know the shelf life. It might be all right, but the sooner, the better."

Yes, he knew it was best to get the shots administered right away. He heaved a sigh. He couldn't let ranch business go. And he wouldn't waste resources. But he also wasn't inclined to blow off his commitment with Caroline. "All right, see if Denny can finish the job today. I've already made other plans, but let me know if he can't do it."

"Will do."

Jack grumbled to himself as he pulled produce from the refrigerator. He'd just told Roger that ranch business was taking a backseat to *other plans*. If necessary, Jack could have lunch with Caroline and then leave her to the pool. Maybe they'd have a chance to talk tomorrow. He didn't like feeling uncertain and undecided.

Whatever Roger thought about Jack's response, he didn't share. Jack had the feeling people liked Caroline. But he couldn't help wondering if things would change as she started making a difference in his life. He'd been so available, so predictable for the past few years. And now the possibility of this nature preserve was floating around again. Would they be on opposite sides? The implications of that pressed against him. Would she be considered the enemy by his friends and other townspeople if she was cheerleading the preserve? He didn't worry for himself, but he'd hate to see others regard her as bad news.

He was still mulling the situation when he got the text from Roger.

—No worries. Denny and I will finish up today.—

Relief shot through Jack, and he couldn't contain a grin. *Back on track.* By the time Caroline arrived, Jack had sliced some fresh fruit and mixed the eggs for scrambling—and was nervously rehearsing a conversation starter about her future.

"Knock-knock," she called out at the door.

"Come on in." Jack peered around the corner, and his heart bounced.

Light radiated from the bright smile on her face. Any guilt he felt about not helping with the inoculations floated right out the door. He'd made the right decision.

"What can I get you to drink? Tea? Mimosa?"

"Mmm, a mimosa sounds lovely." She set her swim bag near the door and moved toward him.

Jack poured the drink and handed her the glass. "I've got everything ready for omelets or scrambled eggs. We can go ahead and eat, or maybe you'd like a tour of the house first?"

****

Caroline's pulse jumped. He was ready to show her his house? She'd seen only the main living space connected to the kitchen—and the wine cellar. But he'd mentioned all those bedrooms. An office? His own room? No denying she was curious about the rest of the space.

"I'd love to see the house. But we can eat first. Scrambled eggs sound great. What can I do to help?"

He shook his head. "Not a thing. This is one meal I can handle."

She watched as he went to work, his hands busy with a cook's tasks. He moved quickly from stove to counter to fridge as if juggling, and she had the feeling he was burning nervous energy. Maybe he wasn't a hundred percent comfortable having her in the house. Yet he'd already invited her to stay on her next visit. She couldn't do that if they were walking on eggshells.

Determined to make her presence feel natural, she moved into the kitchen and nudged him. "Jack, I don't need to be waited on. How about you do the eggs, and I'll take charge of the toast?"

"Uh, sure, that's fine."

"And plates?" She gestured toward the cabinets.

"Top right."

She removed the plates and swung around as a thought occurred to her. "Hey, what about side dishes? Are we supposed to take something to share to the dance?"

He stopped his hands and stared at her like a deer in the headlights. "Umm. That's a good question. I haven't been in a long time. No one's mentioned it, though."

"I better text Nora. I don't want to show up empty handed if everyone else is contributing."

"I'm sure it'll be fine. There's always a ton of food."

Ah, no way would she look like a freeloader in front of the community. Caroline tapped out a quick message to Nora. A moment later, the phone dinged with a message.

—Oh, gosh. You're a guest this time. Don't worry about bringing anything.—

—It's a potluck?—

—I'm bringing enough cake and cookies for all of us.—

—OK thanks.—

"It's potluck," she told Jack. "Nora's bringing desserts. What could we do?"

"Can't imagine we have time to pull something together. It's not—"

"You have potatoes and eggs? We could whip up some potato salad. That's easy."

Jack gave a laugh. "For you, maybe."

"Seriously, the potatoes can boil while we tour the house. Easy-peasy. As long as you have fresh mayo and mustard." Without waiting for his assessment, she opened the refrigerator and perused the contents. Looked like it held all the necessary ingredients. Decision made. "We got this."

He turned from the stove and shot her a smile. "Okay. There's a bag of potatoes in the pantry."

She pushed down the lever on the toaster then went in search of the spuds. The kitchen and pantry were well-stocked, and Caroline had no trouble finding the necessary pots and bowls for the task. Of course, on a ranch, cooking was part of daily life. No stopping for a quick bite at a favorite restaurant on the way home from work or a school activity. Rosalyn had probably prepared three meals a day. A different lifestyle than what Caroline was used to, for sure. She'd bet half of her family's meals had been eaten at restaurants or were made easy with carryout. She didn't mind cooking, but never had time for long, drawn-out meal prep.

"Just about ready," Jack said a few minutes later.

She popped up the last of the toast then carried the plate and jam to the table, moving around as if she belonged there. Jack didn't seem put off. If she read the clues correctly, his body language indicated he was more relaxed than he'd been earlier. *Mission accomplished.*

"Guessing someone who likes well-done steak also likes crisp bacon," he said, brows raised.

She peeked at the skillet then patted his arm. "That's good guessing."

He placed the platter of eggs and bacon in the center of the table then pulled out a chair. "Have a seat."

"Thanks. This looks great," she told him.

"Pretty good teamwork, I'd say."

"Yes, and just wait until we get started on that potato salad. It's going to rock."

****

After cleaning and cutting the potatoes, Caroline let Jack carry the large pot to the stove. Then he took her hand.

"You're now well acquainted with the kitchen. Want to see the rest?"

"Absolutely."

He led her through a wide opening into a formal living space complete with vaulted ceiling, slate fireplace, and tall windows. The hardwood carried through, but the floor of the main seating area was covered in a plush wheat-colored rug.

"This is beautiful." She moved to his side, arms touching. "Did you use it much?"

Jack shrugged. "We had holidays and family gatherings in here." He pointed to the windows. "Used to put a big Christmas tree right there."

"I bet that was spectacular."

"Library in here," he said as they continued down the hall.

Inside, Caroline was surprised to see a spacious room full of natural light with white bookshelves and a window seat. She thought of her library at home—the smallest room in the house—crammed with books double stacked on the shelves, a desk, and one armchair. She could spend some time in here. "What an inviting space," she told him. "It's lovely."

Jack cleared his throat. "You're more than welcome to use it when you're here." He took her hand and moved along the hallway. "We could bring your things over this afternoon. I mean…if that's…you're staying…" He stopped talking and rested his forehead against hers. "I sound like a stammering imbecile. You get my thoughts all tied up in knots."

She pulled back and sent him a soft smile. "I think we have enough going on today. Let's deal with that tomorrow."

Nodding, he took her arm and a couple of steps. "Guess I'm wondering about your timeline."

She bumped against him as they began walking again. She sensed he needed to keep moving, to have something to do, while having this conversation. "I thought I'd stay through next weekend. I'd like to see Dylan and company again, but then I need to re-focus on this book project. It needs to be well underway, maybe a first draft to the publisher, this summer if I intend to retire." She glanced his direction. "I don't trust the new dean of biology not to find a way to sabotage it."

"He's that bad? Aren't there others who can help you? You're a tenured professor, after all."

"Sure, I still have a lot of friends there, but I can't ask others to run interference for me. Everyone is busy, has their own problems to deal with. And, yes, he's that bad." She blew out a long breath. "Or maybe I'm in a rut, and it's time to move on."

Jack slid his arm across her shoulders. "Maybe a little of both?"

"Probably. The longer I'm away, the less I miss it. That man makes me grumpy. I'm enjoying the book project, the freedom of being out of the office, and managing my own schedule."

Jack opened another door and ushered her inside. "This is the ground-floor guest room, which I thought you could take over when you're here."

The room featured a queen-size bed, an accent chair, dresser, and a small desk. "Oh, my. This is a nice room—almost as big as the cabin."

"Think it would work for you?" His voice carried a hint of strain.

She turned toward him. "I'm sure it would." She glanced away, still thinking of their conversation. "The thing is, this may be silly, but I don't want to feel as if I was pushed out of my job. I want to leave on my own terms."

Jack smiled. "Exploring other opportunities?"

Caroline grimaced. "Sounds like I was let go."

He pulled her against his chest and spoke into her hair. "If you're gone and you're happy, does it really matter?"

She sputtered a laugh. "Good point. No, it doesn't. Regardless of how or when I leave, eventually it won't matter. I'll just be part of the history."

He placed his hands on her shoulders. "We…we've got something here. I don't want to keep you from the things you love, but I don't want to lose you. I guess my question is, can you do the things you want to do from Texas?"

Her throat clogged. "I think so," she whispered.

His lips met hers in a deep, slow kiss.

She melted against him, and strong arms wrapped around her, pulling her closer. As if his hands conducted electricity, heat sizzled through her. This was worth some back-and-forth travel.

"I'll need to figure out the logistics," she told him long moments later.

"Yeah." He took her hand and turned toward the door. "We can do that."

Back in the kitchen, he handed her a glass of iced tea. "Where are you off to next?"

She took a much-needed gulp before answering. "I'm not sure. I still need mountains and desert, so maybe Colorado." She looked at him and couldn't help if he saw longing in her eyes. "Maybe Sedona. It's…it's such a beautiful place." She placed a hand on his arm and lowered her voice. "Jack, you'd love it."

She arched her brows and watched an array of emotions flicker in his eyes. He obviously knew what she was asking.

He squeezed her hand. "I'll be here waiting for you when you get back."

Caroline glanced away as her throat burned. The man had feelings for her, but he was unwilling to budge.

He tipped her chin and looked into her eyes. "Hey, is that not going to work for you?"

She didn't yet have an answer as to how many times she'd be willing to travel back to Texas. One more question loomed in her mind. Would he ever meet her halfway?

"I...I don't know, Jack. I enjoy my own company, but I have to say, it's nice to have a companion sometimes, too. I mean, think about it, how often do you go up to Sunset Ledge by yourself? Some things are meant to be shared."

"True." His Adam's apple bobbed, and he looked past her.

She waited in silence.

Finally, he glanced back and brushed a thumb across her cheek. "What does this relationship look like for you? At this stage in our lives, we both have families and obligations. We've got roots."

But her foundation had hit shaky ground. Everything she'd built seemed to be waving in the winds. Could Jack offer a solid base?

"Maybe for now, we go with the flow and see where it takes us?" she offered, her eyes searching his.

A slow smile spread across his face. "That isn't my strongest suit, but it sounds like our best option. Can we...for now, can we say we're in a relationship?"

Tears welled in her eyes, but she shot him a sassy smile. "Sounds like you don't want me going out on dates with other men while I'm traveling," she said in an airy tone.

He pulled her to him. "That's right, we're…we're a couple."

With a light laugh, she lifted her face. "We can say that."

Chapter Twenty-One

The beating of Jack's heart sounded louder to his ears than the taps he gave the cabin door. He stepped back and waited for Caroline to appear.

A moment later, she opened the door, and heat flooded his veins.

She stepped onto the porch wearing a sparkling smile, a denim skirt, and a bright turquoise blouse that fit low on her shoulders and sparkled as well.

Tongue-tied, Jack stared at the vision before him. She would turn heads tonight.

"Hey, Jack. You look nice."

He'd gone so far as putting on a pressed dress shirt and cologne with his jeans and boots, but that was nothing compared to her. "You, my lady, are breathtaking."

She cocked her head and gave a little curtsey. "Why thank you, sir."

"I hope you didn't buy those fancy boots just for tonight."

The caramel-colored boots featured a design with light stitching and inlaid pieces of turquoise leather. "No, but I'm thrilled to have someplace to wear them. They were an impulse purchase several years ago. On sale. I've only worn them a few times, but don't worry, they're comfortable and broken in so I should be able to dance in them."

"Pretty swanky for our little country shindig."

Caroline laughed and patted his arm. "I have a feeling you underestimate the style of the women around here."

He might not be the most aware of men when it came to fashion and hairdos. Rosalyn had often called him clueless. He didn't care about those things, but he had no doubt Caroline would make a statement tonight. And he'd be proud to have her on his arm—and in his arms on the dance floor. He smiled inside with anticipation. It'd been a good long while since he felt like this. He took her hand and helped her down the steps then opened the car door for her.

She turned. "You've got the salad?"

"In the backseat. Complete with serving spoon, as instructed."

"Excellent."

Inside the car, he glanced her way. "Looks like all systems are go for a perfect evening." The day had been warm and sunny, and with bonfires lining Main Street, he expected the evening to be plenty comfortable.

"The weather couldn't be nicer."

A few minutes outside of town, Caroline swiveled toward him. "What do you know about the band?"

"Not a lot, but Roger says they put on a good show and play lots of familiar dancing tunes. They're out of Fort Worth."

"Sounds great."

Jack pulled the SUV into a parking spot along one of the side streets off Main. "It's just a short walk," he told Caroline. "You can leave your wrap in the car. If you need it later, I'll come back. But once the sun goes down, there'll be fires lit all along the street. Gotta check in first. Then we can find Roger and Nora."

"I'd like to meet your other friends, too."

"Sure. Lots of folks will want to say hello." He checked his phone. "Roger and Nora are here. You ready?"

"Yes, let's go!"

He opened the back door and retrieved the salad then offered his arm to Caroline. They were stopped almost immediately as a few other couples made their way toward the roped-off portion of the street.

"Jack, great to see you." Chuck Anderson slapped him on the back.

Jack introduced Caroline and before they could move on, Paul and Lucy Kline stopped as well. Paul held out a hand. "Hey, Jack. Long time no see." The man spoke to Jack, but his eyes lingered on Caroline.

After introductions were made, Jack took Caroline's arm and practically tugged her toward the street. "This could go on all night," he told her, his voice low. In fact, it probably *would* go on all night.

Caroline laughed. "Would you rather be ignored?"

He shot her a look that spoke for him. The answer was yes. Thankfully, he spotted Roger and Nora coming toward them.

"Hey, friends," Nora squealed and waved. They both greeted Caroline with smiles and hugs, and Jack had to fight to keep a silly grin from his face as pride swelled inside him.

"You two look great," Nora said. "Caroline, that top is darling. And those boots! Wowza, you're a regular cowgirl fashionista. Oh, listen." She whirled around in the direction of guitar strings reverberating at the microphone. "The band's warming up," she said.

"Let's go find drinks and get this party started."

As usual, they all followed Nora's lead, her energy and enthusiasm bubbling around them. Roger fell into step beside Jack as Nora tugged Caroline ahead. Jack would have preferred to enter the main area with Caroline on his arm.

"What's in the bag?" Roger asked.

"Oh, uh, our contribution. Say, Nora, any idea where this goes?" He held up the bag.

"We made potato salad," Caroline added.

"Troughs of ice on the west side."

To Jack's great pleasure, Caroline took a step back and linked her arm through his. "Let us drop this off, and we'll meet you at the bar."

"That's a generous description." Nora waved her hand with a laugh. "You mean the keg station?"

"Oh, is that all—"

"Don't worry, there's wine and hard seltzers, and plenty of non-alcoholic options, too. See you there."

Jack grinned. "Come on. Let's get in there so you can see we aren't total country bumpkins."

Caroline stopped and rested a hand on his arm. "Jack, I hope I never gave you that impression."

"I didn't mean anything other than you're a city girl. We're not as refined around these parts."

"Not true. Everyone I've met has been lovely."

Still, he felt warm under the collar. He did wonder if they measured up in her eyes. She was a university professor, smart, sharp. Around here, most people finished high school then went to work. They were smart about ranch business but not book smart. Some might have a hard time finding Nashville on a map. Not the kind of people she was used to socializing with.

Only a little farther, they turned onto Main Street.

Caroline gasped. "Ooh. This is beautiful. The town really puts on a show."

Lights twinkled in the trees and along the serving tables, and the seating tables were draped with colorful cloths. Already, the rich, smoky scent of Texas mesquite hung in the air.

"Not too shabby, huh?" Jack said. "Wait 'til it gets dark. It'll be even better."

"I can imagine. The whole street will glow."

They checked in at the front table and got wristbands then Jack spotted the troughs for side dishes. "Let me drop this off," he told Caroline.

He approached the table just as a couple of women did.

"Hey, Jack." Darla Schmidt touched his arm. "You brought a dish?"

"Some potato salad." He nestled the bowl into the ice alongside some other salads.

"Well, aren't you the handyman," she said in a sing-song voice. "Yum, it looks delicious."

"Well, I can't take the credit. I had some help." He held out a hand to Caroline.

The woman turned, and her face froze.

Jack cleared his throat. "Darla, this is Caroline Tate."

"Pleasure," the woman said stiffly.

The other woman reached across Darla and tapped one of the other bowls. "Oh, my. That looks like Arlene's potato salad." She nudged Darla. "You won't want to miss that."

Jack's face warmed. Was that a personal dig? Were they not interested in the salad after he mentioned

Caroline had made it? He couldn't wrap his head around that.

"Nice to meet you," Caroline said. "Enjoy the dance."

It was Jack's clue to keep moving, and he did so eagerly. Caroline didn't appear put off. Maybe he'd imagined the slight.

Holding on to her, Jack kept an eye on his date while also observing the stares she generated. They could hardly take three steps in a row without being stopped. She dealt with the interest with poise and grace, smiling the whole time.

He knew it wasn't only the fact that he'd come out of his hermit shell and shown up with a date that had the town mesmerized. Caroline was a beautiful woman who would capture attention no matter what.

He leaned in. "You're making me look good," he told her.

"Oh, pshaw." She nudged him. "You don't need me for that. It's really great how happy people are to see you, Jack. You're obviously a leader in the community."

He shrugged. "I've lived here forever."

"Sure, but it's more than that. I feel privileged to be your date."

Her words were accompanied by a bright smile that took away his breath. Jack had half a mind to scoop her up and head home, away from all the people and commotion. Then again, he enjoyed showing her off. "I believe it's time we offer you a cold drink. This way." He needed one for sure.

At the "bar," they met up with Roger and Nora.

"You made it. We were starting to wonder if you'd

changed your minds," Nora said.

"We're drawing a crowd," Jack told her. He stepped up to the table with Caroline.

She opted for a flavored seltzer, and he ordered a beer. The cold liquid went down just fine.

"Want to find our table or mingle for a while?" Nora asked. "It'll be hard to talk once the band starts."

"I'm fine mingling," Caroline said. "Nora, did you help with the decorating? It's amazing how transformed the whole street is."

"I helped with the planning, but lots of people pitched in to string the lights and set up."

"It really has a fabulous ambiance. The flowers on the tables and all across the stage are a nice touch."

Potted yellow flowers lined the area in front of the bandstand at the far end of the dance area. Jack smiled inside. Caroline seemed genuinely impressed with their little event so far. That was encouraging. It might not matter in the whole scheme of things, but he wanted her to like the town. He wanted her to want to spend more time here.

****

Caroline took in the scenery and pushed the strange encounter with the women out of her mind. While most people had been friendly, she could understand the local women—the single ones—being disappointed to see Jack with an outsider. There could easily be a few hopefuls who'd been waiting for him to be ready for a romantic relationship again. She couldn't fault them for that.

Thankfully, she seemed to have an ally and champion in Nora. Her easy laughter and ready smile gave Caroline an extra dose of confidence to socialize among all those strangers who might or might not be welcoming and accepting.

Nora joined conversation after conversation. The woman knew something about everyone—who had a medical issue, who was taking a trip, and who had a quilting or home project under way. She must've pledged six meals in the coming week. As if she were the town scribe, calendar, and caretaker.

"Nora, you're amazing. How do you remember all of this?"

"It's just what I do. We look out for each other." She stopped walking and turned to Caroline. "Speaking of amazing, I can't tell you what good it's done my heart, and Roger's, to see Jack so happy. When I saw you two riding yesterday, it brought tears to my eyes. Not even kidding. It's been a long, long time since I've seen him look relaxed and refreshed." She tipped her cup to Caroline's. "And it's your doing."

Caroline took a sip of her drink and contemplated how much to tell her new friend. Not everything, certainly. "I enjoy his company," she said. "We had a fun day yesterday. Even went up to Sunset Ledge. It was spectacular."

Nora's smiled widened. "Ahhh, I wondered if he'd take you up there. Good. That's good."

"Speaking of, we'd better find the guys before Jack thinks I abandoned him." Caroline searched the crowd. Didn't take long to see Jack standing with a couple of other men. He was tall, sure, but more than that, he had a commanding presence about him. He didn't blend in.

"There you are," Jack said when she moved beside him. He gestured toward her drink. "How are you doing on—"

"Hey, guys and dolls, we're gonna get this party started." A booming voice spoke into the microphone, causing Jack and Caroline to swivel toward the stage.

"That's Bill Conroy, the town mayor," Jack said.

"He has a great voice."

"Has an auctioneering gig on the side."

"Oh, fun. My grandpa did that, too."

Jack shot her a look of disbelief. "Really?"

"Yes. See, I'm not totally ignorant of small-town life."

"I knew you were a woman of—"

"First, I've got a few people to thank for all their hard work to make this swinging time happen," Bill continued. "Band's gonna start playing here in a short minute. You can start your dancing or hustle on over and fill your plates."

Jack leaned in. "What's your pleasure? Feel like twirling?"

She flashed him a grin. "I think I do. I doubt they'll run out of food anytime soon."

As soon as the band struck its first notes, Jack took her arm. "There's our cue."

Along with several other couples, they made their way to the open blacktop. The men were dressed in typical jeans, boots, and western cut shirts, but the women were decked out in fancy blouses, a few dresses, and jewelry. The dance was obviously a big deal—a rare opportunity to put on their glitz.

Caroline said a silent prayer that she wouldn't embarrass herself by tripping over her feet—or Jack's. Despite her earlier assurance to Jack, she'd never danced in cowboy boots before.

Jack swung her onto the pavement. She let out a

little squeal as he quickly spun her around then pulled her back again. Roger and Nora moved in beside them, and before Caroline knew it, they were a foursome. A moment later, Jack handed her off to Roger who twirled her under his arm while Jack whirled Nora and in one smooth motion sent her to Roger at the same time he released Caroline.

She nearly doubled over laughing. "Oh, my gosh! The band is great," she hollered. "This is perfect dance music."

He squeezed her hand. "You're a good dancer."

"Thanks. What a great event. It's fun to see so many people enjoying each other and having a good time." The smiles and laughter were energizing, uplifting.

Thirty minutes later, they were still on the dance floor, and she was nearly breathless.

When the music slowed, Jack placed one hand on her waist and pulled her close. As they swayed together in time with the music, Caroline realized the sky had turned a dusky blue and gold and the lights shimmered in the trees. It was romantic. With Jack's cheek brushing against her hair, the motion was mesmerizing. There would be no doubt in anyone's mind tonight that she and Jack were a couple.

As the music ended quietly, she pulled back and was caught in the force field of his glacier-blue eyes. She blew out a soft breath. "You getting hungry?" As soon as the words left her lips, she groaned inside. His eyes had answered that question, and food wasn't the subject.

"I am." Warm amusement laced his words.

She dropped her hand from his arm. "Me, too.

Let's get in line." As she filled her plate, she couldn't help a quick look at their potato salad. The bowl sat almost as equally empty as those around it. She breathed a sigh of relief and helped herself to a generous portion.

"You having fun?" Roger asked when she arrived back at the table with a heaping plate.

She settled into the chair Jack pulled out for her. "This is a blast," she told Roger. "I'm so glad I didn't miss it."

He bobbed his head and shot a glance toward Jack. "Nice to knock off work and let loose every once in a while."

"Yeah, yeah, whatever. Take it up with Human Resources," Jack responded. He looked at Caroline. "How's the food?"

"This brisket is delicious. Too bad I'll be too full for seconds."

"And there are about a million desserts over there," Nora piped up. "You can't miss those. In fact, we can probably rummage around and find some foil or a bag and make a little sampler to-go."

Caroline laughed as she pictured Nora doing just that. "Now that's not a bad idea."

"Hey, do you need another drink?" Nora asked.

Caroline jiggled her seltzer, which was nearly empty. "I do. And maybe we could—"

"I'll get it." Jack stood. "Same thing or a glass of wine?"

"White wine would be great." To Nora, she lowered her voice. "And perhaps the ladies' room?"

Nora stood and lifted Jack's arm from Caroline's shoulders. "You guys stay here and talk about bulls or baseball or something. We've got girl stuff to tend to."

With that, Nora whisked her away from the table. "Also, I want you to meet Doug Peterson. He's the science teacher at the high school and leader of our 4-H group. I told him all about you and how you got your friend out here lickety-split to take care of that poisonous weed."

"Oh, fun." She tucked that bit of information in the back of her mind. Sounded as if there could perhaps be additional opportunities for getting involved on a local basis.

When the man turned, she smiled and extended her hand. He was younger than she expected, possibly doing a rural gig to get some experience before moving on.

"Pleased to meet you," he told Caroline. But his words carried a blasé tone and weren't accompanied with a smile. "You just moving to the area? Gotta say, science jobs are kind of hard to come by around here."

"Well, I may look for some volunteer opportunities, but I'm getting ready to retire from teaching college. Not looking for a full-time job for sure."

He looked at her for a moment and nodded. "Good. Nice to see you, Nora. Enjoy the dance."

Caroline had the distinct feeling the high-school teacher had dismissed her. She almost laughed. *Whatever.*

Nora took her arm again. "So, there are the portables down the next street, but I know a better option. Stella's Diner keeps the doors open for this.

When they arrived at the diner, Nora gave her a little nudge. "You go on ahead. I'll wait out here."

Inside, Caroline stepped into the ladies' room. Both stalls were occupied. She turned to wait outside but stopped when she heard a voice ring out.

"And what the heck is Jack Armstrong thinking? All this time he's played the reclusive widower, then he shows up strutting around with some outsider. And have you seen the floozy? Trying a little too hard. That off-the-shoulder blouse and fancy boots?" The woman gave a little laugh. "Hope it's worth the blisters she'll have tomorrow."

"It's a shame," a voice from the other stall agreed. "But Nora really likes her."

"She probably feels like she has to make an effort for Roger's sake," the first woman responded. "We've got plenty of great single gals right here in the community. Such a waste."

"And what's with the pearls? For a street dance?" The woman laughed. "Does she think she's the queen or what?"

"Can't you imagine poor Rosalyn rolling in her grave? She was such a class act."

Caroline's face flushed hot, and she hurried out of the room. *Now what?* She couldn't go back outside. She'd have to wait until the women came out, then pretend she was just coming in and hadn't heard a thing. And ignore the burning in her ears. She hated this kind of petty drama. And here she'd told Jack how friendly everyone had been. And *she* had been friendly to everyone she'd met.

She blew out a breath. Did these people even matter? Did Jack's true friends feel the same way? Couldn't she be in a relationship without all this nonsense? She flicked the hair from her shoulder. She was having a great time and wasn't about to let those women ruin her evening. They could just get over it.

****

Caroline regrouped with Nora and pasted on a smile. "Hey, want to hit the dessert line?" Was there anything a little chocolate couldn't fix?

"You're talking my language," Nora told her.

The selection of desserts was nothing short of overwhelming. "Wow." Caroline shook her head and reached for a plate. "I want one of each."

"Go for it," Nora said with a laugh.

With a plate full of cookies and cakes to share with Jack, Caroline made her way back to their table, hoping the promised glass of wine was waiting for her. As she approached, she saw that several men had pulled up chairs and were in conversation with Jack and Roger. As soon as she placed the plate on the table, Jack stood and pulled out her chair.

"Thanks." She settled in and pushed the plate between them then cut a lemon bar in half. "Help yourself. I got enough for both of us."

He slid an arm across the back of her chair, his hand resting lightly against her shoulder.

A conversation was already in progress. Caroline listened in but gave most of her attention to her wine and dessert since the band was on break.

"Simmons said he had some dirt weasel contact him last week," one of the men said.

"What's that mean?" Roger asked. "A call or did someone actually come out?"

The man leaned forward and waved his hand for emphasis. "Showed up in his fancy three-piece suit. Came sniffing around right up to the house."

When Jack's head jerked up and he stared at the man she hadn't met, Caroline paused her hands.

"Man, those bloodsuckers are relentless," Jack said. His voice turned hard. "I'm not buying more land." He shook his head. "Someone else can ante-up this time. I'm tapped out."

Caroline frowned. "What in the world are you talking about? Dirt weasels? Bloodsuckers?"

He waved a hand as if shooing away something bothersome. "Dirt weasel's a term we use for the developers who come out here and try to get their hooks into the ranch land. Turn it into a resort and golf course. Bring city slickers out to play cowboy for a weekend. They feed on guys a little behind on payments or over-mortgaged."

"That's the nice term," the other man added with a grin.

Caroline nearly choked on her wine. They assumed all developers were bad guys? Anyone from the city was a nuisance? She wanted to slap the stupid grin right off the guy's face. Instead, she forced a humorless laugh. "Easy there. You're looking at a city slicker."

Jack leaned in. "Present company excluded."

"Oh, thanks." She couldn't help a little sarcasm creeping in.

"They come out here with their suits and ties and fancy college degrees and think they can con people into their projects," another joined in.

"Won't take no for an answer," Jack added. He gestured toward the man. "What are they looking for this time?"

"Not sure of the details. Somebody musta made some money on that project over there outside Abilene or they wouldn't be back."

"Yeah, somebody did, but it sure wasn't Hawkins. They ran the operation into the ground and ran him out. Now the city owns the whole shebang. Public golf course and trails. So instead of producing anything, it's sucking up tax dollars."

"We've fought 'em off before. We can do it again," another man sitting beside Roger said. "Is it that same guy who's been out here before? What was his name?"

"Mr. Suave, dark hair, white teeth…always looked like he just come from vacation."

"Right. Who was that weasel?"

"Henderson? Was it that guy again?"

"He was slicker than a boiled onion."

"Nah, that one died in a plane crash," Roger said.

The air whooshed from Caroline's lungs.

"No kidding? One of you guys tamper with that plane?"

"It was an act of God," the balding man said with a laugh.

Another one let out a snort. "See? God's on our side."

Their words pounded in Caroline's ears.

"Hendricks was his name," Jack said.

"Doesn't matter. There's always another one ready to take over. Can't take a hint."

Caroline gasped, and her entire body went cold. *Hendricks.* They were talking about Andrew? *Laughing* about Andrew. *About his death.* Bile rose in her throat. She stared at Jack, shaking her head.

His eyes narrowed. "Something wrong?"

Caroline looked around the table, and her throat tightened. No words formed to answer his question. She willed herself not to cry. So cavalier about someone's death. A simmer sprang to life inside her. *Dirt weasels.* These small-minded rulers of the land brushed with a broad stroke their disdain and dislike of people they didn't even know.

She dropped the lemon bar onto her plate and stood. "I can't listen to this."

Every eye around the table stared at her. Frowning, Jack sprang from his chair and reached out to her. "Caroline?"

The words of the women in the diner rang in her ears. *An outsider.* "I don't belong here." She pushed back her chair and stepped away from the table, moving around the people milling about.

A moment later, Jack stepped in front of her. He placed a hand on her arm. "Caroline? What's wrong?"

Concern laced his words, but his laughter rang in her ears. She heard his participation in the sickening conversation around the table. She sucked in a deep breath, clenched her hands, and looked straight past him. "Andrew Hendricks. That *dirt weasel* you're joking about? He was my husband."

Chapter Twenty-Two

Jack stared at Caroline, unable to comprehend what he thought he'd heard. *"What?"*

She faced him, but her eyes were distant. Why wouldn't she meet his eyes? Though people jostled around them, he stood still, staring, waiting.

Finally, she glanced at him. "He was my *husband*." Her voice was raw, barely more than a whisper. Tears glistened in her eyes.

Could it really be true? What reason would she have to lie? How could— "That's why you're here? That's how you knew about my ranch? Did you take over his business? Is that what this is all about? I don't—" With the weight of a freight train, a thought slammed into his brain sending shockwaves through his system. "Holy hell, are you casing my ranch?"

She faced him with a hard glare. "Are you kidding me? Paranoid much? Get real, Jack. Here's a news flash for you. Not everyone is out to get your land."

He nudged her away from the tables and spoke in a low, hard voice. "But *he* was. He kept close tabs on all the ranchers out here, just waiting for an opportunity to swoop in and launch an attack."

"Oh, please. How would you even know that?"

"We look out for each other around here." He fought to keep his voice from rising. "We know when someone's being hassled, pressured. Hell, some prime grazing land not far from here barely produces anything. It's all for show—more like a playground now. And he did his part."

Caroline gasped. "How dare you? Not everyone considers these fields to be holy lands. Ranching is a business, too, right? You and your cowboy partners hole up here in your little backwoods cocoon and pass judgment on people you don't even know and businesses you know nothing about—"

"Oh, I know about this business. And your husband's business. Make no mistake—"

"You arrogant, overbearing cow*baby*. My husband. Was. A. Good. Man." She ground out the words. "He didn't hurt people. He didn't take advantage of people. He didn't steal their land. In fact, he gave people new hope, a fresh start. When they were about to lose their land, he gave them a way out."

Jack laughed. "Stop. Don't insult my intelligence. Don't try to tell me his projects were altruistic."

"No. But he was honest and fair." She took a step back. "He was not a vulture. And he was not a *dirt weasel*."

****

Caroline flinched when someone touched her arm. She turned to find Nora at her side, her other hand resting on Jack's arm.

Nora leaned in. "Hey, friends, folks sure are getting their money's worth tonight," she said in a hushed tone. "Dinner, dance and a free floor show."

Caroline hugged herself around the middle and scowled at Jack. His face was hard, his lips a thin line. He clearly wasn't giving her the benefit of a doubt. As if she had anything to do with Andrew's former business or knew which properties he'd ever looked at. She knew some business associates and about some of the big deals, but certainly not the day-to-day operations.

Jack stood shaking his head. "I don't know what you're playing at, but you're here under false pretenses. Don't even think about using my ranch in that book of yours. If you're even writing one."

Before Caroline could respond, Nora broke in. "Might I suggest moving this conversation to the parking lot or waiting until it's time to go," Nora said.

Caroline turned to face her. "You know what? It *is* time to go. And I need a ride back to the cabin."

Nora's mouth dropped open, and she glanced between Caroline and Jack. "Okaaaay. I guess—"

"I will drive you," Jack cut in.

"Absolutely not. You just go on back to your buddies." Her voice shook with the anger coursing through her. "Go hang out with your little insider clique of cowboys. You seem to be comfortable there."

He swore under his breath. "You're gonna run off? Can't handle an honest conversation?"

"Oh, is that what this is? Funny that's not how it feels." She grabbed hold of Nora. "Please. I need to leave *now*."

Nora hesitated, and when Caroline glanced back, she saw Nora put a hand to stop Jack from following. "I've got this," she told him.

As quickly as Caroline could move through the people without knocking someone over, she hurried away from the tables with Nora trailing behind her.

At the edge of the roped area, she turned. "Where's your car?" She hadn't considered that they may have parked on a different street.

Nora jerked a thumb. "Next block, but we can go down the alley and skip the crowd. And it's the truck. We had a lot of stuff to haul over."

"That's fine." She'd ride a scooter if that's what it took to get out of there. As soon as she climbed into the truck, she remembered the scarf she'd left in Jack's car. *Oh, shoot.* Her brand-new scarf from Lauren. Maybe Jack would have the decency to give it to Nora and she could mail it.

"I just need to get away from here. Time to go home."

Nora pulled the truck onto the main road. "Now listen here, you're not thinking of leaving the ranch tonight, are you? I know you're upset, but I also know you've had a couple of drinks. And it's getting late. That's not a good combination for driving."

Caroline bit her lip. Nora was right, but, oh, how could she stay another night there, unwelcome and under attack? "Does Jack have a key to the cabin?"

Nora let out an audible sigh. "He does. But you don't have to worry. There's no way he'd use it to get in tonight. He would never do that."

But Caroline wondered. *His land, his rules.*

"Hey, you want to tell me what this is all about? What happened back there? One minute you two are wrapped in each other's arms like there's no one else in the world, and the next your eyes are shooting daggers at each other. And now I'm the one driving you home."

Caroline looked out the window at the darkness that enveloped them. It would be better to leave in the dark—that way she wouldn't have to see the green and gold fields she'd come to love or the clear blue skies.

Or Jack's house and the barn. *The barn*. Tears pricked her eyes. She'd miss the horses.

She swallowed hard. "Maybe I could crash at your place tonight."

"Really? It's that bad? I mean, of course—"

"Oh, never mind. I can't put you in a position like that. I know you and Roger are loyal to Jack."

"Whoa, there. Jack is a good friend, but that doesn't make him a saint. He can be as stupid and stubborn as any other rancher in a ten-gallon hat. But if it's the only way to keep you from driving tonight, I'll tie you to my sofa."

Caroline sputtered a laugh. "That won't be necessary."

"Come on. What gives? I've got a good ear."

She sucked in a deep breath and gave Nora the condensed version of the story. "So now he thinks I'm here for some clandestine purpose. Spying on him. Out to get his property."

"But you didn't know your husband had ever been out here."

"No clue. I knew Andrew visited Texas sometimes and had some projects. But Texas is a big state, right? It's ridiculous. Believe me, I didn't have time to keep close tabs on his work. I had my own career." As tears threatened, she turned away. "They laughed. Jack, Roger, all of them. They laughed about Andrew's death."

Nora reached over and squeezed Caroline's hand. "I'm sorry. I'm so sorry, honey."

They lapsed into silence until Nora turned the truck into the Armstrong ranch. A few moments later, the car's tires crunched on the gravel driveway in front of the cabin. A familiar sound Caroline would miss. She picked up her purse and opened the car door.

"Thank you, Nora. For everything. I've truly enjoyed my time here. I'm sorry to leave on this note, but it's time for me to move on. You take care."

Nora caught her hand. "You take care, too. Listen, Caroline. Remember the good times, okay? I know there was a spark. You...you looked so happy yesterday. And this evening. Maybe give Jack some time. Let things calm down? Things might look different in the morning."

Caroline shot her a wan smile. "Goodnight, Nora. Go back and enjoy the rest of the evening."

The only thing that would look different in the morning is that all this would be in the rearview mirror.

She stepped inside and bolted the door behind her. Anger still coursing through her, she marched into the kitchen. At least the packing would be easy since she'd only been back one night and hadn't fully unpacked or gone to the market. She picked up the few items that were hers but left her Vandy travel mug for the morning. "Darn straight," she muttered to herself. "I don't have to take this kind of nonsense." She rolled her eyes, thinking of the frosty attitude from the science teacher she met. "Sure, buddy, as if I'm out to get your job. Ha!"

Time to get back to where she belonged, where people valued her. True, she had a crummy boss at the moment who didn't exactly sing her praises, but she'd already made her mark in the world. She had a legacy, a reputation. And she didn't need to prove anything to the people around here.

Next, she marched to the bedroom to retrieve her

big suitcase. But she hesitated at the closed door as memories of last night assaulted her. What a sad, crazy turn of events. Pressing her lips together, she slowly opened the door. The rumpled bedcovers greeted her when her glance strayed to the bed. Her breath caught. No way could she sleep there.

She turned to the closet and began tossing clothes into the suitcase. There were more than she remembered leaving when she left the first time. Unfortunately, the extra pair of boots were impossible to cram in. She'd have to wear them—spend all day in a constant reminder of the street dance. *Erg.* She looked forward to putting the whole thing behind her. When the closet was empty, she retrieved the extra blanket and pillow then switched out the light. She pulled the door shut with a hard snap and tossed the bedding onto the sofa. It wouldn't be comfortable, but she didn't plan to be there long. At first light, she'd be kicking up some dust outta there.

****

Jack stood at the kitchen window clenching his coffee mug. He couldn't explain why. Insanity was the only explanation that came to mind. The first glow of morning shone pink against the horizon. And he waited for the scene he knew was coming.

He wanted to see it. Wanted to see her go—to close the brief, absurd door he'd mistakenly opened. He'd let someone in. Let himself feel again. And now he felt every gut punch. And he deserved to. *What a fool.*

He added more sugar to his coffee and took a gulp. But it couldn't wash away the bitterness that enveloped him.

A thin plume of dust appeared first, and his throat

tightened. A moment later, the silver rental car bounced into view in the ghostly light. And the woman who preferred sunsets to sunrises would be out the gate before the sun rose. Well, fine. Then he could get on with his day. Nora could clean the cabin and wipe the electronic entry system clear of Caroline's code.

He watched until the taillights went out of sight. Then he sagged against the counter and blew out a long breath. *Door closed.* When he straightened, he squared his shoulders, refilled his mug, and headed for his computer. Last night he'd been too keyed up, too angry, to sit down and do research. *Last night.* He shook his head as images from the dance flashed in his brain. Last night, she'd embarrassed him in front of the whole town.

By now, he suspected everyone knew he'd been duped. She'd been married to one of their chief antagonists. That was going to rankle a while.

He'd tried to play off Caroline's departure as a health issue. As if she weren't feeling well. But he'd felt every stare and knew it was a flimsy line. Knew few bought it. The story of her leaving would have spread like burning fields—without the controls. He'd forced himself to stay until Nora returned so he could play the part of concerned partner. But he didn't have the best acting skills. And he could hardly choke down a swallow of beer. What a debacle.

At his desk, he logged into the computer and searched Andrew Hendricks. What had become of his business? Had it carried on without him? Had his ownership or shares been turned over to his wife? Jack could not believe that Caroline had innocently stumbled across his ranch. The odds were too far-fetched. She'd likely come out to try and scope the territory for the proposed wildlife refuge.

Peeling back the layers, he discovered the company was still in business, still eating up property with hotels and golf courses. Probably still harassing landowners. He read the history of the company and viewed dozens of photos of their developments. But found few references to Hendricks. And no one by the name of Hendricks or Tate currently held a position in management. Didn't mean she wasn't scouting for them as a consultant. It'd be impossible to track down all their vendors and associates. Had she ever gone by Hendricks?

He returned to the search results and kept reading. Apparently, the man was a big hit with City Hall. Numerous awards for redevelopment projects involving blighted areas. Jack blew out a long breath and ran a hand across his jaw. According to a couple of articles, Hendricks and his company had championed green space in their urban projects and contributed financially to community centers and libraries.

Looked like his projects were welcome to some people. Caroline's words rang in Jack's ears. *My husband was a good man.*

Jack was about to type another search field when he glanced at his hands. His stomach clenched. In the short time since he'd removed his wedding band, the white line that had been there for years had faded. He stared at the tanned skin, then squeezed his eyes closed as pain shot through him. *He'd taken off his ring for her.*

When he opened his eyes again, his gaze strayed to the drawer in which he'd tucked away the ring. He could put it back on. But he couldn't turn back the clock. The truth hurt, but he was not a married man. His throat clogged, and several moments ticked by before he could face his computer again. With a heavy heart, he pushed back and was about to go for more coffee, but the peal of his phone stopped him.

Ah. Here was a much-needed distraction. He squared his shoulders and picked up. "Hey, kid."

"Hi, Grandpa."

"What are you up to?"

"Eating breakfast. I have a soccer game today."

A pang of guilt rushed through Jack. He'd never seen Dylan play ball of any sort. "Sorry I won't be able to see that." Now that he thought about it, he realized with a jolt they'd stopped asking. Reed had stopped sending schedules. For some reason, that fact settled hard in Jack's stomach.

"Me and Dad can come to the ranch on Friday."

"Is that right? How's Kristen doing?"

"Good. But Dad says we better come this weekend 'cause it might be the last time before the baby comes. Can we come?"

"Sure, you can. I'll look forward to that."

"But we have to leave Sunday morning in time for my afternoon game."

"That'll work."

"Is Miz Caroline still there?"

Jack ran a hand across his jaw. She'd certainly made an impression on Dylan in a short amount of time. Her knowledge and enthusiasm had been obvious—and contagious. "No, kiddo. Sorry, she had to go home. But we can still go riding and explore the creek if you want." Dylan didn't need to know the particulars, but Jack didn't look forward to Reed's questions, which he knew would come after Dylan went to bed.

"Okay."

Dylan agreed, but Jack heard the disappointment in his grandson's voice. And he knew he'd be a poor substitute for Caroline in the science fun-and-games department.

Jack spoke with Dylan a few more minutes while memories of their day at the creek with Caroline ran through his mind. Caroline had been so good with the kid. It'd seemed natural to have her there. After he said goodbye to Dylan, Jack pressed his folded hands against his lips, and let out a deep, weary sigh. From now on, he'd measure time a new way—before Caroline and after. He stood and shoved the chair into place with a little more force than necessary. Might as well get *after* started.

Chapter Twenty-Three

Standing at the curb outside the Nashville airport, Caroline waved down her daughter then nearly stumbled as she hitched her carry-on bag onto her shoulder. The early hour and restless night were taking their toll. Not to mention the hours of waiting around for a flight at the Dallas-Fort Worth airport.

She couldn't wait to get home and get into comfy clothes and slippers. And sleep. She desperately wanted to sink into a long, deep sleep. All day she'd stewed about the events of the last two days—the extreme highs and lows. From the feel of Jack's arms around her to the sound of his laughter and the ugly words. It was exhausting, and a heaviness had settled in her heart and every muscle in her body.

"Hey, sweetheart." She forced an upbeat tone and called to Lauren.

"Hi, Mom!"

She moved in, and Caroline hugged her close. "Thanks for fetching me."

"Sure. I wasn't expecting you back so soon."

Caroline shoved her bags into the car, ignoring the question in Lauren's comment, and climbed inside. She sensed her daughter's eyes on her. "Hope I didn't interrupt your day."

"Nope. I had nothing going on. Have you eaten anything?"

"Oh, you know how travel days are. I've had an odd assortment of snacks."

"Okay, let's stop somewhere."

"I think I'm just ready to be home." And not ready for a deep heart-to-heart conversation with her daughter about a certain cowboy.

"But, Mom, there's no food at the house."

"Ah. You're right. Yes, let's stop." Getting out again and making a trip to the grocery store sounded like way too much trouble.

"How about the Clock Tower Cafe?"

Caroline perked up. The cafe was one of their favorite places. She couldn't resist that. "Sure." In fact, she'd get an order to go and have it tomorrow.

"Let's split one of their lemon bars," Lauren said as she pulled the car into the parking lot.

Ugh, no. Caroline climbed out of the car. She might never eat another lemon bar as long as she lived. "You know what sounds better? Their key lime cheesecake."

"Mmm, yes. That's amazing, too."

"I've made a decision," Caroline said after they ordered, hoping to take charge of the conversation. "These past few weeks I've discovered there's a lot of exploring out there for me to do. And new opportunities. So, that tells me I'm ready to leave the university, but not retire from working."

The university didn't feel like a good fit anymore. Why not branch out and try something new? All across the country there were 4-H programs and science camps and zoos and nature preserves. She didn't need middle-of-nowhere Texas.

"Oh, my gosh. That's huge, Mom. Would this have

301

anything to do with events in Texas?" She leaned closer with a conspiratorial smile. "Come on, tell me about the dance. I see you're still wearing your fancy boots. So they're pretty comfortable? Good for dancing?" Her voice pitched up with expectation.

"The boots were great. They looked good with my outfit, which—"

The server delivered their food, giving Caroline a moment to pause. She couldn't help but salivate at the beautiful chicken salad before her. She picked up her fork and smiled at Lauren. "The dance had its ups and downs. It was quite an affair for the locals."

"Yeah? What made you leave so soon?"

"Well, if I'm going to announce my retirement from Vandy, I need to make a lot of progress on this book project first."

Lauren cocked her head, a puzzled frown on her face. "But I…are you…what about the cowboy? Jack. I thought things were heating up there."

Caroline reached for her water glass, but her throat clogged, and she set the glass down without taking a drink. "That isn't going to work out."

"But, Mom, you seemed happy. I could hear it in your voice. Are you going back?"

"Not likely."

Lauren stared at her a long moment. "That's too bad," she said softly.

Caroline frowned. "Anyway, Texas is so far away. It's not as if I'd ever intended to stay there."

"But you could. I mean, if you're not at the university, you don't have to hang around here."

Caroline shrugged. "Here is home."

Lauren let out a long sigh and flopped back against

the booth.

"Honey, what's wrong? Why does this matter?"

Lauren looked away before she met Caroline's eyes. "The company wants me to move to Dallas."

"Oh my," Caroline put a hand to her chest. "They've officially asked?"

She nodded. "They'll bring me over as director. That means a big raise and a couple of people under me. Plus, I'd report to Maggie, the VP. And she's great."

"Honey, that's fantastic." Now she understood her daughter's concern.

"Yeah, but like you said, it's so far away. I don't want to leave you—"

Caroline held up a hand. "Stop. You do not have to worry about me. You need to do what's right for your career. This sounds like a wonderful opportunity." She meant what she said. But inside, she had to admit it was a big zinger—another momentous change. Everything familiar was suddenly morphing around her.

Lauren toyed with her silverware. "I…I guess I was hoping you'd want to move to Texas. We could both move and still be close. Have some new adventures. There's a lot to do. It could be fun."

"Dessert, ladies?" the server interrupted.

"Oh, yes." Caroline waved a hand. "We're celebrating. Let's go crazy and get two desserts. Something chocolate, too?"

Lauren cracked a smile. "Sure, Mom."

"Okay, we'll have one of those walnut fudge brownies and a slice of key lime cheesecake."

"Be right back," the woman said.

"Mom, did you like Texas? I mean, I know the

traffic's bad around Dallas. But you like warm weather. You could live in a suburb or farther west and stay out of the traffic mess."

Could she move to Dallas for her daughter? At least she wouldn't have to worry about accidentally running into Jack Armstrong. Since he never left the ranch, there was absolutely zero chance of that happening. Her face warmed as she remembered her silly daydreams about working near Stockton, about staying at Jack's house. She reached for her water and chugged several gulps. And she honestly thought it would happen. She knew the man was deeply connected to his land, but the paranoia, the animosity toward others shocked her. Had she not listened carefully enough?

"Mom, you seem sad. Did something happen?"

"I'm just tired, sweetie." Maybe not the whole truth, but not a lie.

The desserts arrived along with the check and carryout order. Caroline appreciated the cafe's efficiency. "These look amazing." She cut both desserts then sank her fork into the cheesecake and let out a soft groan.

"Way to make good choices, Mom."

Caroline sputtered a laugh at her daughter repeating the Mom-words she'd so often heard from Caroline. "Why, thank you. I think I deserve a gold star."

"You got it. Hey, if I move to Dallas, maybe you can help me find a place, and your cowboy friend can visit. I'd like to meet him. I mean, if you were closer, maybe things would work out."

My cowboy. Caroline stopped chewing and put

down her fork. The words tugged at her heart, but she willed herself not to show any emotion.

"I know there's more to the story, Mom. Remember Mother's Day dinner? You were practically giddy telling me about going back for that dance. Did Jack turn out to be a jerk or what?"

Caroline met Lauren's eyes and let out a long sigh. Might have to give her the condensed version to stop the interrogation. "Yes, I thought there might be some potential with Jack. But it turns out the people there are really close-minded. They, Jack included, have a huge issue with developers wanting to use the land for anything other than a ranch."

Lauren's brow furrowed. "I don't get what that has to do with you and Jack."

"He knew who your dad was and some of the people out there had dealings with him." She took a gulp of water. "And they weren't positive."

"Seriously? They knew Dad?"

"A city slicker out to steal their land." That's all she would repeat.

"What?" Lauren's mouth dropped open. "They said that?"

"Pretty much. So. Regardless of where I decide to live, that relationship is over."

****

Jack wiped an arm across his brow then yanked a few more weeds and tossed them into the bucket. He checked his watch again. Only fifteen minutes had passed since he last looked. He glanced at the rows of plants around him. There were not enough weeds to keep this up. He'd have to find a project. Staying busy and keeping his mind focused on a task was the only way he knew to avoid drowning in a mire of unwelcome thoughts. To keep last night in the past.

But that was impossible. Every encounter he'd had with Caroline in the last month replayed over and over in his mind. And based on the new revelation, he found himself questioning everything she'd said. Heck, he wasn't even sure about her book project. Was that just a front? Bottom line, he felt used. She'd exploited the ranch for her personal gain.

The questions gnawed at him as he moved down the row, pulling weeds and picking vegetables. He jumped when his phone pealed from his back pocket. He wasn't expecting a call, but he couldn't not look. Holding his breath, he pulled out the phone. Hmm, local number. He picked up. "Jack Armstrong."

"Jack," a high-pitched female voice crooned. "Hi, it's Darla. So glad I caught you. Listen, I'm out running around, and I've got the bowl you left last night. Thought I'd just drop it by your place."

Jack rolled his eyes and considered telling her to drop the bowl into the nearest trash can. The fewer reminders he had of last night, the better. When would he learn not to answer every call? He pinched the bridge of his nose. "Very kind of you, Darla. Thanks. You can just leave it at the gate, and I'll grab it next time I go out."

She gave a light laugh. "Why, Jack Armstrong, what kind of lady do you take me for? I would never return a bowl empty. I've got some homemade beef stroganoff with your name on it. And I won't be leaving it at the gate for the varmints to get into."

Jack looked at his watch again and groaned inside. Almost five. Was she hoping for a dinner invitation?

Was it arrogant to think so? Could he stand her idle chatter in the interest of not being rude? It might at least eat up some time. He cleared his throat. "I appreciate that. What time do you think you'll be over my direction?"

"Want to say five-thirty? That's about thirty minutes."

"I'll meet you at the gate. Thanks, again."

He raked a hand through his hair. What had he gotten himself into?

Thirty minutes later, as promised, he strode to the ranch entrance. A car already sat on the other side of the gate. He gave a wave and opened the gate then stood back as the car pulled through.

Just inside, Darla put the car in park, opened her door, and hopped out. "Hey, Jack."

"Darla." Though she wasn't wearing dress clothes, it was obvious she hadn't been out working in the garden. She opened the back car door and retrieved a bag.

When she turned, she flashed a wide smile. "Here you go. Now you can just heat this up in the microwave. Easy-peasy."

He took the bag. "That's great. Thank you."

"And there's enough for two meals."

She didn't say two people, but the expectant expression on her face conveyed the thought. Jack wasn't so dense he didn't get the hint.

"Very generous of you." He willed himself not to choke as he extended the invitation. "Listen, um, if there's enough for two, you might as well join me. If you don't have other plans." It wasn't the most eloquent or heartfelt invitation, but it was all he could manage under the circumstances.

"Why, Jack, thank you. How lovely. I'd be delighted."

"I can probably rustle up some vegetables to make a salad."

"Great. Looks like you walked. Hop in, and I'll drive you to the house."

When the car door closed, it sounded like a trap to his ears. Felt like one, too.

"Around back, right?" she asked.

"Yep. That's fine."

Inside, Jack moved to the kitchen. "What can I get you to drink? Wine? Soda? Iced tea?"

She followed him to the counter. "Iced tea would be great if you already have it made."

"Sure do." He gestured toward the table. "You go ahead and have a seat and make yourself comfortable."

"Oh, goodness, no. Let me help with that."

In the awkward silence, he poured her drink then busied himself with the vegetables. After the longest ten minutes of his life, she removed the dish from the microwave.

"That should do it. Ready?"

"You bet." *Ready to get this ordeal over with.* Jack slid a plate of sliced cucumbers and tomatoes onto the table.

"Your house is so lovely, Jack."

"Thank you," he said around bites. "This is delicious."

"After LeRoy died, I couldn't keep up the house. Moved into one of the smaller places on the property. It's cozy and manageable."

The minutes ticked slowly by, and Jack forced

himself to feign interest and stay engaged in some conversation. He threw in a few mm-hmms and nods at what he hoped were appropriate intervals. Offered an occasional smile. She was a good cook. When he let his gaze rest on her face a moment, he acknowledged that she was an attractive woman. Her clothes and tanned face were all Texas. She belonged here. But he had no desire to touch her. No interest in her life. And he would not be doing this a second time. Manners be damned.

He frowned when she waved a hand in front of him. "Hello? Jack, I just told you my daughter's having surgery this week."

He sat straighter. "Oh, I…uh…"

"And you said, 'that's nice.' "

Her tone wasn't whiny or angry, but Jack heard the admonition and felt like a schoolboy who'd been sent to the principal's office. He sat back in his chair and shook his head. "I'm sorry, Darla. Guess I'm distracted. Hadn't planned on having a dinner guest tonight."

She quietly studied him. "You're pretty sweet on that Caroline gal, aren't you?"

The soft words delivered a hefty punch. And naked truth. There was no getting around it. He'd fallen in love with Caroline Tate, and regardless of the circumstances that brought her to him or made her leave, he couldn't just get over it.

He clenched the fork in his hand and blew out a harsh breath. "I suppose I am. Or *was*."

She nodded. "It's not always a smooth road, you know. Sometimes you have to give a little. Sometimes you have to fight a little."

She pushed back her chair and lifted her plate then

reached for his.

Jack stood. "Please, I'll clean up."

She set the dishes on the counter. As she passed him, she patted his arm. "Thanks for keeping me company for dinner. Don't let happiness slip through your fingers, Jack. Now, how do I get myself out?"

Guilt mixed with gratitude inside him, and Jack gave her a genuine smile. "Thank *you*, Darla," he said. "Just push the green button, and the gate will open."

He followed her to the door and gave a final wave as she climbed into her car. Instead of going back inside, he leaned against the porch railing. With a heavy sigh, he shoved his hands in his pockets and looked west. A line of high clouds made a dramatic formation across the sky. Sunset was probably an hour away, but already the sky glowed with a golden hue.

He watched the sky. He could read any number of things into the coming spectacle. It could be a sign that the sun still rises and falls, and he should go about his business. Or it could be a reminder of Caroline sent from above. Either way, it was going to be a beautiful sunset. And he'd be watching it alone.

Accept that...or fight it?

Chapter Twenty-Four

Monday morning. A new day. A new week. A fresh start. And, boy, did she need it. As Caroline sipped a strong cup of tea on her patio, she made a mental list of tasks to accomplish. Of course, the book was her top priority, and she'd need to get to her next location soon—as soon as she found the energy to get up and go again.

Back in her own bed, she'd expected to fall into a fast, deep sleep. But that turned out to be impossible. If she pieced together the snatches of sleep, would it even equal five hours? She had her doubts. The tangle of emotions from her hasty departure from the ranch both wore her out and kept her up. Anger, sadness, and frustration mixed into a kind of hollow restlessness. She took another sip of tea, closed her eyes, and forced her shoulders to relax.

She had other things to think about. Based on her conversation with Lauren at dinner last night, Caroline needed to add more items to her to-do list—including contacting both her financial advisor and a friend in real estate.

Caroline had a vague idea of the market value of her home based on the tax bill she received every year, but she'd need expert advice on what kind of work would have to be done to bring top dollar. Even though she wasn't set on moving, she'd promised her daughter to at least explore the idea.

Besides, a few meetings would get her out of the house, and keeping busy would limit her time to dwell on events of the past few days. She sent a quick text to Nora about the scarf—friendly, but specific, with no other chit-chat. As much as she'd looked forward to being friends with Nora, it couldn't last now, and there was no point in prolonging a relationship. She couldn't help a rueful smile. They could've had some good times.

She'd also miss out on connecting with Kristen, watching where Dylan's love of wildlife took him, and...oh, the baby. Caroline pressed her lips together and blinked hard. She wouldn't hold that baby, and she wouldn't see Jack hold it either. In her mind, she'd already captured adorable, emotional photos of the two.

With a heavy sigh, Caroline went inside and refilled her mug, then settled at the table with her laptop. *Focus on your work.* Determined to crank out a couple of short essays, she opened a new blank document then clicked on her photo folders. Each essay needed to connect with three or four photos. Butterflies would be a good topic for today. Something happy and cheery. She'd seen so many varieties on the ranch. The yellow one, Cloudless Sulphur, so pretty against the brilliant blue sky with, ironically, white puffy clouds... *Oh.* Her throat tightened as she remembered how Jack had come upon her taking the photo of the butterfly and the sky. How—

She burst out laughing. Apparently, she'd made quite a scene lying in the road, had him running to her aid when she'd only been— Her breath caught, and without warning, her laughter turned to crying. A moment later, her shoulders shook, and she sobbed into her hands. He'd been so concerned, afraid for her. And that was because… She squeezed her eyes shut…because he cared for her. The screen blurred, and she lurched from the chair and blindly went in search of tissues.

Still sniffling, she hugged herself and sagged against the kitchen counter. How was she going to get this project done if she couldn't even look at the photos? If she broke down into a blubbering mess every time a memory crashed in? Every single picture would draw a memory.

She sucked in a shaky breath. Many tasks awaited her attention. She should move on and come back to this later. She had to keep making progress. Colorado was the next place on her list. No reason she couldn't make that trip this week. She opened her notebook and found the name of the lodge she'd considered. Then she took her laptop into the office for a change of scenery.

Thirty minutes later, she had plane tickets and reservations for lodging and car rental. At the desk, she switched to researching and planning her route. She expected to see deer, small mammals, and hummingbirds, but she hoped to also see elk and coyotes. And mountains, of course—with babbling streams and colorful meadows. At least she wouldn't be distracted by memories of sunsets. The sun would probably go behind the mountains before it could turn the sky brilliant colors.

The buzz of her phone jerked Caroline from her work. She glanced at the screen and smiled to see her daughter's face. "Hey, honey. How's your day going?"

"I did it, Mom. You're speaking to the new

Director of Environmental Impact."

The excitement in Lauren's voice came through loud and clear. She'd made the right choice.

Caroline put a hand to her chest. That kind of happiness and opportunity was what all parents wanted for their kids. "Oh, that's fantastic. Congratulations, sweetie! I'm so proud of you."

"Thanks. Sorry, I didn't wait longer to give them my decision. I had a call today, and it ended up feeling like the right time. But I'm not trying to rush you into anything. I'm not moving to Texas tomorrow."

"No worries." She'd take time to explore her options. Maybe she wouldn't even buy a house and put down new roots right away. While she wouldn't want to be far away from her daughter forever, the idea of being a rolling stone for a while was appealing. And a little time on her own would give Lauren a chance to spread her wings a bit first. "When do they want you there?"

"Soon, but they understand I have a lease and need a little time. They'll put me up in one of those long-term-stay hotels for a while."

"That's perfect. You'll be able to explore and figure out which area you want to live in and what the traffic patterns are like. I just made reservations for going to Colorado on Thursday, but when I get back, I'm totally available to go apartment hunting with you."

"Okay. Be sure to text me your itinerary."

"Yes, Mother, will do." Caroline rolled her eyes but infused her voice with humor. She glanced around the room then reached to the bookcase for one of her favorite photos of Andrew.

"Guess I'd better run," Lauren said. "But I'll talk to you before you leave again."

"Of course. Maybe dinner Wednesday night."

"Sounds good."

"Bye, honey. Enjoy the day."

The diplomas on the wall caught her eye. Her husband had so many degrees, licenses, and certifications, they used to laugh about the alphabet soup of letters between the two of them. Her gaze dropped to the photo in her hand. While some memories had faded, she could never forget Andrew's image. Seemed as if the older she got, the more Lauren bore resemblance to her dad. Probably because her hair had darkened over the years. "We did good, Andrew," Caroline whispered. "Our little girl is a wonderful young woman. You'd be so proud of her."

Caroline smoothed a thumb over the photo. Andrew had been dressed in a tux for the Chamber gala they were going to. Andrew was a handsome man—and always sharply dressed. Even as his temples grayed prematurely, he'd always had a full head of hair. And he'd been drop-dead gorgeous wearing anything from shorts and a T-shirt to a tux and bow tie. She could see how he might come off as a little too polished or arrogant to Jack and the rancher crowd.

With a snort, she placed the photo back on the shelf. Jack also could be described as arrogant. Certainly not cause to disparage a man or laugh about his death. Funny how different yet alike the two were. Both men knew their stuff and commanded respect in their fields. Both had presence. And both had stirred something inside her.

She'd been on her own so long, she'd forgotten how nice it was to share meals with someone, to have a companion for riding or taking walks or watching

Darlene Deluca

sunsets. Sadness stole over her. She would miss Jack—
or the man she'd thought he was.

She turned to the window and let her thoughts drift.
It was always hard to see—or acknowledge—the other
side of the coin. Those Texas ranchers didn't see that
Andrew had given people another option. All they
could see was that a friend was no longer one of them.
They saw the change, and it scared them. She
understood that what Andrew did was business to him.
To them, it was personal. And it made them fearful,
bitter.

But Jack wasn't stupid. He should be able to
understand another viewpoint. Would he regret his
words? Would he miss her? And the biggest question—
could he ever humble himself enough to apologize?
Didn't seem like his strong suit even if he admitted
being wrong. She checked her thoughts. That wasn't
entirely fair. He'd been quick to apologize that night at
the barn when the foal was born, and he'd hurt her
feelings.

She flopped into the cozy reading chair and
drummed her fingers against the fabric. What if he did?
Could she accept an apology knowing how he felt?
Even if she did, she'd still be on her own for travel.
He'd be a part-time companion. He'd be part of her life
on his terms when it fit his lifestyle. Jack wasn't
budging on that. But in a relationship, two people were
supposed to share each other's lives and interests—it
couldn't be only her sharing his.

She rubbed her temples. Here he was still taking up
space in her head. She'd told Lauren her relationship
with Jack was over, but when would she convince
herself?

****

At the sound of wheels on the road, Jack looked up from the field and spotted Nora's truck coming his direction. He braced himself. This would be their first encounter since the dance, and he wasn't sure of her position on the whole mess. If she even knew any of the details. Had Caroline confided in her? He'd love to know, but it might be best to steer clear of that topic. He didn't need to re-hash the weekend yet again.

She stopped the truck and got out then pulled a small cooler from the back.

Jack waved.

"Hey, there," she said as she approached. "I've got lunch."

Jack checked his watch. Sure enough, lunchtime by the clock. He hadn't had much appetite the last couple of days. He met her at the road. "Great. Thanks. You just missed Roger. Went to have a look at the foal."

Nora waved a hand. "No worries. He can eat when he gets back. I'm not tracking him down. Enjoy."

Jack nodded. "Thanks for the delivery." Apparently, she wasn't keen on sticking around to chat, either.

He started to open the cooler, then Nora turned back around.

"Oh, I need to go down there, anyway. Is your car locked?"

"My car?" Jack echoed.

Nora looked past him. "Yeah, Caroline left a scarf the other night."

The breath whooshed from Jack's lungs. He remembered that now. She'd never gone back to the car. And he hadn't seen it in the dark—or in his state of mind when he left the dance. It should still be there.

"Told her I'd mail it," Nora added.

In the awkward silence, a number of thoughts raced through Jack's mind. Did the scarf hold sentimental significance to Caroline? Was this an opportunity? Did he want a reason to contact her, or should he simply let go?

"Jack?" Nora cocked her head and regarded him quizzically.

He made a quick decision and met Nora's eyes. "I'll take care of it."

She studied him again, and heat crawled up the back of his neck.

"You sure about that?"

"Yep."

Nora opened her mouth as if to say something, then closed it again.

"Something else on your mind?"

"You know, what's between you and Caroline is between you and Caroline."

"Yeah, thanks."

"But I want you to know that I talked to my niece Gabby last night."

Nora placed her hands on her hips, her hard stare pinning Jack in place. What did her niece have to do with anything?

"She confirmed that she'd mentioned the cabins to some of her friends, including Caroline's daughter, when they were thinking about places for a girls' getaway. That's how Caroline heard about the ranch, Jack."

Jack opened his mouth, but Nora didn't stop for a breath.

"She mentioned it the first time I met her at the cabin. Said the personal recommendation had enticed her."

What? She had to be making this up.

She slanted her eyes. "I double-checked. To satisfy your suspicious nature."

Jack put his hands on his hips and stepped forward. "You're telling me that Caroline's daughter is friends with your niece?"

"Right. Small world, huh?"

Stunned, he blew out a harsh breath. "Yeah."

"On the other hand," Nora continued with an airy tone of voice. "Like Caroline said, Texas is a big place. And she didn't keep tabs on her husband's projects. Imagine not knowing every move your spouse makes, right? Oh, wait, how did I not know Roger wouldn't be up here? I guess he forgot to give me his daily itinerary." Sarcasm dripped from her words, and her brows rose.

Jack got the message.

"By the way, the other cabin is rented this weekend, so guests will be roaming around."

Jack nodded. "Reed and Dylan are coming, too. So, we'll need Star Friday and Saturday."

"Got it. I better scoot along. Don't forget about the scarf, okay?"

"I won't," he murmured. He had half a mind to go get it right this minute, to feel something tangible of Caroline's. But he needed a few minutes alone to ponder Nora's revelation. The truth hammered in his brain. And when he glanced at the cooler again, he knew whatever she'd brought wouldn't sit lightly in his stomach.

They'd been wrong. And even if the man hadn't been Caroline's former husband, the conversation, the laughter, and name-calling, had been out of line.

Later that afternoon, as soon as he latched the last gate, as soon as he could get away without arousing Roger's curiosity, Jack headed home. He went directly to the car in the garage and yanked open the passenger side door. Caroline's scarf dangled from the seat onto the floor. He snatched it up and wrapped it around his hands.

He couldn't help a reluctant smile as he visualized the scarf around her shoulders with the sparkly teal top she'd worn. The scarf suited her—bright coral and teal with some blue and white. Of course she'd want it back. A tremor of sadness surged through him. She knew it was in his car, but she'd contacted Nora, not him. He shook his head. Couldn't blame her for that. And she wouldn't be coming back to fetch— The craziest idea flashed inside him, and blood rushed to his head. Where had *that* come from? He must be more tired than he thought. *No. No way.*

But what if he did? What if he delivered the scarf?

****

As of Friday morning, the same crazy notion stirred inside Jack just as it had been all week. It had kept him up at night, had Roger questioning Jack's health.

"Jack," he complained the day before. "I keep losing you. You feel all right?"

"I'm fine," Jack lied. Again. But his focus on the tasks at hand was zilch.

By the time Reed and Dylan arrived on Friday, Jack couldn't think straight. He hated this wishy-washy feeling, this not knowing the right thing to do—it went against his grain.

He caught Reed watching him multiple times. Finally, he set down his after-dinner bourbon and scowled at his son. "Why are you looking at me like that?"

"Like what?"

"Like I've grown horns. Is something wrong?"

"Dad, you seem off. Distracted, like something's bothering you."

Jack ran a hand over his jaw. He hated being so transparent. He picked up the drink again and looked into the amber liquid. "I'm thinking about going to Caroline's."

"What do you mean?"

He looked up. "In Nashville."

Reed's eyes widened. "You're joking."

Jack stood and began pacing. "Guess I'd have to go to Dallas and catch a plane."

Reed held up a hand. "Wait a minute. We've asked you a hundred times to come to Dallas to visit and you never have. Now you're ready to get on a plane to visit this woman you've only known for a few weeks?"

"Well…I…I said I'm thinking about it. Maybe I could…"

"Why did she leave, anyway? Thought she had an open schedule."

"Long story. Bottom line is, I made a mistake, and she left. If I want to straighten things out, I've got to make a move. She's not going to just show up at the ranch again."

"So, you had a fight. She left. And you want to win her back. Is that what I'm hearing?"

Jack braced against the table and blew out a breath. "Close enough."

With a slight frown, Reed folded his arms and tilted the chair on its back legs, studying Jack through puzzled eyes. "Huh. This is a pretty big deal for you. So you really like her? She's...ah, special?"

He met his son's eyes. "She is."

"Wow. You thinking long-term...marriage?"

Boom. There it was. The word Jack had not uttered. But now that Reed had ventured there, the idea didn't sound completely crazy. "I don't know. You have any problem with that?"

"Not if you love her and she loves you back, Dad. It was obvious the weekend we met her that you felt something. I wasn't expecting it to develop so fast."

"I...yes. It was unexpected." He ran a hand across his jaw. "Maybe I—"

"Mom would want you to have a life again, you know."

Jack swallowed hard and met his son's eyes. "She can't be replaced, you know."

"Yeah. But you can have a new life."

They sat in silence a moment.

"We like Caroline," Reed said. "We don't know her well, but Dylan, Kristen, we all talked about it. Had a good feeling about her."

Jack nodded. A new life and all that went along with it was the sort of thing he'd avoided considering because it meant changes. Big changes—a new outlook, a different future. Letting go of the past.

****

At breakfast the next morning, Jack poured himself a cup of coffee then joined Reed and Dylan at the table.

He drank slowly, letting the strong brew fortify him. Finally, Jack broached the subject he'd been stewing over. "I've got an idea. What time is this soccer game of yours tomorrow, Dylan?"

Dylan and Reed looked up, wide-eyed.

Dylan's glance shifted to Reed then back to Jack. "Three o'clock."

"How about I come see it? They still let grandparents in, right?"

Dylan grinned. "Yeah, lots of grandparents come. That'd be cool."

Jack turned toward Reed. "Then maybe you can get me to the airport on Monday."

Reed gave a slow nod. "We can make that happen. You booked your flight already?"

Jack cleared his throat. "No. Thought we could do that this morning. I guess all I need is a computer and a credit card, right?"

Reed chuckled. "That should do it. I can walk you through the process."

"I suppose once I get to the airport there are plenty of signs. I hear that place is a zoo."

"We can help, Grandpa," Dylan piped up. "Just don't take a bunch of stuff. And remember, you have to take off your shoes and take all the stuff out of your pockets."

Jack raised his brows.

"Security," Reed said.

"Right." For the first time, Jack felt a little foolish that his nine-year-old grandson knew more about air travel than he did. He sucked in a deep breath. Could this old dog still learn some new tricks?

Chapter Twenty-Five

With the instructions from Reed and Dylan playing in his head, Jack exited the plane and followed the crowd down the jetway. Head toward baggage claim and ground transportation. That's where the rental car counters will be.

All right. Should be easy enough. The only luggage he'd been able to scrounge up was a beat-up black duffel. He hoisted it over his shoulder and skirted around a woman with two kids and a roller bag. He dodged a couple of other travelers and tripping hazards then stopped to read the signs and get his bearings.

"Sir! On your left."

Jack heard the words and leapt out of the way in time to avoid being mowed down by a vehicle resembling a golf cart. What the heck? How could anyone distinguish that beeping from the noise and commotion in the terminal?

Careful to check behind him every few steps, he started down the hallway again. He'd rather not have an injury or not-so-funny anecdote to tell at this point in his journey. The signs were clear enough, and with some minor jockeying, he found the rental car company he'd booked without further incident.

At the counter, he presented his credit card, driver's license, and insurance card and signed or initialed at least five times on the papers the attendant handed him—and wondered what exactly he'd agreed to. He didn't bother to ask or read the fine print. With that completed, he took the key fob the attendant dangled in front of him. "Thank you."

"My pleasure, sir. We'll see you in a couple of days."

Or a couple of hours. Hard to say which.

Inside the stuffy, fume-filled garage, he located the mid-sized black sedan and tossed the duffel in the back seat. Inside, he fumbled through the navigation settings and typed in the address Caroline had listed on her rental application. Might as well get to it. In about thirty minutes, he'd know whether or not the trip had been a colossal waste of time.

With a little luck, he'd manage to arrive without getting lost. According to Reed, the navigation would be aware of accidents or road construction and steer around it. A lot to ask of a computer, but Jack put the car in drive and eased onto the street, checking the mirrors while he watched the traffic and listened for instructions.

Fifteen minutes later, fists clenching the steering wheel, his stomach growled, reminding him that it was lunchtime. But would food settle his nerves or make his stomach churn more than it did already? Eating a little something might be the best course of action. He eased the car into the right-hand lane and kept an eye out for some kind of fast-food chain. That would do.

Only moments later, a retail center appeared. He quickly signaled and exited the roadway, startled when the navigation system objected. He had no idea how to pause the route. The complex was nothing short of a maze. By the time he made his way to the restaurant, he'd been honked at, flipped off by an impatient woman in a minivan, and nearly rear-ended by a kid who barely looked older than Dylan. Welcome to the city.

He downed a small burger then set out again. After waiting through three traffic lights, he finally resumed his journey, to the relief of his cyber guide. He spared the screen a glance. Seventeen minutes to go.

As he got closer to his destination, it wasn't the mechanics of the travel that most concerned him. It was the welcome he'd receive.

His hands went clammy on the steering wheel as he turned the car onto Caroline's street. He followed the directions of the robotic voice about halfway down the street and parked at the curb of a stately stone-and-white-clapboard house with trim lawn and shrubs. A metallic-blue car sat in the driveway. He breathed a sigh of relief. Looked like she was home. He climbed out of the car and retrieved the scarf from a small plastic bag inside his duffel. He refolded it then wanted to kick himself. In his hurry to get there, he hadn't thought to bring flowers or chocolates—an offering of something besides her own belonging. He glanced at the house. Probably too late to leave and come back. She may have already noticed the car.

He rolled his neck as he approached the house then jogged up the porch stairs. He raked a hand through his hair then rang the doorbell.

When the door opened, his heart stuttered—a younger version of Caroline stood before him, brows raised.

"May I help you?" the young woman asked.

"I…um…yes. I'm here to see Caroline Tate."

Her curiosity turned to a frown. "Was she

expecting you?"

Jack cleared his throat. "No. I…uh…" He held up the scarf. "I wanted to return this to her. She…well, she left it in my car."

The woman's expression changed again, and Jack had a hard time reading it.

"You're Jack," she said flatly.

His stomach clenched. So, she knew of him, but he wasn't picking up positive vibes. What had Caroline told her daughter about him?

"Yes. Jack Armstrong. You must be Lauren." Thankfully, from somewhere in the depths of his brain he recalled her name.

"Right. Sorry, my mom isn't home."

"I see. Any idea when she'll be back?"

She quietly studied his face while he stood waiting for an answer and feeling like a fool the size of Texas.

She crossed her arms and leaned against the door casing. "Not really."

He clutched the scarf, unsure what to do next. He wanted to deliver it in person, but should he leave it with the daughter? At least Caroline would know he was in town.

"All right. Well, I'll go on—"

"You hurt my mom," Lauren said softly.

The accusation hit like a slap in the face. And like a blowtorch to his collar, heat seared the back of his neck. He shifted uncomfortably and met her eyes. "I did. I'm real sorry about that."

He endured her glare until she finally straightened and gestured toward the two white rockers on the porch.

"Have a seat, Jack."

She disappeared into the house, and he did as he

was told, sinking into the farthest chair. He ran a hand across his jaw. Now what? Did he need to sit here for a butt-chew from Caroline's daughter?

A few moments later, Lauren reappeared with two bottles of lime-flavored mineral water.

He gratefully took the bottle she offered. "Thank you."

"You could've mailed the scarf," Lauren said.

Jack took a long drink of the cold water while he processed her comment. Her voice had softened. The curiosity was back.

"Yes. I could have. But I wanted to apologize in person."

"That's why you want to see her?"

"It is."

"She hasn't come close to having feelings for anyone since Dad died. And that's been ten years. But I could tell she liked you. She was excited about the dance."

"And I can't imagine why she picked me, but I don't want to lose her. She's an amazing woman."

"Why do you think an amazing woman would be married to a jerk? That's what you thought of my dad, right?"

So, Caroline had shared that information with her daughter. Regret washed over him. "We didn't see eye to eye on his business ventures. I'm sorry about the way it got communicated."

In the silence that followed, Jack watched her face. She looked toward the street as if deep in thought.

"She's in Colorado."

Jack blinked. "Excuse me?"

"Mom came home for a few days then left again. I

think she was upset and needed to stay busy, so she's focusing on her book project."

He closed his eyes and groaned inside. Just like him. Doing things to keep his mind occupied, to keep from relentlessly stewing over his loss. He should've known she might not be here. She'd talked about several other trips to finish the material for the book. He'd come all this way for nothing.

He set the water bottle on the small table between them and stood. "Please tell her I was here. And I'm sorry I missed her."

Lauren rose also.

With as much dignity as he could muster, Jack squared his shoulders and gave her a nod as he walked past. "Thanks for your hospitality. I'm sorry about the loss of your father. You're lucky to have such a wonderful mother."

He grabbed the railing and started down the steps.

"Okay, Jack. I'm going to tell you where she is."

He swiveled around, his heart pounding.

She stepped toward him. "Do not make me regret this."

Chapter Twenty-Six

Finally, Jack spotted Caroline coming through the automatic lobby door. His throat went dry. She looked as lovely as ever. Her hair was tucked behind her ears and held in place by the familiar straw hat with its red flower.

Though he wasn't at all sure of this course of action, he set his drink firmly on the bar, grabbed hold of the small bag that contained her well-traveled scarf, and strode toward the entrance. "Caroline?"

She stopped abruptly and stood as if she'd been frozen in place, then she whipped around toward the bar, stunned disbelief on her face.

Eyes round as dinner plates stared at him, and her mouth hung open. After what seemed an eternity, a puzzled frown replaced the surprise. "Jack?"

He moved toward her, belatedly realizing he didn't look his best, scruffy and rumpled from the crazy, unexpected hours of travel—probably not the best way to sweep the lady off her feet.

"What on earth are you doing here?"

"Looking for you." He cleared his throat and withdrew enough of the scarf from the small bag for her to see. Then he held it out to her. "You left this in my car."

She took the bag and stared at him some more. "You left the ranch and came all the way to Colorado to give me my scarf?" Her voice was flat.

Jack shoved his hands in his pockets. "No, not really."

Her brows rose, and he knew she was waiting for more.

He blew out a long breath. "I owe you an apology." He watched her face for any signs of softening. Had enough time passed?

She looked down and fiddled with the strap of her camera bag before meeting his eyes. Hers were full of challenge. "Yes, you do," she said quietly.

He ached to pull her into his arms, but knew it was too soon for that. He held her gaze and spoke firmly. "That night at the dance, I said some dumb things. Hurtful things, and I'm sorry."

A family burst through the door, laughing and chattering as they brushed past. Jack looked around the lobby then gestured toward the seat he'd vacated at the bar. "Could we sit a minute? And talk?"

Caroline shifted her stance.

Jack held his breath.

"I suppose so," she murmured. "But not here. Let's go out to the patio."

Jack trailed behind, hoping Caroline couldn't hear the thundering of his heart.

****

Caroline stopped a waiter and ordered an iced tea then dropped into a chair at a table in the far corner of the lodge's back patio, still wondering if the altitude was messing with her mind. Was this an apparition or was Jack Armstrong actually here in the flesh? She glanced at the bag in her hand and touched the scarf. Seemed real enough.

331

But *Jack*? Jack had left the ranch. She lurched upright. *Wait*. How did he track her down? She frowned his direction. "How did you find me?"

"I, uh…went to Nashville first. Your daughter was at your house, and—"

"Lauren told you I was here?"

Jack leaned forward. "Don't be mad at her. She's a nice young woman who took pity on me."

Caroline put a hand to her mouth as the significance of his words sank in. He'd gone to Nashville first. He'd gone to Nashville then got back on a plane and flew to Denver. Navigated both of those airports in one day. And driving? The lodge was more than an hour from the city.

"Jack, did you drive here from Denver?"

His chest heaved. "I did."

"Oh, my gosh. I can't believe—"

"I miss you."

Caroline's heart slammed into her ribs, and she gaped at the man across from her. His brilliant blue eyes held sincerity. He missed her? She'd only been gone a week. And there'd been no contact between them since she left. No late-night video chats or text messages. Nothing like the week she'd been gone to North Carolina when she'd sent photos and updates and had looked forward to ending the days by connecting with Jack.

"I don't know if you can forgive me," he said. "But I had to come here and try to set things straight. I know I jumped to some conclusions and said some harsh things." He studied his hands a moment then glanced at her again. "You were right to be angry. If anyone ever talked that way about Rosalyn, I'd want to rip them to shreds. I shouldn't have spoken ill of your husband even though I didn't know who he was."

Tears sprang to Caroline's eyes. Remorse was etched in the lines on Jack's face. He got it.

"You…you brought color and life back to the ranch. Back to my life. You…your hat…your pearls…the way you dance…the way you look at the world…everything about you makes me smile. And I don't want to lose you. It's a lot to ask, but I hope you'll forgive me and come back to the ranch again. Start over. Let me do better this time."

She toyed with the straw in her tea, thinking. How to put this? "You know, Jack, I can understand that every sell-out is personal to you. It's a change to the community. But not everyone is out to do you a dirty deal. You can't label everyone who comes from a city as a bad person."

Jack blew out a breath and nodded. "You're right. The boys were out of line that night at the dance. And so was I." He leaned closer and folded his hands on the table. "I got on the computer. I saw some of the projects your husband's company did. I know they won awards for contributing to the communities where they did business." His voice dropped. "I saw the good side I hadn't seen before."

He looked into her eyes, and she saw the man she'd fallen in love with. Giving him a second chance would give her one, too. *Remember the good times*, Nora had urged. They had some good times. Heat washed over her as she remembered the feel of his arms holding her.

He must've sensed the direction her thoughts had taken. His lips turned in a slow smile, and he reached across the table and brushed a thumb over her hand. "Is there any hope for me?"

His hopeful expression combined with a gleam of light in his eyes sent tingles along her spine. He'd gone to great lengths to find her. Here he was. Jack, minus the cowboy hat. Jack, with the Rocky Mountains—not the fields of Texas—the backdrop behind him. "I can't believe you're here," she murmured.

"Exactly where I want to be at this moment." He glanced around then gestured toward the walkway and adjacent garden path leading from the patio. "Let's take a walk."

"Sure." She stood, and Jack tossed a few bills on the table then took her elbow. As they moved from the patio to the sidewalk, Jack fell into step beside her—close but not touching. On the path, they were surrounded by Alpine wildflowers and the buzz of hummingbirds.

"This is pretty," he said. "Are you getting some good pictures?"

"Yeah. Some really nice hummingbird shots."

"You know, of course, you can use any of the photos you took at the ranch for the book. That was never in question."

It'd been in her written agreement, but nice to have him acknowledge it.

"Where to next?" he asked.

Caroline stopped walking and turned to face him. "Maybe Sedona."

A slight nod was his only reaction.

She sucked in a deep breath. "Here's the thing, Jack. I love the ranch. Yes, I want to come back. But in the last few weeks, I've discovered that I still have things to do and places to see. I don't want to be stuck somewhere. I can't live like a recluse."

"I know that." His voice was deep and sure.

And so? "Jack," she whispered. She glanced away from his face and gasped. "Jack, look!"

He turned.

Behind him, the sun had begun its descent, lighting the sky with streaks of purple and changing the clouds to breathtaking hues of pink and orange.

"Ooh, it's beautiful." Caroline clapped her hands. "That's the prettiest sky I've seen the whole time I've been here."

"It's stunning," Jack murmured.

Caroline slowly turned to him. "It is. Even in Colorado." She shook her head. "It's a long way from home. From Sunset Ledge."

"Mm-hmm."

"You came all this way…so many miles…"

Jack smiled and lifted a lock of her hair. "Sometimes you have to go an extra mile or two for the people you love."

Her mouth formed an "O," and Jack closed the small gap between them, pulling her into his arms. He held her close and let her process his words. It felt good to have her in his arms, but also to admit the love he never thought he'd feel again. When she loosened her grip, he pulled back to see her questioning eyes.

"Jack." Her voice wavered. "I love the ranch. It feels comfortable, and I know there's always work to do, and it's hard for you to leave. But if you can leave it to track me down in Colorado, couldn't you go with me to have a glass of wine on the French Riviera? Or at least at a vineyard in California? Or watch a sunset on the beach?" She rested her hands against his chest.

"Sometimes? Couldn't you?"

He held her gaze a long time before nodding. Then he brushed his thumb across her cheek. In the next moment, their breath mingled. "Yes," he said as his lips touched hers. "I think I could."

Epilogue

One Year Later

"Mooooom!"

Lauren's shriek came from the top of the stairs.

Jack looked at Caroline, and their eyes met. *This was it.*

In the next instant, Lauren clambered down the stairs, letter in hand, and flew into her mother's arms.

Jack took a step back and pulled a surprised Dylan against him.

As Caroline rocked Lauren in her arms, the rest of the family and Lauren's boyfriend, Tommy, followed down the stairs. They'd all come to the ranch for a fun Memorial Day weekend full of swimming, horseback riding, and cooking out.

They didn't know they'd also be attending an intimate wedding and reception—until now. Jack and Caroline had kept their secret for weeks. To reveal it, they'd left notes for their children in their respective bedrooms to be read as soon as they made their way upstairs to freshen up and store their bags.

In the family room, Reed handed little Amber Rose to Kristen. Then he moved forward and wrapped Jack in a hug. "We're happy for you, Dad."

Jack held onto his son then looked past him to lock gazes with Caroline. This was an emotional moment for all of them. They couldn't turn back time or replace all the people they'd loved and lost, but they could hold those memories in their hearts and keep living. Keep loving. As Rosalyn used to say, *you can keep giving love away and never run out.*

Reed loosened his grip, and in a flash, arms were everywhere as they all took turns hugging each other, laughing, and crying and squealing.

Jack pulled Caroline's daughter into his arms. He'd had a soft spot for Lauren since that first encounter in Nashville when she'd trusted him with Caroline's whereabouts.

Tommy held out a hand to Jack. "Congratulations, sir."

Jack blinked as his eyes misted. He clasped the younger man's hand. "It's Jack. You—"

"Stop!" Dylan yelled.

All heads turned toward him.

He flailed his arms in the air. "Why is everybody crying?"

Grinning, Reed ruffled the kid's hair. "Because Grandpa and Miz Caroline are getting married, and we're happy."

"Cool!" Dylan said. But he looked around the room uncertainly. His glance shot to Kristen. "Am I supposed to cry?"

Laughter erupted throughout the room.

"No, you don't have to cry," Jack told him. "But you can if you want to," he added quickly. He knew better than to suggest boys can't cry.

"Whatever you feel like." Kristen brushed a hand across her cheek and sniffled. "We're just excited to add Caroline and Lauren to our family."

Finally, Dylan grinned. "Me, too."

Jack held up his hand to Dylan for a high-five. "How about some drinks and snacks?"

"Oh! We need to get the coolers," Lauren said.

"On it," Tommy told her as he and Reed headed for the doors.

Caroline pulled glasses from the cabinet while Jack opened a bottle of Prosecco.

"Mom, this is so fun," Lauren said. "I love the dress and sandals. But where on the ranch can we wear them? You're planning the ceremony here in the house?"

"Poolside, sweetheart. It's all set up. Don't worry. The sandals will be fine there."

"Should we go out and pick some wildflowers while we still have our boots on? For a bouquet?"

Caroline grinned. "All set. Nora and I had lunch in Abilene yesterday and picked up armloads of amazing fresh flowers. They're keeping cool in buckets of water down in the cellar."

"She's thought of everything," Jack chimed in. He leaned down and planted a quick kiss on her lips. The sparkle in her eyes reflected his own delight. They were both enjoying their surprise.

****

Caroline took a sip of the bubbly drink Jack handed her. So far, everything was unfolding perfectly.

She and Jack had enlisted Nora and Roger's help with the planning. Roger had been particularly eager to assist, which Caroline attributed to his chagrin over his part in the laughter and name-calling at the dance. Over dinner several months ago, the four of them had worked through it, but she could tell Roger remained remorseful.

So now, an arbor stood near the pool, flanked by two potted yellow rose bushes. New outdoor lights were strung across the entire pool deck. Matching simple summer dresses in light teal hung in the closets for Kristen and Lauren along with fancy jeweled flip-flops. For Kristen and Reed's adorable baby Amber, Caroline had found an outfit with a teal-and-yellow floral pattern. Crisp white dress shirts were steamed and ready for all the men and Dylan. None of them would have known to bring dress clothes for a weekend on the ranch, of course.

She checked her watch. Joe and Lisa should be here soon. Renaissance Man Joe had gone through the online ordination process a few years earlier and would perform the ceremony. Roger would pick up Joe and Lisa from the airstrip in Stockton this afternoon. Nora was contributing a beautiful white cake and a variety of other desserts including her amazing fresh strawberry shortcake.

Nora arrived first, and after another round of hugs, the women gathered around the table and arranged the bright mixed flowers into colorful, whimsical bouquets.

An hour later, tires crunching outside signaled the arrival of the remaining guests. Before she had a chance to properly say hello, Joe took Caroline's arm and waved something in front of her. "Caro, I've got a surprise for you." A huge grin covered his face.

His excitement was infectious, and she couldn't help laughing. "Let me see. What is it?"

He unrolled a printed copy of the university's magazine that featured Caroline and her book on its cover. "Hot off the press."

So far, Caroline had seen only the digital version of the magazine. The university had done a lovely job of covering the publication of the book, along with excerpts from a couple of her essays and quotes from a few glowing reviews. Caroline's glance shifted to the copy of *Nature Everywhere You Look* that held a place of honor on the coffee table. She still pinched herself over the initial reception by the ecology community. That the praise had spilled over into general non-fiction book territory was more than she could've hoped for. "Joe, thanks so much. This—"

"But wait, there's more." He pulled out his cell phone and held it in front of her. "Ah, you should've seen the look on Hanson's face."

Caroline looked at the photo and grinned as pride and satisfaction rushed through her. *Dear Joe.* He'd snapped a photo of a staff meeting, and almost everyone around the table had a copy of the university news magazine. The sour expression of Dean Hanson in the background was priceless.

Still laughing, she shook her head. "Oh, my gosh. Jack, come look at this."

Jack moved in beside her, his warm hands gently kneading her shoulders. Then he let out a low chuckle. "Might need to frame that one."

The book project had opened so many new doors, expanded her life. Her time at the university would always remain special to her, but she didn't miss it. New adventures and opportunities awaited her—as well as a new lifestyle. She was giving up proximity to shops and restaurants and longtime friends, but Jack's love and companionship, and the vast peacefulness of the ranch more than compensated.

They'd agreed that the ranch would be her home base, but she'd still travel for professional opportunities as well as personal enjoyment. Jack would accompany her occasionally. She reached up and squeezed Jack's hand.

When his gaze met hers, she leaned closer and let her hand slide down his arm. "Hey, fella, want to get hitched?"

****

Caroline's words shot adrenaline straight to Jack's veins. "Darlin', that's the best proposition I've had all day. Is it time?"

She nodded. "Let's start getting ready." She clapped her hands. "Hey, guys, go grab your things. The ladies are taking over the upstairs, and you all can have the main floor. We'll see you poolside in about an hour."

A little after five, Jack got the signal from Nora. He stepped into place beside Joe in front of the arbor, his dress boots clacking against the concrete deck. He adjusted the collar of the new white shirt and watched the back door while blood whooshed in his ears.

Nora took her seat beside Roger. A moment later, Lauren opened the back door, and Caroline stepped outside.

Jack's throat clogged immediately. In her white dress and pearls, with flowers in her hair and a soft smile lighting her face, she looked radiant. Early evening sunshine bathed the pool area in a warm glow and reminded Jack of all the sunsets to come, all the sunsets he hoped to enjoy with Caroline at his side, whether at Sunset Ledge or a distant sandy beach.

Caroline hooked her hand through Lauren's arm,

and together they walked the short distance to the arbor. After the two embraced, Jack stepped forward and offered Caroline his arm.

He listened as best he could while Joe told stories of his friendship with Caroline and his first adventure at the ranch. Then Jack repeated the marriage vows as Joe instructed. Finally, Reed stood and handed him Caroline's ring, a slim circle of diamonds set in gold. Jack smoothly slid the ring onto her finger. When she pushed a new gold band onto his finger, it felt like coming home, like the most natural thing in the world. Like it belonged there.

There wasn't a doubt in his mind that he would love and cherish this woman for the rest of his life. As everyone who mattered most to him cheered, Jack kissed his bride.

A word about the author…

Darlene Deluca writes contemporary romance and women's fiction, and likes to explore relationships – what brings people together or keeps them apart.

Her intent is to bring to life interesting characters that will leave you cheering or sighing with a satisfied smile as you turn the final page.

With a degree in Journalism, Darlene started her career as a newspaper reporter. She currently has ten published novels, which are available in paperback and ebook versions.

She writes day or night, whenever the words/mood/deadlines strike, and almost always has a cup of tea and a bit of dark chocolate nearby.

http://www.darlenedeluca.com

www.ingramcontent.com/pod-product-compliance
Lightning Source LLC
Chambersburg PA
CBHW051134030726
47504CB00004B/865